THE LUPATUS STONE

The LUPATUS STONE

RACHAEL BELL-IRVING

RACHAEL BELL-IRVING
The Lupatus Stone

Published by Firelight Stories Publishing
Copyright © 2021 by Rachael Bell-Irving
First Edition

PAPERBACK ISBN 978-1-7770481-2-9
E-BOOK ISBN 978-1-7770481-3-6

COVER & INTERIOR DESIGN Jazmin Welch
EDITOR Tara Avery
PROOFREADER Michelle Parker

This is a work of fiction. All characters, organizations, locations,
and events portrayed in this novel are either products of the
author's imagination or are used fictitiously.

To Matthew

CHAPTER 1

Nathan

Nathan sprinted through the trees, dodging branches without slowing his pace as the burn in his thighs drove him on. Sweat pasted his t-shirt to his chest, and the wind pierced his exposed skin like needles. Soil-stained snow clung to his joints and weighed down his sandy-brown hair.

Faster.

Though it was early November, he didn't need to wear more than a pair of shorts, even in the thick and frozen woods. Running was the only time he felt alive, and he didn't want nuisance layers of clothing slowing him down; after all, he was suited for the cold.

The icy chill of night still hung in the air, not yet chased away by the early morning light creeping through the dense trees above. The sky was a soup of grey clouds, releasing a thin dusting of snow. The few snowflakes able to break through the treetops settled gracefully onto the rocks and sodden logs peppered across the forest floor. Nathan spotted every obstacle with perfect clarity, easily avoiding the debris that could have slowed him down.

A small animal darted away in his peripheral vision, breaking Nathan's focus and causing him to lose his momentum. With a loud curse, he stumbled through four large, awkward steps before stopping. A low growl consumed his mind. "Shut up," he snarled at himself. The protest quieted but never fully subsided.

"I don't care," Nathan muttered, his ribs stretching as exertion strained his lungs. Even though he wasn't hungry, his inner wolf was spurred to chase whatever had run from him. His human thoughts were constantly at war with the wolf instincts living inside the mind they shared.

The uncomfortable itch under his skin would be scratched if he shifted into his wolf form and let go of the reins that kept his canine nature under control, but Nathan ground his teeth against the idea. Steam curled from his body where his burning skin met the chilled air. If he hung around too long, his muscles would seize. He was tempted to let them tighten, to feel the fight in his legs when he hiked back up the mountain.

I'm too far already. He glanced over his shoulder. Having lived in these woods for three years, he knew he was dangerously close to the highway, a mistake he wouldn't have made had he been able to focus. But he still had far too much energy, and if he didn't burn it off throughout the day, he wouldn't be tired enough to avoid the nightmares that hadn't let up since before Halloween.

The shadows of the past flooded his mind, blurring his present. He was twelve years old again, running through the woods with the skin-tingling feeling that he was being followed. In his memory, he rounded a corner and came face-to-face with a pair of silver-blue eyes surrounded by the shadows of the forest. Nathan hadn't been afraid at first — he hadn't even thought to run — until a massive set of jaws burst from the darkness and lunged for him, and by then it was already too late.

Nathan's breath caught, disrupting the rhythm of his lungs and throwing him into a painful cough. Once he caught his breath, he inhaled the frosty air and reached his hands overhead, stretching the muscles between each vertebra. He'd moved to the dense forest of northern B.C. to outrun the nightmares and the werewolf that caused them. Today his antidote of exercise was failing. He would just have to keep running.

Rather than heading north toward his den, Nathan turned east, planning to continue his run through the forest. A hiccup in the mosaic of forest smells caught his nose. His body tensed. After he had been cursed, his senses had been continuously overwhelmed, resulting in a constant headache. It took years for his brain to understand how to sift through the scents, to file the observations efficiently in his mind. The regular flow of scents had been interrupted, like a rock cutting through the flow of water. Something nearby lacked any smell whatsoever.

That's not possible.

A tingling sensation tickled the back of his neck, and the skin tightened as he turned sharply to the left. The scentless thing shifted, moving farther away. Curious, Nathan pursued it, his footsteps silent as he prowled across the forest floor.

The void spot disappeared.

Nathan's forehead creased as he scanned the bark along the trunk of the large pine where he had last detected the anomaly. Though his sharp eyes traced the tendrils of dense shadow, they found nothing but wood. When the scentless spot didn't move again, Nathan huffed and turned the way he had come, tilting his chin as he found his bearings.

As he took a step away from the tree, the wolf under his skin surged forward to fight for dominance, its presence throbbing in Nathan's mind. Nathan bit the inside of his cheeks but couldn't block out the wolf's anger. It urged him backward.

Nathan looked over his shoulder at the pine. "What are you—?"

His heart lurched into his throat as a figure in black leapt from the darkness. Nathan locked hands with the attacker and threw them to the ground. A spray of frozen leaves burst into the air from the impact. Nathan's jaw dropped when he registered what had attacked him.

It wasn't a person — it was a shadow, a humanoid creature with no recognizable features except beady, blood-red eyes and a gaping mouth filled with black fangs. The creature's claws dug into the back of Nathan's hand as it snapped at him.

Nathan wrenched one hand free, closing it into a fist he drove into the creature's abdomen. The shadow reverted to a smoky form, and Nathan lost his grip on its other wrist. His hand dropped through the creature's body, slamming into the dense, cold earth as the smoke slipped like a snake from underneath him, slithering across the ground to re-form behind him.

"That's cheating," Nathan snarled as he turned around, mirroring the creature's stance. He tilted his head, looking it up and down. "What are you?"

The shadow's mouth curled into a smile as its body swayed back and forth.

Nathan lunged, one hand outstretched to grab the creature's throat. The monster turned to smoke, but Nathan's heightened vision caught the change quicker this time. He dug his toe into the dirt and pivoted to the right, heat pulsing through his muscles as he attacked again, catching the creature by the throat as it solidified.

With a low growl, Nathan squeezed the shadow, easily pushing himself past human levels of strength. Wisps of smoke tickled his skin as the creature's red eyes widened to the size of golf balls. Moments later, the shadow crumbled into ash that fluttered to the ground.

After glaring at the dirt until he was sure the creature was dead, Nathan rolled his shoulders and lifted his chin to the sky. As adrenaline sizzled through his blood, a victorious howl instinctively poured from his lips, a warning to anyone else who might challenge him. Feeling the wolf surging to the surface, Nathan cut off the howl and swallowed its remains.

I'm in charge, he reminded the wolf bitterly.

Movement in Nathan's peripheral vision caught his attention. Crouching low, he spotted three more shadows standing behind him. Before he could move, the incorporeal creatures swarmed him, engulfing him in darkness. Invisible hands struck him from all directions, their claws raking across his skin and drawing thin lines of blood. Nathan's fingers shifted into claws, and he swung back wildly but was unable to hit anything solid. Blood pounded in his ears, mixing with the low hissing from the creatures.

Nathan stumbled down a slope, unable to tell where he was putting his feet as the shadow creatures overwhelmed his senses. The snow and twigs crunched beneath his heels until his feet hit pavement. The clouds of darkness dissipated into the air with a lingering snicker, leaving Nathan swatting at empty air.

"Come back and fight!" he demanded, unspent energy coursing through his body.

Screeching tires answered him. Nathan turned sharply to see a black truck riding its brakes toward him. He jumped back at the same time the truck groaned to a halt.

There was just enough time for him to shove his clawed hands behind his back before the passenger door of the truck opened and a young woman popped her head out above the door.

"Are you alright?" she asked. Her long blonde ponytail settled down her back as her bright green eyes watched him with tense concern.

He located her scent. It was soft, like the smell of rain with a hint of something floral, but an unrecognizable layer was woven through it. It had a … texture, like tiny bubbles in a fizzy drink, which Nathan had never experienced before.

"Yeah, sorry," Nathan replied, holding up his hands defensively once his fingers had shifted back to normal. "I wasn't paying attention."

The woman eyed him with the same apprehension he felt toward her. "What are you doing out here?"

"Running." He knew it was strange to see someone running in a t-shirt and shorts at this time of year, and he didn't see the point in lying. "Long-distance training." He tried to sound nonchalant even though he couldn't pull off harmless if he wanted to. At six feet four, with toned muscles, Nathan often made humans nervous.

The woman turned to the man in the driver's seat. Through the glass, Nathan saw broad shoulders, curly dark hair, and brown skin. Nathan's heightened hearing picked up the man's deep voice as he asked, "What do you think?"

The woman shushed him before he finished. "He's fine." When she turned to Nathan, he was surprised to see her scrutiny soften. "Have a good run." She slipped back into the cab of the truck.

Nathan moved to the side of the road, scrunching his forehead as he watched the truck drive off. *Did she know what I was?* He discarded the thought a second later. Humans were ignorant of the existence of werewolves, which suited him fine. The last thing he wanted was to find himself the focus of an angry, pitchfork-carrying mob.

Looking back at the trees, Nathan knew he was lost. Cheeks burning, he scowled as the wolf chuffed mockingly in the back of his mind. Being lost wasn't a big deal for a werewolf—he could follow his own scent back to the den—and he felt silly for having the thought.

He lifted his nose to the breeze wafting down the mountain, searching for any hint of the shadows' lack of scent. Though he knew other magical creatures probably existed, he had never encountered any. Especially nothing like that.

The sound of a man grunting in the distance caused the back of Nathan's neck to prickle. The snowflakes seemed to still as an unsettling calmness filled the air. There was a pause—like the split second between an inhale and exhale.

When the silence passed without consequence, Nathan let out a strained exhale and turned away from the direction the sound had come from. He must have imagined it; even the most avid hikers didn't come into this dense part of the woods. *Stupid.* Muscles bunching, he bent his knees to launch himself into another sprint up the incline.

A scream split the air.

CHAPTER 2

Nathan

The scream's vibration bounced off the trees and rippled across Nathan's skin as it died away. He sprinted toward the source.

As Nathan got closer, he picked up the strained sound of heavy breathing, quickly drowned out by a loud groan. "Get up! We don't got time to waste," a gruff male voice snapped.

Slowing his pace, Nathan kept his body low to the ground and prowled nearer. He crawled onto a large boulder looking down on a stretch of flattened terrain. The elevation was easy to tread, but the fallen trees and dense bush would be challenging for any human.

Nathan flattened himself against the rock as the sounds of footsteps closed in.

A girl stumbled through the thicket of trees, her movements clumsy and desperate. She stopped at the base of the rock, using it to steady herself as she readjusted her glasses with a shaking hand, and glanced back over her shoulder. The scent of paper and honey wafted after her, partially masked by salty sweat and body odour—the scent of fear.

Tilting his head curiously, Nathan frowned at the state of her gear. The seams of her purple winter jacket were coming loose, and the toes of her brown hiking boots were so scuffed they had gone white. She was tiny among the towering trees; with a curvy, stout frame, she couldn't be taller than five feet four.

She must be freezing.

Two men stomped through the bush after her. Both wore thick winter jackets, dirty jeans, and steel-toed boots. The shorter of the two, ghostly pale with bushy eyebrows, crossed his arms while his bearded, olive-skinned friend stomped toward the girl.

"The sooner you get us to the treasure, the sooner you'll be rid of us," Beardy said, his words spraying spittle onto his beard. He waggled a small paper notebook as the girl, light-brown curls falling in front of her face, turned to face them. "Stop wasting our time with excuses."

She flinched as he smacked her with the notebook and pressed it into her collarbone until she grabbed it. Holding the book protectively against her chest, she glared at the men with revulsion. "I told you, I don't know—"

"Shut up!" A crack split the air as the bearded man struck her cheek with the back of his hand. Her body keeled to the left, thrown off balance, and she fell awkwardly onto her knees.

"You're the one who wrote the thing, so stop complaining and start leading."

She sniffed loudly, readjusted her glasses, and glared up at the men. "No!"

Nathan joined the two men in flinching at her firm tone. She wiped her nose with the back of her fist and got to her feet.

"I-I am tired and c-cold and have told you *multiple times* this endeavour is useless. This is *one* clue, and it doesn't tell us *how* to get there!" She waved the notebook at them. "You have no supplies, no provisions, and no basic common sense. I demand you take me back. Now."

Nathan grimaced. While he was impressed by her bravado, the shaking in her voice diminished her credibility. She was about as scary as a mouse.

The thugs glanced at each other briefly. Beardy smiled as he faced the girl. "We only get paid when we find the treasure, so I don't care how long it takes or how many bones you break getting there." He approached slowly, and the girl's shoulders crept toward her ears as she curled inward.

"Matter'a fact," he continued as his smile shifted into a sneer, "we could break you right now and get it over with.

Maybe that'd stop your complaining, hmm? I could start with your fingers. You don't need those anyway."

The girl backpedalled, sending sprays of soggy snow in all directions. "I'll scream again!"

He barked a rough laugh. "And who'll hear you? We're in the middle of nowhere. There's a lot we could do to you all the way out here."

Nathan had heard enough. Rising into a crouch on the boulder, he launched forward and landed in a squat between the thug and the girl. Both yelped in alarm, the girl falling to the ground.

The bearded man jumped back, raising his fists and scowling at Nathan. "Who the hell are you?"

Nathan glowered as he rose to his full height. Beardy's eyes bulged as he craned his neck to meet Nathan's gaze.

"Leave, or I'll break more than your fingers." This was one of those rare occasions when Nathan and the wolf were on the same page — these pieces of dirt had to go.

Beardy glanced back at Bushy-brows, who shrugged in reply. He didn't offer any assistance.

The bearded man put his hands on his hips. "This is none of your business. Keep walking and you won't get hurt."

"No."

The man sputtered, shook his head, and shifted into a fighting stance. "You asked for it." He charged, fists raised.

Nathan blocked the attack with his left hand and countered with a right cross. Despite pulling back his strength, the smack of his fist hitting the man's cheek resonated up to the canopy.

Stumbling, the thug cradled his cheek as he stared at Nathan in shock. With a guttural yell, he charged again, this time aiming to tackle Nathan around the waist. After waiting until the last moment, Nathan used his superior speed to step out of the way, and he grabbed the man by the collar before he could barrel into the girl on the ground. Nathan spun and tossed the bearded man at his bushy-browed friend; they fell to the ground in a tangle of limbs and groans.

"Last chance," Nathan warned, crossing his arms.

Bushy-brows leapt to his feet and, with his fists raised like a boxer's, inched forward.

Upper lip twitching, a low snarl rumbled up Nathan's throat. He held still, waiting until his prey was within reach. Then he reached out like a viper, grabbed one of Bushy-brow's hands, and twisted it violently to the side with a loud crack. The man fell to the ground, wailing in agony as he held his injured wrist.

The bearded man's brow glistened with sweat. All it took was a narrow-eyed glare from Nathan, and he was quick to haul his companion to his feet and guide him back through the forest the way they had come. They shouted threats as they hustled away.

With a deep exhale that fogged the air, Nathan eased the tension in his shoulders. The wolf was surprisingly quiet, satisfied by the brief adrenaline rush. When he turned to deal with the girl, he saw she had dropped the notebook. Scooping it up, Nathan frowned at the red paperback. Slightly bigger than a deck of cards and only a quarter as thick, it was an unremarkable thing to be fighting over. Slipping the notebook into the pocket of his shorts, Nathan focused on the girl.

She huddled at the base of a tree a metre or so away, the root system creating a protective cage around her.

Smart. "You okay?"

She replied with a weak whimper but didn't move. He frowned and stepped closer. Watching him through slitted eyes, she cowered deeper into her hiding spot. The reaction sent a spike of pain through Nathan's heart.

"I'm not gonna attack you or anything," he said, holding his hands up defensively. Her body wouldn't stop shaking. "You, um … you gonna be okay to get out of here?"

She grimaced, tucking her chin close to her chest. The dark brown frames of her glasses were a startling contrast against her skin, which had turned pale from the cold.

"Hey." Ignoring her fearful quivering, Nathan crouched beside her. Up close, the girl was younger than he initially thought. She couldn't be older than sixteen. Her soft chin and the freckles across her cheeks reminded him of his own. The scent of paper and honey was even more prevalent. The eerily familiar smell shoved into his nostrils like it was trying to remind him of something.

Hesitantly, he stretched out a hand. "Come on," he urged her. "I'll get you outta the cold."

Finally, she peered up at him. Her glasses slipped down her nose as her warm hazel eyes pinned him with a fearful, confused look.

The air rushed out of Nathan's lungs, and his skin iced over. He struggled to inhale, fighting against the shock that struck his chest like a freight train. As his legs lost the strength to hold him up, gravity pulled him to his knees.

For the first time in seven years, the wolf inside of him was silent. It had never met this girl face-to-face because, when Nathan had been cursed at the age of twelve, he had abandoned her.

His little sister Abigail was lying half-frozen in front of him.

Before he could escape, she grabbed his extended hand. He gasped, his muscles locking into place. Her chin dipped, but her grip stayed strong.

It can't be her.

The wolf barked loudly, snapping Nathan's attention back into focus. Neither half of him could be sure it was really Abigail, but she could die if he left her in the woods. It was too far to town; in her condition, it would be dangerous to keep her outside much longer. The closest place for her to warm up was his den.

Cursing to himself, he squeezed her hand and pulled her away from the tree's protective roots. Her head lolled, eyebrows trembling as she struggled to keep her eyes open.

"Come on, get up," Nathan said curtly, his voice like sandpaper scraping his throat. He turned around and hiked her onto his back. *It's not her,* he repeated as he gripped her thighs to shift her higher.

"You're gonna have to hold on. Loop your hands — not there!" He gagged as she wrapped her arms around his neck with surprising strength. He grabbed one of her wrists to free himself from her vise-like grip.

"Loop this one under my arm," he suggested so her arms would cross his torso and not his windpipe.

"D-d-don't growl at me," she mumbled, her words slurring, but she did as she was told. Her knuckles dug into his sternum as she held on tight, but the pressure loosened as she was jostled on his back while he hiked. Her expression altered between peaceful and tightly scrunched, as if trying to hold onto consciousness. Her cracked lips were turning blue.

How long did they make you hike? A low, burning heat ignited in Nathan's gut. If he ran into those thugs again, they wouldn't be walking away.

Silently praying she would keep her eyes closed, Nathan ran through the woods as fast as he dared. Her weight was insignificant; he could have been carrying a ghost. The girl needed help, and he would do what little he could to provide it … or the Abby he remembered would never forgive him.

CHAPTER 3

Nathan

Nathan charged into the front room of his den, skidding on the smooth stone floor. Sweat trickled down the long strands of his hair and into his eyes, but he knew his way around without sight, and desperation kept him moving. The girl had lost her grip halfway through the run, forcing him to cradle her in his arms; his whole body buzzed with panic.

The den was split into two sections. The front entrance was a wide, stout cave about six metres deep that then narrowed into a smaller tunnel leading to a hidden entrance on the other side of the mountain. To the right of the foyer was an archway that led to the large circular room he used as his living space. It was a spacious room because Nathan didn't have much to fill it. All he owned was a duffel bag of clothes. He'd added a small cooler for food and a ratty old mattress with cheap sheets he picked up at a yard sale in town.

Kneeling awkwardly, Nathan lowered the girl onto the bed as gently as he could. Her face relaxed a fraction.

Carefully, he removed her soaked jacket and set it on the end of the bed. Then he wrestled the sheets out from underneath her limp body and piled them up until only her head stuck out from the small mountain of fabric. Her limp curls were splayed out like a fan on his lone pillow.

Nathan placed her glasses next to her head, triple-checked that she was still breathing, and slumped onto the floor with a heavy sigh. *What were you thinking?* He ran a hand through his hair, shaking out the snowflakes that clung to the strands. He watched the sheets rise and fall with her breath, his foot twitching impatiently.

The wolf's instinctual curiosity was keenly focused on the girl. Even though it was a part of Nathan and shared his memories, the wolf couldn't seem to connect with her image. The longer Nathan stared at her, the more he saw his sister. She still had the small nose that used to crinkle when she was frustrated. Her high-pitched, bouncy laugh echoed softly in his mind. He had loved pushing her on the swings in the backyard until she laughed so hard she nearly fell off. Only two years apart, they always had each other for company. Their father would watch them, arms firmly crossed but a smile slipping through, while their mother brought them snacks.

"No!" Nathan growled. He rubbed his face furiously and then slapped his cheeks to match the sharp pain in his heart.

This can't be her.

Being in the same room made it impossible to ignore the resurfacing memories of his past, so Nathan pushed up to standing and slipped into the front hall. The large oval mouth of the cave looked out on a sea of tree trunks with bark darkened from the ever-present dampness of the British Columbia autumn. He often spent hours sitting at the entrance of the cave, watching and listening to the forest. When he could focus, Nathan could be still for hours. Watching the subtle bustle of the woods was better than spending time with his memories.

The chill in the fresh air soothed the ache in Nathan's chest. With a heavy sigh, he leaned against the wall next to the entrance with the toes of his old sneakers sticking out over the ledge and shoved his hands into his pockets.

Oh.

He pulled out the notebook, damp but otherwise unharmed. Wrinkling his brow, he flipped open to the middle. The scribbled cursive made it difficult to make out individual letters, but what he could identify didn't make any sense. He suspected the contents were written in a different language, but then again, he wasn't confident in his English skills.

It seemed like a strange thing to kidnap a girl over, but if the thugs were hunting for treasure, Nathan wasn't all that surprised. People were easily motivated to do stupid things if money was involved.

A fresh wind made him shiver, sending a needle-like sensation rippling down his spine. His cold tolerance was strong, but wet clothes could still be dangerous in winter conditions. A quick scan of the floor revealed a pair of jeans he had discarded earlier. Giving them a quick sniff and satisfied they didn't overtly smell, he shed his shorts. The jeans were cotton-soft from years of use. He swapped out his sweat-soaked shirt for a black crewneck t-shirt.

As he transferred the notebook to the back pocket of his jeans, he wondered how long it had been since he last washed his clothes. They got rinsed regularly, usually in the small waterfall that ran next to the cave, but he couldn't remember his last proper bath. The wolf protested this stupid human thought and Nathan shook his head.

He stiffened at a rustling from the side room. The sheets shifted again. On silent feet, he inched back to the bedroom. His jaw was tight as he checked on the girl.

She rolled to her side, a groan rising into the air.

Crouching next to her, his long arms resting on his knees, Nathan tilted his head curiously. The wolf urged him closer, but Nathan held the desire at bay.

The girl's eyebrows pulled together, and her eyelids fluttered. Nathan's throat tightened, and he leaned toward the exit. Before he could run, the girl's eyes flickered open. She groaned again, her body shifting beneath the blankets as she looked up first, then to the room. Her breath caught on the inhale, and her eyes widened as she spotted Nathan.

Panic erased any words he might have spoken. He expected her to be scared, but he wasn't prepared for her scream.

The sound knocked him onto his back, and his hands flew up to cover his ears against the onslaught. Pain like a thousand stinging hornets ripped through his inner ears. He cursed, unable to gauge his own volume. Sensitive wolf hearing was not designed to take a scream at such close range.

Black spots speckled his vision as he glared at the girl. She was sitting up and her lips were moving, but he couldn't hear her through the ringing in his ears.

"Speak softly," he ordered through gritted teeth, knowing his accelerated healing would dull the pain soon.

Her forehead wrinkled in an expression of fear and suspicion as she considered him.

Tentatively, Nathan lowered his hands from his ears. "That was a hell of a scream."

The girl patted the sheets frantically until she found her glasses and hurriedly put them on. "Wh-who are you?"

His name caught in his throat, and he said the first thing that came to mind. "John."

Narrowing her eyes, the girl pressed her back into the cave wall and pulled her knees into her chest. "Where are we? *John*."

"A cave in the mountains," he replied curtly, regaining some composure. "I found you in the woods getting attacked by some idiots and brought you back here to dry off." He crossed his arms, watching her closely. "Do you remember any of that?"

Her gaze drifting around the den. "It's a bit foggy, but I do remember someone chasing away those men. Thank you." Despite the gratitude, her suspicion clearly hadn't faded. "What were you doing in the woods?"

"None of your business."

She scowled. "Then how do I know you aren't working for them?"

That was a fair question. Nathan shrugged. "You don't."

When he didn't offer more, she gave up on her glaring. "Well, thank you, I guess." She looked around the room again. "I'm afraid to think what they would have done if you hadn't shown up."

Puffing up his chest slightly, Nathan scratched his jaw as he looked anywhere but the bed. "You're welcome. Why were you hanging out with them anyway?"

She scoffed loudly. "It wasn't by choice. They jumped me on my way to school this morning. It feels like I've been hiking for hours." She straightened her legs and reached for her toes in a brief stretch.

"Because of this, right?" He pulled out the notebook and tossed it to her. She fumbled before snatching it with a firm grip.

"This stupid thing," she grumbled as she shook the notebook with both hands.

"*What* is it?" Nathan asked, watching her skeptically.

Her cheeks flushed a rosy pink against her fawn-toned skin. Even her freckles had brightened now that she had warmed up. "They're research notes," she said, her voice softening as she stared thoughtfully at the book. "I study mythology and history at the university. Sometimes I investigate mythical treasures, but it's just for fun." She shot Nathan a defensive look. "I don't know why those idiots thought any of this was real."

"Well, they seemed pretty convinced. I'm guessing they grabbed you to translate whatever language that is." He gestured at the book.

She let out a surprised chuckle. "It's Latin," she explained. "I use it to take notes to keep up my proficiency. I just wish I knew what they wanted with …" She frowned at the book.

"… 'With'?"

With a polite smile, she shook her head. "It's nothing."

He snorted. "Obviously it's something."

"Well, it's nothing *you* need to concern yourself with," she corrected in a firm tone.

With a huff, Nathan shrugged off the comment. "Fine, then. What are you doing studying in university? Aren't you, like, sixteen?"

She was quick to correct him. "Seventeen. I skipped a grade in high school."

Abigail would be the same age. And skipping a year of high school? Nathan could never compare. When he looked up, she was staring at him. "What?"

"Nothing," she said, diverting her gaze. "You remind me of someone, that's all."

Muscles tightening, Nathan hustled to his feet and headed for the exit, desperate to put some space between him and the girl. "Weird," he muttered. "Come on, I'll drive you back to town."

"Really?" Her hazel eyes brightened as she scrambled to her feet. "You have a car?"

"I've got an old truck down the hill. Takes about an hour to get to town." Though he wasn't keen on being trapped in a car with the haunting scent of this girl who so frighteningly resembled his sister.

"You live up here all the time?"

He thought he heard judgment in her tone. "Yeah, so?"

To his surprise, she nodded with understanding. "Are you the hermit people've been telling me about?"

Nathan's eyebrows pulled together as he glanced at her from the corner of his eye. "Hermit?"

"Sorry," she said quickly, blushing. "Not in a bad way. I just moved here for school, and my place is shabby. The neighbours were saying I could hire the hermit to help fix it up. Sounds like you do odd jobs and stuff?"

Both Nathan and the wolf bristled. "Yeah." He rubbed his jaw. Last week, he had traded a few hours of yard work for a haircut and shave when his beard had grown matted and irritating. He hadn't known he had a reputation, though. "When I need cash." *And a proper meal.* Even being part-wolf, he could only survive on wild game for so long.

"Thank you. I'd appreciate the ride." She grabbed her jacket and cringed as she slipped one arm into it. The water-soaked fabric squished faintly. Reluctantly, she slid her other arm in, but she left the coat open.

"Great," Nathan said. "Let's go."

She hurried after him, her feet scuffing dirt across the cave floor. "Don't you want a jacket?" She stopped, pressing her hand against the wall for support.

Nathan stumbled to an awkward stop. "Oh, yeah." They awkwardly shuffled around each other with a mumbled chorus of *excuse me* and *sorry*. He grabbed a faded red crewneck sweater from a pile of clothes next to the bed and threw it on.

"Alright, let's go," he said gruffly, ignoring her creased brow and concerned eyes as he pushed past her and took the lead through the skinny back tunnel.

"Miranda."

He froze, an icy chill rushing across his skin. "Huh?"

"My name is Miranda," she explained, her voice closer to his back. "I should have introduced myself sooner."

He clenched his hands, digging his nails into the rough skin of his palms. *It's not her.* He shouldn't be surprised. It had been seven years since he had last seen Abigail, and they had been children. Their hometown was a country away. There was no way the girl could have been her.

"John?" Her hand pressed gently into his back.

Her touch sent a shock of electricity through him. Nathan jumped out of her reach and marched toward the rear exit of his cave. His throat felt like it was coated in sandpaper as he spoke. "Let's get going."

CHAPTER 4

Nathan

Nathan's stomach churned with regret as they stepped out onto a sheer ledge and immersed themselves in the sharp chill of the forest. The foliage was thicker on this side of the low peak, creating the perfect cover for the back entrance to his den. It was also a steep climb down and, while easy for his long legs and superhuman strength, would be a challenge for Miranda.

The truck was hidden in a small alcove off the side of an abandoned logging road that snaked through the dense wood. Normally, getting down to the car would take him a few seconds.

A headache knocked on his temples as he glanced warily at Miranda. She eyed the drop with her lips pulled into a thin line. Her gaze shifted across the landscape, clearly trying to plan her route down.

He wouldn't have worried about letting her figure it out for herself, but the smell of honey and paper surrounded him like a cage. He couldn't escape the old memories it dredged up of Abigail's bubbling laughter, of the wall of books she had in her tiny square bedroom, of how angry she had been when he snuck in to make a fort with them.

Turning his back, Nathan bent his knees and stretched his arms to catch her. "Get on my back."

"What?" She retreated a step, stumbling on a tree root and grabbing onto a nearby branch to stop herself from falling.

Nathan shook his head. "Ab—" He bit the inside of his cheek before he finished the word and tried again. "Miranda." The name tasted oddly sour in his mouth. "There is no way you can make it down there."

Her confusion turned into a glower. "I am perfectly capable of getting down myself."

Nathan met her glare for glare. "I got you up here, I can get you down." He turned around again, bending lower so she wouldn't have to jump far. "Now get on."

When she stubbornly refused, Nathan turned around to face her. "Fine."

Her eyes went wide as he reached for her, and she held out her hand in a feeble attempt to stop him. "Don't you dare."

Ignoring her, Nathan grabbed her hand and pulled her onto his shoulder, cringing at her cry of alarm. Once he had a good hold on her, he began climbing down the hill. The fists smacking his back were nothing more than light taps, and her weight was easy for him to carry. He ignored her impressive vocabulary of curse words until eventually she used them all up.

When they got to the road, Nathan put her down firmly on her feet. Turning away to avoid her furious glare, he unlocked the truck and slipped inside, leaning across the cracked leather bench to unlock her door.

With her nose scrunched, Miranda climbed into the truck. She clipped her seatbelt with a huff and stared intently at the front windshield.

Nathan tried to apply the same concentration to his driving, but it was impossible when her presence was drowning him. Even cracking the windows open did nothing. Parasitic guilt ate away at his insides as he wondered what his Abigail would think of him had it been her.

"Are you alright?" Miranda asked after half an hour of driving and silence.

He grunted, trying to clear the lump of emotion from his throat.

"You look like you want to kill someone," she added quietly.

Shit. He didn't want to scare her. "You don't get outside much, huh?" he asked curtly, gesturing at the state of her jacket.

She uttered a sharp *humph*, pushing up her glasses. "I go hiking regularly," she corrected. Her tone made him wince.

"Sorry." he mumbled. "Your gear is so bad, I figured—"

"I'm a poor student. It's not like I can get new stuff every year."

Think before you speak, idiot. "Why go to school in Prince George?"

Miranda leaned her elbow into the car door and propped her chin on her fist. "I like small towns. I grew up in a tiny town in the States," she explained. All the air rushed out of Nathan's lungs. "When I got the scholarship to come up here, it felt like a good fit. Sounds cheesy, huh?"

"No," he said hoarsely. He could sense her watching him, searching his face for something.

"Why are you living in the mountains?"

"It's quiet." Back when he had been on the run, he'd regularly slept in the woods. He'd always preferred it to sleeping under bridges or in alleys as he passed through cities on his way north. When he settled in the cave, the stillness of being in one place had fuelled his restless curiosity, leading him to explore the town. Because of his physique, it hadn't been hard to pick up labour, and when Nathan realized he could earn money that way, he afforded himself some small human comforts. He even managed to trade in a few months of work for the beat-up old truck so regular work and human food would be more accessible.

He paused, risking a glance at her. She was still staring at him. He wished she would stop. "Are you gonna throw away the notebook? Those guys'll probably come after you again if you still have it."

She frowned, and her gaze finally pulled away. "If they come again, I'll be ready," she said firmly, turning the notebook over in her hands. The faint scent of sweat soon filled the cab of the truck, followed by the drumming of her quickening heartbeat.

"If it's just a bunch of notes, why hold onto it?"

"They're important!" Catching her composure, she settled back into the seat. "I like trying to prove myths are real, but it's just for personal interest. I never thought anyone would be convinced the riddles held any validity." She shook her head, her curls swishing across her jacket. "I'm not going to throw away all the effort I've put into this because some people think they can abuse my hard work."

"You're pretty brave," Nathan conceded. He'd expected her to be more shaken by the assault, though perhaps she was hiding her fear behind a thick skin. When her eyebrows shot up in surprise, he added, "Or stupid. You should go to the police."

Miranda scoffed. "They wouldn't take me seriously. I mean, maybe with the kidnapping, and I'll tell campus security, but ultimately those thugs are on a wild goose chase." She sighed heavily. "I've never had good experiences with the police. It's a waste of time to involve them."

"You're still being stupid."

With a huff, she tilted her chin up. "I don't need your opinion."

"Doesn't make it wrong."

"I don't care what you think."

"Fine."

"Fine."

Anger sizzled across his skin. Not at her, but at the stupid ideas she had in her head. *Whatever, it's not like you owe her anything.* "What *is* this treasure they're after?"

"It doesn't matter. It doesn't exist. As soon as they realize that, they'll come to their senses."

"Men like that have no senses," Nathan said with a condescending laugh. "They follow the money, and if the money says 'find the golden goose,' then they'll search for Atlantis trying to capture it."

"The golden goose has nothing to do with Atlantis."

Nathan rolled his eyes. "My point is guys like that will go after any ridiculous treasure if it means getting paid." He was about to continue when her heart rate picked up. "Unless you believe in this treasure too?"

She flinched and gave him an appalled look. "Not in the slightest," she assured him. "The Lupatus Stone is as real as Excalibur."

"The Lupatus Stone?" He had the sense he should know that word, but couldn't place where he'd heard it before.

"It's a mythical talisman supposedly created by the first werewolf of King Arthur's reign. I found a lead that suggested the Stone might be hidden in these very mountains, but it's all theoretical." She let out a loud sigh. "Who knows where those thugs got the idea."

She sounded convincing enough, but her fidgeting could be felt through the seat.

"Well, try not to get yourself killed." He wasn't sure how time had passed so quickly, but they were already in Prince George. At Miranda's instruction, he pulled off the main road and onto a residential street.

Just a few more blocks.

They rolled into the lane belonging to a row of skinny, identical townhouses. She pointed him to a specific unit midway down the row.

"This is me," she said quietly.

Nathan shut off the engine, keeping his hands on the wheel.

Miranda didn't move right away. She stared out the window in silence, the time dragging on around them until Nathan was sure even her human hearing must be able to pick up the sound of his heart pounding. Finally, she offered him a weak smile. "Take care of yourself."

Nodding robotically, Nathan kept his gaze on the road. "You too." The words came out in a croak.

She slipped out of the car. Nathan flinched as the door clicked shut. Silence crawled down his throat. He finally looked over, just in time to see her curls vanish into the house.

It wasn't her.

His body sank into the seat, a thousand-kilogram weight pressing into his chest. *Wasn't that what I wanted?*

Remorse dug its claws into his heart. He'd been seeing a ghost; his sanity was finally cracking. It had only been a matter of time. The nightmares had bled into his conscious mind, making him see things that weren't there. Even the wolf was silent, baffled by the conflicting emotions.

Nathan leaned his forehead against the wheel and sucked in a desperate breath as the ghostly impression of paper-thin hospital sheets pressed into his skin. Whispers of soft voices wafted through the air, but he couldn't picture the faces they belonged to. Memories of the time before his first transformation were blurred, as if coated in a thin film that kept them out of focus.

The memory of that first night's pain, however, never faded.

Every muscle in his body clenched as he remembered writhing, clawing at his skin and wishing he could rip it off. He'd felt like hundreds of sharp-taloned bugs were crawling under his skin. The sound of his joints popping sporadically interrupted the blood pounding in his ears and made him flinch every time.

The taste of salt on his tongue brought Nathan back to the present. He sat up and scrubbed the tears away with the back of his hand, sniffling aggressively. The *what-ifs* were what hurt the most. What if he'd listened to his mother when she told him to stop playing in the woods past curfew? What if he'd been able to outrun the werewolf who cursed him?

What if he'd died that night?

After starting the car with stiff movements, Nathan pulled away from the curb, aimlessly moving forward. The wolf fought against the anguish, making Nathan's skin tighten. While it didn't understand the guilt about Abigail, it felt the same rage toward the werewolf who had cursed Nathan, the same crippling fear of those silver-blue eyes in the darkness. The wolf's insistent snarling slipped from Nathan's lips, filling the truck, demanding he let it take over.

He slammed on the brakes and pounded the wheel with his fists. "Why won't you shut up?"

A car honked behind him, and with a jerk Nathan pulled the truck to the shoulder, letting the other vehicle pass. In his rear-view mirror, he noticed a car pulling up in front of Miranda's place. Three men got out of the truck and headed toward the townhouse.

He threw the truck into park and hopped out of the cab in time to see them disappear through the side gate. Gritting his teeth, Nathan tossed the keys onto the seat and stalked toward the townhouse.

As he got close, the lingering smell of the men's body odour hit his nose. Nathan curled his upper lip. Two of the scents were familiar—likely the same thugs he'd dealt with earlier. This time, Nathan didn't question the instincts that told him to follow the men.

CHAPTER 5

Nathan

The handle to the back door lay in pieces on the dewy grass. Nathan slipped silently into the townhouse, and his muscles cramped immediately. *How can anyone live in this box?* The open living and dining room was only as wide as he was tall.

An old leather two-seater couch with a rectangular wooden coffee table and a similar square dining table with four simple chairs were the only furniture. The musky scent of the men tainted the softer feminine smell lingering in the air. With the wolf's help, a calm focus settled Nathan's frayed nerves, just as it did when he was hunting. He shifted deeper into the house, searching for his prey.

Someone's low muttering came from the kitchen. He hesitated, assessing how many people were present, before inching to the edge of the archway. With a quick glance to establish the intruder's position, Nathan lunged.

The bearded man who had kidnapped Miranda was rummaging through the kitchen. *Looking for the notebook?*

Nathan hit him in the back of the head, hard. Beardy let out a surprised gasp before falling to the floor, unconscious.

After nudging the thug roughly with his foot, and confident he wouldn't be up for a while, Nathan stalked back to the living room to search for the others. Footsteps on the stairs, heading away, drew his attention. *A basement.* Nathan found the door at the back of the living room and followed the sound.

"This is stupid. It's nothing but storage," an unfamiliar man complained, his gruff voice followed by shifting cardboard as he searched through a stack of boxes. His blond hair was tied in a ponytail at the base of his neck and the sweat coating his cream-coloured skin left a potent stench in the air. He filled the basement with curse words, unaware of Nathan's presence at his back.

Nathan lunged forward and struck Blondie on the back of the head, just as he had done with the first, and the man crumpled to the ground.

One more.

A scream rattled down the stairs, coming from the main level of the house.

Nathan's heart spasmed. He sprinted up the stairs in three large steps. "Abigail!" Terror pulsed in his veins. "Abby!" He slid into the kitchen and came to an abrupt halt, nearly tripping on his own feet.

Miranda stood in the middle of the kitchen with a frying plan clutched in her trembling hands. Bushy-brows lay at her feet, sprawled out next to Beardy.

With wide eyes, she spotted Nathan and raised the pan again. Her hair was wet, the tight curls bunched around her shoulders. Her fogged glasses perched crookedly on her nose. She had traded her earlier clothes for dark jeans and a grey, long-sleeved sweater with the scent of laundry detergent still clinging to it.

"What did you call me?"

"What?" Nathan blinked.

The frying pan was still raised, ready to swing. "'Abigail.'" Her voice cracked. "You called me 'Abigail.'"

Heat rushed to his cheeks. "Sorry!" he blurted, raising his hands defensively. "You … you look like someone I used to know. I, uh, I—"

"How could you know that?" Her body trembled as the pitch of her voice rose. Her heart was beating dangerously fast. "That's not possible."

"Miranda," Nathan corrected firmly. He tried to take a step forward, but her grip tightened on the frying pan. He wasn't worried about the improvised weapon; he feared she was going to hurt herself. Her panic was potent in the air, sour and sharp. If she went into shock, he would be helpless. "It was a mistake."

She shook her head furiously. "I haven't used that name in years. Not since I was a kid," she said. "I started using my middle name after ... since then ..."

Finally, she lowered her arms.

Nathan's breathing went shallow and his expression slackened. *Abigail Miranda Duncan.*

She looked like she was about to speak again, and Nathan's shock turned into panic, unprepared to face the truth. He took a step back, waving his hands at her to stop. "Don't. Please don't."

"I thought ... I thought it was just a coincidence that you looked so much like my dad, like what my brother might have looked like by now. But you can't be him. He's dead. They all died in the fire."

The wolf was silent, abandoning him when he most needed its strength. Abigail's breathing was as shallow as his and her brow furrowed as she studied his face.

"His eyes were hazel, like mine. But you know my name. Y-you scowl the same way he did. Your freckles and your hair ..."

The lump in Nathan's throat doubled, making it difficult to speak. A single word escaped his lips, desperate for freedom. "Abby."

Her eyes widened as she whispered, "No." She dropped the frying pan and ignored it as it clattered to the ground. She took a step toward him. Nathan backed away, but he hit the wall and there was nowhere he could run.

"What is your name?" she demanded.

Nathan stammered, shaking his head.

"What is your real name!" Her clenched fists trembled at her sides and her eyes glistened with tears.

Nathan cringed and tried to answer, but his mouth only opened and closed like a dying fish desperate for oxygen.

Abigail let out a shaky exhale, but there was hope in her voice as she said, "Nathan?"

Without his wolf hearing, he would have missed his name. But there it was, the inescapable truth laid out in front of them. Tears pooled along his bottom eyelids, and Abigail choked back a sob.

Nathan whimpered, the words falling short on his tongue.

"Tell me if it's you!"

The voices of doubt and guilt raged inside of him, reminding him how much safer she would be without him. She would see him as a monster if she found out what he was, what had happened the night of the fire that killed their parents and so many others.

The hope in her eyes made all his fears irrelevant.

Nathan nodded. "It's me, Abby. I'm so sorry—" He could barely get the words out.

Abigail ran at him. Instinctively, he opened his arms and she crashed into his torso, hugging him with strength enough to push him into the wall. Warm tears stained his sweater, and he wrapped his arms around her to protect her shaking body. She was the little ten-year-old girl again, and he was as lost and helpless as the day he'd left her behind.

"They told me you were dead!"

Another stab of guilt struck like a knife and twisted in his gut. "I'm sorry, Abby. I never forgot about you. I-I mean—"

"Why?" she shouted, her head still pressed against his chest. Her nails dug into his skin where she gripped his top.

The delirious joy of having his sister back warred with the guilt, painfully squeezing his heart. He squeezed Abigail harder.

Then he heard a rustling near the front door. Clear, articulated footsteps across the sidewalk stopped in front of the house.

Nathan took Abigail by the arms and held her in front of him. "I'll try and explain everything, but right now we have to get out of here. You're in trouble." She glanced back at the kitchen, her jaw dropping when her gaze fell on the two unconscious men lying on the floor.

"Do you have the notebook?" he asked. She nodded and pulled it from the back pocket of her jeans.

"Good." He nodded. "Let's go."

He marched out of the kitchen but stopped when he realized Abigail wasn't following. "Abby," he warned. He reached for her hand, but she recoiled.

"How do I know it's really you? You were supposed to be dead. D-did you fake it? Why are your eyes different?" She pressed a hand to her forehead. "I must be dreaming. This can't be real."

Nathan eyed the men lying on the floor. "I owe you a lot, but—"

"I am *furious* with you and … and I'm confused."

Nathan nodded. "You should be mad at me, but we need to …" The hairs on the back of his neck rose. The wolf barked in alarm, aware that they weren't alone.

"Nathan, I— *Umph!*"

Nathan covered her mouth and put a finger to his lips to signal her to be quiet. Then he listened. There was a whispering outside the house. It sounded like wind, but it was articulated, unlike the sweeping of a natural breeze. The strange sound prickled his skin.

Motioning for Abigail to stay put, Nathan inched over to the window that faced the front yard. Black smoke curled across the grass, moving with a mind of its own. The smoke parted to form three wispy streams that diverged for a moment before fusing back together. It hovered over the lawn but didn't move toward the house. The possessed smoke wasn't nearly as terrifying as the man standing at the end of the walkway.

Nathan's heart thrashed inside his chest as a growl reverberated through his mind.

Silas.

He was tall and lean, standing casually with his hands in the pants pockets of his crisp, black suit. He wore black leather shoes and a dark-red tie. His black hair was shaved along the sides but kept thick across the top, tousled like he had just rolled out of bed, though Nathan would bet every hair had been placed with intention. Though he was five decades older than Nathan, Silas didn't look older than thirty-five. The man's silver-blue eyes shone with anticipation.

Silas caught Nathan's gaze. A white smile stretched across his face; his eyebrows lifted, intrigued; and he gave a small wave. They had crossed paths a few times over the years, but Nathan couldn't think of any reason Silas should be here. Except for—

The Lupatus Stone. Abigail's research.

Nathan clenched his jaw as he stepped away from the window and turned back to Abigail. "Is anyone else home?"

"No. My roommates are away this weekend. They went to see their— *Oh!*" she squeaked when he pushed her back to the living room, toward the back door.

"We have to get out of here. *Now!*" he ordered. Abby was too stunned to resist.

They were steps away from the back door when Nathan noticed the wisps of smoke seeping into the house from under it. Glancing over his shoulder, the same thing was happening at the front, with some pouring in through the cracks in the window as well. The wolf had its hackles up, jaw tight.

"Is there a fire?" Abby asked in alarm.

The unnatural smoke wasn't rising. It crawled across the ground like a snake looking to bite.

Nathan pulled his sister to the wall in the centre of the living room, positioning himself between her and the living smoke. The wolf's frustration at not having a physical threat to fight seeped into Nathan's muscles, making them twitch. He tensed them to keep himself in place.

One trail of smoke slipped into the kitchen while another disappeared down the stairs to the basement. From his position, Nathan could see the legs of the bushy-browed man. The smoke crawled over the man's shoes, up the rest of his body, and then seeped into his skin.

The smoke's whispering stopped, leaving the house full of silence. Nathan's pounding blood echoed in his head.

To his horror, the man's foot twitched. Bubbles rippled across his ankles as if bugs were running under his skin. Then he sat up, and Nathan got a clear look at him.

Abigail gasped, a hand flying up to cover her mouth. Nathan's jaw dropped.

Bushy-brows turned his head mechanically, looking into the living room. From lid to lid, his eyes were covered in inky blackness. Bushy-brows smiled as he pulled himself to his feet, standing with a soldier's straightness as he waited for his friends to join him. Beardy twitched on the ground beside him.

Nathan pushed Abigail as close as he could to the wall, shielding her from the horror he couldn't prevent her from seeing. They jumped as the basement door swung open, hitting the wall with a bang. Blondie stood at the top of the stairs, the same black eyes and creepy smile plastered on his face.

"N-Nathan," Abigail said in a shaky voice. "W-what's happening?"

"So glad you asked."

Silas's eloquent voice came from the front door. Nathan's stomach twisted. Abigail clutched the back of his shirt with trembling hands.

The scent of iron mixed with pungent musk and leather swept up Nathan's nose. His memory was stained with Silas's scent, never to be forgotten.

Leaning against the doorframe, Silas remained infuriatingly at ease. He regarded them with a half-smile. "They have been possessed by demons, sweetheart."

"What are you doing here?" Nathan demanded, his voice deepening, sounding more animal than human.

Silas regarded him nonchalantly. "I wish I could say this was intentional, Nathan, but I'm as surprised as you are. What has it been, three years since we last ran into each other?" He looked Nathan up and down as if he were a stray dog. "I'd say you look awful, but you always did enjoy living in the mud."

"Get out," Nathan said. Instead, Silas stepped inside, and the room shrank.

"You know him?" Abby whispered.

"Indeed, he does," Silas cut in, his smiling growing. "Aren't you going to introduce us, Nathan?"

Nathan bared his teeth, too angry to form words.

Silas rolled his eyes and slid his hands back into his pockets. "Never one for small talk, were you?" He sighed. "There's no need for such hostility, Nathan."

Though he sounded bored, Silas's gaze glittered with a hungry desire Nathan was all too familiar with. Bloodlust oozed from him as potently as his confidence did.

Nathan flashed him a feral smile. "Your lackeys couldn't get the job done, so you hired some demons?"

Silas's forehead creased. "Yes, good help is hard to find." He sized up the demons, and his expression brightened. "But I've contracted with a new business partner. One who is very used to dealing with demons. Apparently, if you find them a weak-willed host, a curse isn't necessary. *And* I don't have to pay them." He shrugged. "It's all business. I wouldn't expect you to understand."

"And what's your side of the deal? Glorified errand boy?" Nathan spat.

Silas's smile held a dangerous edge. "It's a *loan*, Nathan. I get to use demons as my enforcers while I find the Lupatus Stone." He turned his attention to Abigail. "Which this beautiful young lady will be kind enough to locate for me."

Abigail sucked in a sharp inhale. Nathan blocked her line of sight to the werewolf. "She's not going anywhere."

Silas laughed. "There are three demons here. They will fight endlessly until the human's body gives out or you kill their innocent host, which you and I both know you're too weak to accomplish. And your track record against *me* certainly isn't in your favour. What makes you think you're walking out of here alive?"

"Leave him alone!" Abigail shouted, startling Nathan and Silas both.

Silas raised an eyebrow. "Happily, if you agree to come with me and cooperate."

"Abigail, don't move," Nathan ordered. To his surprise, she shoved him from behind.

"I can make my own decisions."

"*Abigail.*"

"You were dead as of ten minutes ago!"

"Well, this makes things interesting," Silas mused.

Nathan glared at Abigail. "He will kill you the moment he's done with you. Or worse."

Silas shook his head, pressing a hand to his heart. "You've always been so resentful, Nathan. It hurts me deeply." His eyebrows lifted as he looked back and forth between the siblings. "But she doesn't know, does she?"

Abigail's brow furrowed. "Know what?"

"Shut up!" Nathan snarled.

Silas's jaw went slack for a moment. He gathered his composure swiftly and returned to smiling. "Fine by me. All I ask is for a front-row seat when your little bubble implodes." The glee in his voice made Nathan's skin crawl.

Silas gestured the demons toward Abigail and Nathan. "Take her alive. Do whatever you want to him."

CHAPTER 6

Nathan

Nathan lunged at the same time as the three demons, crashing into them in the centre of the living room. In a whirlwind of limbs and claws, Nathan managed to knock two of them back before taking a right cross to the jaw from the third. He stumbled, momentarily stunned that the demon had hurt him. Even trapped in human bodies, they were stronger than they had been in the woods.

Nathan quickly returned the favour, striking Beardy in the larynx. Despite the loud wheeze that squeezed from the man's throat, he showed no hint of pain. While he regained his equilibrium, the other two attacked.

Every time Nathan pushed one aside, the other two filled the void. No matter how hard he hit, they kept getting back up. Then one of them got behind him, and before Nathan could react, two clammy hands boxed his ears.

Black dots erupted in Nathan's vision, and a deep ache throbbed against his temples. There was a distant female scream. He pried his eyes open and, through his blurry vision, saw Silas dragging Abigail by the arm toward the front door.

Nathan roared his fury and swung wildly, hitting the demon closest to him with an openly clawed hand. The faint resistance of skin against his fingers did nothing to slow the carnage. The metallic smell of blood bloomed in the air.

As the ringing in his ears receded, Nathan saw Blondie on his back at his feet, gasping. He hadn't meant to kill him, but he would deal with that later.

I can't lose her again.

Black smoke rose from the man on the ground. Blondie's eyes widened as the darkness melted away to reveal his blue irises again. The expression of fear was frozen on his face as Nathan stepped over the body and tackled another demon on his way to the front door, grabbing his opponent's shirt to pull him toward the ground. The final demon jumped on Nathan's back and wrapped his arms around his neck.

Gagging, Nathan released his grip on the demon's shirt, clawing at it with one hand while digging his claws into the forearm around his neck with the other. Nathan pitched his weight backward, running the demon on his back into the wall. There was a loud crunch, and the demon released Nathan's neck.

Turning for the door, Nathan made it two steps before the other demon dived across the ground and tangled itself in Nathan's feet. Outside, a car started, muffling Abigail's cries.

Backhanding the demon behind him before it could strangle him again, while simultaneously trying to stomp on the one clutching his ankles, Nathan's mind raced for a way out of the scramble. His skin burned as the wolf surged forward, urging Nathan to let it take over. Desperate for the strength, Nathan tore off his shirt and sweater in one motion as he prepared to shift.

Before he could take on his wolf form, a golden light burst through the door. It swept across the room in a powerful wave, and a surge of energy coursed through Nathan as if someone had filled his insides with helium. The force threw him back. The drywall cracked as he struck it, and his knees made a similar sound as he landed awkwardly on the floorboards.

Though the golden light blinded him, shrill, inhuman demon screams vibrated across the room.

Nathan rubbed his eyes, blinking furiously. When he sniffed the air, he sensed two new figures entering the house.

"That worked fine," a man with a deep voice said. "I don't see what you were worried about."

"I told you, I haven't tried exorcism magic in the field before," a woman scoffed, her tone light.

Nathan got to his feet cautiously, trying his best not to appear at a disadvantage as he angled his body toward their voices.

"Isn't that the werewolf from before?" the woman asked.

Nathan went rigid. Taking another whiff of the air, he recognized the floral scent with its strange, sparkling texture.

The man smelled of cedar and musk, with a hint of the concrete that usually came from city living. He must have been the driver.

"Hello again," she said.

Nathan squinted through the fading gold as the strangers' tense expressions came into focus. The woman's gaze was unwavering as she stared at him with big, green eyes; she looked unimpressed. Nathan guessed he could get past her skinny body easily. The man behind her could put up more resistance, given the linebacker physique emphasized by his crossed arms. His impassive expression gave Nathan no clue how much of a fight he might put up.

"On the highway," the woman added into the silence.

Nathan snarled.

The woman exhaled, slow and controlled. "We're not here to fight you," she assured him. "My name is Jessica. This is Damien. We were following the demons."

Or they were also working with Silas and were here to kill him.

"What is your name?"

Now he could make out the stitching of her grey zippered jacket and pick up on the faded threading of the man's jeans. Nathan loaded like a spring and launched himself forward.

Jessica reacted faster than he'd expected, jumping out of the way like she'd anticipated his attack. Damien moved to intercept him, despite Jessica shouting at him not to.

His mistake.

Nathan tried to barrel through him, but Damien grabbed him under the arms and twisted their bodies. Nathan fell to the ground with Damien on his back. Damien's free hand grabbed Nathan's wrist and twisted it behind his back.

Stunned that a human tackled him to the ground, it took Nathan a minute to register what had happened and get his breathing back under control.

Damien tightened his grip. "Calm down."

Nathan could no longer hear the car outside, which meant Silas had already gotten away. Using his full werewolf strength, Nathan pushed off the ground with his free hand and fell backward on top of Damien. The man groaned and loosened his grip, allowing Nathan to pull away easily.

He was about to drive his claws into the man's throat when his body suddenly froze.

Looking out of the corner of his eye, Nathan spotted Jessica with her hands wide in front of her and feet balanced in a fighting stance. She lifted her hands and

Nathan's body rose into the air. He tried to struggle, but his muscles were locked in place.

When she lowered her hands again, Nathan was also lowered to the ground — away from Damien, who scrambled back to his feet.

"Let's try this again," Jessica said, positioning herself directly in front of Nathan. "You're going to tell me what I want to know, and then we'll let you go. Understood?"

Nathan tried to thrash, but Jessica didn't even blink. Her calmness surprised him. He swallowed the lump in his throat, managing to find his voice. "Why should I?"

"Because I saved you from the demons."

Maybe they're not here to kill me? "I had it handled."

"Not from where I was standing." Her fingers flexed and the magic tightened around his muscles, compressing his body.

Was she trying to piss him off more? "What are you, some kind of witch?"

"Give the man a prize," Damien muttered, rubbing the back of his head. Nathan bared his teeth, but Damien wasn't riled.

"Just tell us your name," Jessica said, raising her voice.

Nathan growled.

"Or at least put a shirt on," Damien suggested.

"I'm going to gut you," Nathan snapped.

"Lower the testosterone, boys." Jessica rolled her eyes. "Now, look …" She glared at him expectantly, the magic tightening a fraction more, as if squeezing him in an invisible fist.

"Nathan," he admitted reluctantly.

"Nathan," she said with a curt nod. "We are trying to find the individual summoning the demons. Did you see a man with tan skin, black hair, and a creepy smile? Speaking with a Spanish accent?"

Nathan raised an eyebrow. Creepy smile and black hair, yes. Silas had bronze skin, but he didn't have an accent.

"I don't know who summoned the demons," Nathan said. "But they were working for a werewolf."

"A werewolf you know?" Damien guessed, coming to stand beside Jessica. Nathan didn't miss the man's protective position, only a step behind Jessica, but enough to the side he could easily shove himself in front of her if Nathan attacked again.

Damien's presence distracted Jessica for a moment. Nathan tried to use the opportunity to break out of the spell, but her attention snapped back to him instantly. She flexed her hands, and again the magic squeezed.

"Something like that," Nathan answered, groaning against the tension in his body.

Jessica's grip on the magic loosened slightly. "He was just here, wasn't he? You were about to go after him?"

"He has my sister!" Nathan shouted. "And you got in my way!"

Jessica cringed, eyebrows creasing over her expressive eyes.

Damien slipped his hands into his pockets. "That looked like an attack to me."

He wasn't wrong. Nathan would hurt anyone who got in his way.

After getting a confirming look from Damien, Jessica lowered her hands. The tension evaporated from Nathan's body and his knees buckled as he suddenly regained control over his body.

"I'm sorry," Jessica said sincerely. "We saw a car drive off, but we didn't know. The demons were our priority."

"They're not mine." Nathan grabbed his clothes off the floor as he marched toward them. This time they gave him room to pass. "Enjoy your demon hunt and stay out of my way."

"Where are you going?" Jessica called after him.

"To save my sister."

I'm not gonna fail her a third time.

He ran for his truck, sliding the shirt over his head as he did. He turned the ignition, eager to leave them in the dust. As he shifted the clutch, the passenger door opened, and Jessica slipped into the seat next to him.

He slammed his foot back on the brake. "What are you doing?"

"Helping," Jessica said. "Seeing as it's our fault your sister was kidnapped, it's the least we can do."

She stared at Nathan, daring him to challenge her. The green of her irises were freckled with specks of gold that sparkled back at him. Nathan glowered, but she didn't back down.

Who is this girl?

The wolf was as dumbfounded as the man, its instincts uncertain if she was ally or enemy. Nathan checked the rear-view mirror. Behind him was another truck, the same one they had been driving earlier, with Damien in the driver's seat.

"Fine," he said, unwilling to waste any more time. He stepped on the accelerator, and his truck jumped forward.

"Great," Jessica said, reaching for her seatbelt. "Then you can tell me all about this werewolf and where he got the demons from."

I knew there was a catch.

CHAPTER 7

Jessica

Of all the things Jessica had anticipated coming up against, she hadn't imagined an irate werewolf with a kidnapped sister. Nathan careened down the road at a speed that locked Jessica's jaw. The icy air whipped through the open windows, tousling the wavy, light-brown hair that hung to the nape of his neck. His cheekbones were speckled with freckles, and the dark circles under his eyes made the bright blue colour of his irises stand out.

On looks alone, Jessica didn't trust the tall, lanky young man who looked like he slept outside. When she had trapped him with her magic, she had felt the force of his power fighting back. Werewolves couldn't manipulate the magic within them as witches could; instead, that power manifested as physical strength and heightened senses. Jessica had dealt with werewolves before, but she'd never met one with Nathan's level of strength. From his frantic demeanour, Nathan seemed oblivious to that power, which made him unpredictable … and dangerous.

"Can you pick up his scent?" she asked.

"Yeah. I'll never forget that stench." He leaned closer to the open window. "He's leaving a trail on purpose."

Jessica nodded. He wanted Nathan to follow, which made her even more nervous.

"If you're a witch, what is he?" Nathan gestured to the rear-view mirror, where Damien was doing his best to follow them without breaking any laws.

Jessica bristled at the accusation in his tone. "A soldier."

Barking out a humourless laugh, Nathan checked the mirror again. "What good is that?"

"He took you down."

"And then I almost killed him."

"Almost." She smiled smugly.

Nathan huffed.

"Who is this werewolf and why did he take your sister?" she asked, changing the subject.

"Silas is a sadistic antiques dealer. He wants something called the Lupatus Stone. Abigail's got this notebook of clues that's supposed to lead to it, but she wrote the stupid thing in Latin, so he needs her to translate."

"The Lupatus Stone?" She racked her brain for the reference, but nothing came up. Still, anything that involved a crazy werewolf kidnapping a human couldn't be good.

"Yeah. I'm not surprised Silas wants it—I think he's mentioned it before—but I can't figure out how he linked it to Abigail." Fear tightened his features.

"Are you and your sister close?"

"No." His knuckles whitened. "We ... we haven't seen each other in a while."

His tone put Jessica on edge. "How long?"

"Seven years."

"Oh."

"She thought I was dead," he mumbled. His eyes were on the road, but his attention was clearly somewhere else.

This just got a whole lot more complicated. Jessica gritted her teeth as he took a sharp left turn and sped through a stop sign. "Does Abigail know you—"

"No."

"*Great.*" Family drama. Exactly what she wanted to deal with while chasing demons and evil werewolves. "And what's the deal with you and Silas?"

"It's none of your business."

"It is, seeing as I'm running into battle with you," she replied sarcastically.

His nostrils flared. "No one asked you to come."

"Too bad. I'm here now." And if Silas was using Supai's demons to find the Lupatus Stone, then it was something the Incan god wanted. Which meant she had to beat him to it.

"I should kick you outta the truck right now."

"You can try," Jessica said, confident he wouldn't be able to. "Tell me what you know about—"

He veered left, turning into a parking lot with a welcome sign to the university. He threw the truck into park, left the keys on the seat, and leapt out before she could demand more information.

Jessica hurried after him as Damien pulled up and parked.

"You okay?" he asked when he caught up to her, eyebrows pulled taught, no doubt worried after witnessing Nathan's reckless driving.

Nodding, Jessica gripped his arm, his stability a comfort after the stress of riding with Nathan. "The werewolf is after a relic called the Lupatus Stone."

Damien frowned. "Lupus means wolf. Could this be the werewolf artifact?"

Jessica bit her lower lip. "I don't know for sure." When they tracked the demon's essence to British Columbia, she had assumed they would be heading to a museum in Vancouver that didn't know they were housing some deadly power. Being here, in what felt like the middle of nowhere, had already thrown her anticipated plans for a loop. On top of that, she didn't know what the Lupatus Stone *was*. She hated it when she didn't know things. "But we need to find out."

Damien nodded, his confidence easing the tension in her jaw. "Then what are we waiting for?"

Nathan was already stomping across the grass, his hands fisted at his sides. Jessica and Damien sprinted to catch up with his long strides.

"Stay out of my way," Nathan snapped without slowing down.

"If you keep *prowling* like this, someone's gonna call the police," Jessica hissed under her breath, eyeing a group of students across the parking lot.

Nathan grumbled but straightened, shifting to a brisk walk. Still, his long legs meant Jessica had to jog to keep up.

"Why are you following me?"

"Because we might be after the same thing."

Nathan kept two steps ahead of her, throwing open the doors and plowing past a student so startled they dropped the book they were holding.

With the occasional loud sniff, Nathan led them through the twisting hallways of the university. Under different circumstances, Jessica would have complimented his skill. Normally, pack members taught young werewolves skills like self-control and hunting, but Jessica was fairly sure Nathan was a lone wolf. His tracking skills, however, were proving impeccably accurate. As they turned into the self-titled history wing, he stopped.

Jessica sensed the magical energy a second later. The skin on the back of her neck tightened, and a chill ran across her skin.

Sharing a knowing look with Damien, they followed Nathan. The corridor was quiet, which hopefully meant it was empty. A woman's cry cut through the air, coming from one of the rooms up ahead.

A manic expression took over Nathan's face as he bent his knees to run.

His sister.

Jessica slid in front of him, spreading her arms wide and forcing Nathan to stop. He sneered, but she glared back. This wasn't the first time she had faced down an irate werewolf. Nathan didn't scare her, and he seemed to know it. Slowly, he drew back, though fury still flickered in his eyes.

Gesturing for him to wait, Jessica turned her attention to the hallway. *Wall of silence.* She waved one hand from the floor to the ceiling, a finger on the other pressed to her lips, and the tingling sensation of her magic warmed her palms. A black veil grew up from the floor like a wall, cutting them off from the rest of the hallway.

Jessica waited until the veil had set, rippling like a bedsheet as it caught the sound of their breathing and absorbed it. Then she turned back to the boys. "If you rush in carelessly, she'll get hurt."

Nathan eyed the barrier of magic, probably wondering what it would take to rip it apart. "I'm not just gonna sit here."

"We draw the werewolf out," Damien suggested. "Either by getting him away from the hostage or getting them both out of the building so we can rescue her safely."

Nathan's chin dropped. "Her name is Abigail."

Her irritation softening, Jessica said, "I can draw him out." Before they could protest, she placed a finger to her lips and waved away the silence barrier, forcing them to hold their tongues. With a small sense of victory, Jessica began inching down the hallway.

All she had to do was give Silas a reason to leave the room. Since he also exhibited the signs of a lone wolf, a fire ought to do it. Self-preservation would drive him out, and then she could trap him, get the information she needed about Supai, and she and Damien could be on their way.

Jessica bit the inside of her cheek. *As if it's ever that simple.*

CHAPTER 8

Nathan

Nathan's body vibrated as he tightened every muscle to stop himself from following Jessica toward the office. He hated having to rely on a stranger to save Abigail, and the wolf mirrored his feelings with a low growl in the back of his mind. But Jessica was clearly powerful; she'd been able to stop him despite his rage. Maybe she would be strong enough to take down Silas as well.

Jessica stopped two metres from the door and pressed her hand against the plaster wall next to it. Nathan watched, horrified, as the wall beneath her fingertips glowed red. When she removed her hands, the burn flared brightly for a moment before the wall absorbed it.

Damien stepped in front of Nathan, who fixed him with a dangerous glare. He wouldn't hesitate to fight the soldier. So silently his lips barely moved, Damien whispered, "Wait."

How can I wait when the witch is lighting the office on fire?!

Confirming his fears, smoke spilled over the lip of the doorframe. Silas shouted harsh words; Abigail whimpered.

When Nathan tried to charge forward, Damien shoved him into the wall.

Ghostly pain flared up in Nathan's lungs as memories of the fire seven years ago taunted him. The smoke grew thick and black, and the sounds of crackling fire filled the air. A lick of a flame flickered in the corner of the doorway.

Nathan heaved Damien into the opposite wall and ran at full speed toward the door, forcing Jessica to jump out of his way. He made it to the doorway as Silas emerged, using his momentum to tackle the other werewolf to the ground. In a fit of snarling and clawing, they bashed their way down the narrow hallway.

Nathan was taller than Silas and, based purely on size, should have been stronger. But Silas had far more experience and always managed to outmanoeuvre him. Once the surprise subsided, Silas ducked under Nathan's wild swing, moving with an infuriating grace. Even with Silas fighting one-handed — his other hand was wrapped tightly around a small object he held out of reach — Nathan was no match for him.

Silas kicked Nathan in the ribs, forcing him to double over, and then he slipped around and drove his knee into his lower back. Nathan sprawled on the ground, and by the time he looked up, Silas was gone.

"Nathan!"

"Abby?" Nathan leapt to his feet, his fury at Silas forgotten. Abigail stood in the hallway with Jessica's arm around her shoulders, staring open-jawed at him. Like Silas, Damien had disappeared.

Nathan stormed over to the girls. With one hand, he grabbed Abigail's wrist and pulled her behind him. With the other, he seized Jessica by the throat and pinned her to the wall. "I should kill you for that!"

Abigail shouted at him to stop just as Damien reappeared in the doorway, already reaching for Nathan.

Jessica caught him by the wrist against her throat, and the gold in her eyes burned brightly even as her expression calmed. The hand manacling his wrist tightened, and heat built beneath her palm.

When she abruptly twisted her hand, his wrist snapped.

Nathan groaned as the pain reverberated up his forearm. It was like she had taken a hammer to his bones; the impact echoed under his skin. He released her neck, shocked by how much his wrist hurt. Power rippled off Jessica in waves, sending a tremor down Nathan's spine.

They stared at each other silently. Her distant expression refocused on him and then softened, and the glow in her eyes faded. She broke their eye contact to look at his wrist. "At worst, it's a fracture," she told him. The acidic smell of fear seeped from her.

He looked from his wrist to Jessica in awe. It took a lot to break a werewolf's bones. Nathan hadn't imagined a witch would be capable of such strength, but she'd hurt him without uttering a word. The realization left his mouth tacky and dry, and he struggled to swallow.

Abigail shoved his arm, and the present came rushing back. *Oh no*, he thought mournfully as he turned to face his sister. She had a few scratches concentrated around her hands, but Nathan wasn't too worried about that. The curse was only passed through a bite while the werewolf was in animal form, so she was at no risk of being turned.

Abigail's forehead creased in tight lines as her eyebrows pulled tightly together. "Nathan, why are you attacking her?"

He blinked, looking from his wrist to Jessica to Abigail.

Jessica glared at him. "The fire was fake. There was no heat, no real smoke."

Their eyes widened. Abby turned back to the office, her lips parting in awe.

"Which you would have realized if you hadn't rushed in," Damien chastised.

Nathan replayed the last few minutes in his mind. He had seen the smoke, heard the crackle of the fire, but there hadn't been any heat when he got close to the door. The hallway would already have been consumed in smoke if the fire had been real.

He turned to Jessica. "That was a stupid gamble—"

"It was an illusion," she interrupted in a flat tone. "Lone werewolves are driven by self-preservation. That's why they don't function well in packs. I knew he would run to protect himself, and then I could have *caught him* if you hadn't been so reckless. I would never purposefully endanger someone with my magic." She put up a good front, but the flickering in her gaze hinted at something more than what she was saying.

"And if you threaten me again," she said with a merciless warning in her voice, "Silas will be the least of your concerns."

Nathan wanted to stand up for himself but couldn't find the words. His knees grew weak with a dangerous realization. *I've underestimated her.*

Abigail broke the silence. "Magic?" Her voice cracked. "And werewolves?" She was quivering lightly and sweat coated her brow. She sent a pleading glance up at Nathan, her eyes searching his. Her heartbeat was racing.

"I'm a witch," Jessica said, saving Nathan from having to explain. She said it the same way someone might say their age or their name. "Your kidnapper was a werewolf."

Abigail shook her head. "I-I agree he was an animal, but a *werewolf?* And a witch?" She gestured to Jessica, but whatever more she wanted to add didn't come.

Damien glanced at Nathan. "Did you see what Silas took?"

"The thing in his hand?" *How did Damien spot that?* "I didn't see what it was." Skewering Silas had been his primary focus.

"Was that the Lupatus Stone?" Jessica asked in alarm.

"You know about that?" Abigail asked, echoing Jessica's surprise.

"Nathan told us on the way over." The witch gestured to him absently. "But that's not the point. What happened?"

With a stubborn look Nathan remembered all too well, Abigail readjusted her glasses. "He *thinks* he got the Lupatus Stone. I …" Her pride faded as the colour in her cheeks flared and she dipped her gaze to the ground. "I made a replica of what I *thought* the Stone could look like a few days ago. For fun. When Silas demanded that I take him to the Stone, I led him here and gave him the fake." She looked around the group, and her eyes widened. "Don't tell me you believe it's real too?"

When no one denied it, Abigail groaned. "This can't be happening. He is not a werewolf, the Stone is not real, and y-you …" She gestured weakly at Jessica

The witch turned to Damien with a pleading look, and he grinned. "Let's go somewhere less cramped," he suggested, stepping in between the girls. "Then we can get into the details."

Despite Nathan's gut reaction, he didn't stop Damien from steering Abigail back the way they had come.

"Wait," Nathan said to Jessica quietly, stopping her before she could follow the others.

She paused, giving him a sharp look that sent a chill down his spine.

"Why didn't you tell her what I am?"

Turning her shoulders to face him, which he hoped was a good sign, Jessica said, "It's not my secret to tell." She held out her palms.

With some hesitation, Nathan offered her his injured wrist.

She gingerly placed her hands around it. A faint green light glowed beneath her palms, sending warmth into his skin. "*Reversere skaden.*"

After a sharp snap, like his bone had cracked again, the pain subsided quickly.

"Your bone is aligned," she explained. "It'd be better to let it heal on its own. Given who you are, it won't take too long."

Nathan tilted his head. He hadn't been called a *who* in a long time.

"We have tape in our first aid kit. You can keep it wrapped so Abigail doesn't know how fast you heal."

He flinched when Jessica met his gaze again. Her eyes were normal now, but he couldn't get the image of them glowing gold out of his mind. The sadness in her expression made her seem older than she looked.

"I'm sorry," Nathan said. He had obviously crossed some line, and even though her power scared him, she had saved Abigail from Silas. "I don't deserve this." He gestured at the healing wrist.

Jessica held up a hand to stop his self-pity. "We all have our demons," she told him, her focus drifting down the hall to where Damien and Abigail had left. "What's more important is how we deal with them."

Nathan followed her line of sight, his heart heavy.

Easier said than done.

CHAPTER 9

Nathan

"This is absurd!" Abigail removed her glasses and wiped a hand down her face. "This can't be happening."

Nathan leaned his head against the wall, pressing his shoulders into the cold stone. "It's real, Abigail," he repeated for the third time in thirty minutes, looking up at the sky and wishing the conversation could be over. The narrow corridor between the university buildings where they'd gathered was growing more cramped by the second.

"You can't talk," Abigail snapped, pointing an angry finger at him. "You are part of this insanity."

His eyebrows pulled tight. "It's not like it's any easier for me," he said defensively. "I'm as surprised as you are."

He was still struggling to wrap his head around the fact that he had managed to find both Abigail and Silas on the same day, not to mention the strange witch and soldier interrogating Abby about the Lupatus Stone.

Unfortunately, since Abigail's brain had been fried by the discovery that magic was real, the conversation was going nowhere. Though this was also the first time Nathan had seen magic, knowing he could transform his body into a wolf made it easier to accept.

Jessica sighed heavily, arms folded tightly over her chest. She tapped her foot incessantly, which was increasingly irritating, and stared pleadingly at Damien. The soldier remained quiet, watching Jessica with an amused expression.

Jessica jammed her hands into the back pockets of her jeans. "I don't know how else to explain it," she said, her tone growing bitter. "We came here following demons now apparently in the employ of Silas. Presumably, he'll use them to hunt down the Stone for Supai."

"The Spanish god trying to take over the world with old pieces of junk?" Nathan asked doubtfully.

"Incan god, and yes, that *junk* holds a lot of power," Jessica insisted.

Nathan shrugged, his skin scratching up against the wall.

Abigail was still shaking her head. She wet her lips and looked between their faces, her gaze lingering on Nathan a second longer than the others. "I don't … I can't …"

"What more proof do you need?" Nathan asked. At her glare, he softened his tone. "You saw the demons, the fake fire. It doesn't get more *magic-y* than that."

"Are you joking? How are you not freaking out right now? They're saying that magic — *magic* — is *real*, Nathan! It defies the laws of nature."

"As illogical as researching an artifact out of Arthurian legend when Camelot is believed to be a myth?" Damien asked mildly.

"*I* believe it's a myth! I study those stories because they might offer us insight into a historical period without records. Myths reflect culture, but they're just that: *myths*. Only in my dreams could this be real ..." Her voice grew smaller as it trailed off. Just when Nathan thought Abigail had finally had a breakthrough, she groaned and cupped her face in her hands. "My neurons can't handle this."

Damien glanced over at Jessica and nudged her shoulder with his own. "Maybe a gentler demonstration would help?"

Jessica looked at him in dismay, but with a little silent coaxing, she conceded with a stubborn scoff. "Can your *neurons* handle it, Abigail?"

Abigail lowered her hands slowly, giving Nathan a questioning look. It caught him by surprise, and he tried to respond with what he hoped was a supportive smile. It didn't feel right, but it did the trick. Abigail nodded at Jessica.

Halting her ceaseless foot-tapping, the witch straightened her left arm in front of her, her palm facing the cement. Nathan straightened off the wall, equally curious about what the witch could do. The bandage wrapped tightly around his wrist was a constant reminder of her dangerous potential.

Jessica's eyelids fluttered closed, and she began to hum. The ground in front of her toes rumbled, the gentle vibration concentrated in a small circle. Small twinkles of golden light peeled from her hand and drifted down, melting into the cement.

Nathan took a cautious step forward. Abigail's eyes widened and her focus remained pinned to the spot where the lights had vanished.

Suddenly, a crack split the cement, about the length of his palm, and out sprang a small sprout. Nathan jumped back, and Abigail gasped.

Jessica wiggled her fingers. The sprout shuddered and slowly stretched up. Branches sprouted from the stem, followed by red and pink blossoms. Within seconds, they were all standing around a small flower shrub.

Lowering her hands, Jessica looked longingly at the plant for a moment and then sent Abigail a sharp look. "Good enough for you?"

Abigail crouched in front of the bush and readjusted her glasses. She carefully brushed one of the leaves with a fingertip. Her breath caught as she pinched the leaf and rubbed it between her fingers. Then she chose a flower and plucked it from its stem. Her jaw dropped as she stared at the tiny petals. Finally, she placed the flower carefully on the ground and stood, wiping her hands on her jeans. "I-it's hard to argue with that."

"Glad you approve."

Abigail straightened. "I didn't mean to offend you. But you must understand this is a *lot* to take in."

"Then I'm sure *you* understand why you can't tell anyone."

While Abigail nodded nervously, her composure wavering under Jessica's firm tone, Damien pushed himself off the wall and went to the witch's side to whisper in her ear. Nathan strained to hear their conversation but could only pick up the sound of their breath. He gave up with a pout. Maybe Jessica was using her magic to hinder his hearing.

Finally, Jessica's expression softened. She gave Damien a subtle elbow to the ribs before turning her attention back to Abigail and Nathan. "Glad we understand each other."

Abigail nodded insistently. "Was that a spell you were humming?"

Jessica blinked. "Uh … no. That was just humming."

"Does it control the magic?"

The witch shifted on her feet. "No. It helps me focus."

"But then what—"

"Now isn't the time for an interview," Damien interrupted, softening the words with a smile.

The red flared in Abigail's cheeks again, and she shrugged apologetically. "Are you … um … you know?"

A soft chuckle shook Damien's frame. "Nope," he replied. "Plain old human."

I doubt that. Jessica's strength was evident, but Damien's control over his emotions made him a difficult opponent to read. Nathan didn't trust Damien's laugh, either. The soldier was a mystery, and Nathan hated puzzles.

"Right now, we're in a good place," Damien continued, casually leaning his weight onto one foot as he slipped his hands into his jacket pockets. "Silas has a decoy, and you kept a hold of the notebook. If he is working with Supai, they'll probably have to reconvene, which gives us a little time. Well done."

Abigail's face brightened as she pulled out the small paperback book.

"What good does that do us?" Nathan cut in, breaking off Abigail's smile. "I get that you wanna take down Supai after what happened in Toronto, but why is your god helping Silas find the Lupatus Stone in the first place?"

"We don't know," Jessica said. "If I had to guess, it's probably because the Lupatus Stone can only be found by a werewolf." She looked at Abigail. "That right?"

She nodded. "The legend I was studying said the Lupatus Stone was created by a werewolf named Lupus during the Arthurian period. He was a nobleman who abused nature, and as a punishment, Merlin cursed him with lycanthropy."

One of Damien's eyebrows shot up. "That's not the story I've heard. Is there more than one werewolf origin story?"

"There are," Abigail said eagerly. "Werewolves are found in several cultures. Both the Greek and Nordic mythologies describe the creation of werewolves, and there are lots of stories from across Europe that suggest their existence.

The Arthurian myth is a possible origin of the curse for the United Kingdom."

"From what I understand," Jessica added, "at some point in their evolution, the abilities were passed on genetically, making them shapeshifters, technically. Nowadays, most werewolves are born with their gifts and can't pass them on through a bite. Only cursed wolves can curse others. They're not very common anymore." Her focus flickered to Nathan, and he flinched.

"The *curse*," Jessica said with air quotes, "has come a long way since its various starting points. Werewolves now live all over the world. With training, they can shift at will, not only on full moon nights. If they're strong enough to control their instincts, it can be a great power."

Abigail and Damien's eyes widened. Nathan's mind was fuzzy. He had never thought about the origins of his curse before.

"Though," Jessica added, shooting Abigail a curious look, "I've never heard of *that* Camelot werewolf."

"There are a few different werewolf legends in the poems about Camelot," Abby explained. "In this story, when Lupus realized a bite from his wolf form could pass the curse onto others, he purposely spread lycanthropy like it was a disease and built himself a following."

Nathan's stomach churned as the wolf grew agitated. It didn't like being called a disease, but Nathan thought the term was a fitting one.

"Supposedly, he was terrified of being forgotten. He worked with a warlock to create the Lupatus Stone by using pieces of his soul. The warlock may or may not have been Morgana." From the excitement bubbling in Abigail's tone, she subscribed to this belief. "The Lupatus Stone increases a werewolf's strength and, with it, the wielder can coerce other wolves — even unwilling ones — to obey. It's suggested that the Stone can steal another wolf's abilities to strengthen its effects. The Stone provided a way to make werewolf supremacy a reality, even after Lupus died."

Nathan stilled as Abigail's words rolled through his brain like a bulldozer. If the Stone could steal a werewolf's ability completely, then maybe he could be cured. Suddenly dizzy, he leaned into the wall for support, though it didn't stop the flush of adrenaline that tingled through his body.

The others didn't seem to notice Nathan's sudden shock. "So Silas becomes a super werewolf, and Supai gets an army of powerful soldiers," Jessica concluded grimly. "Why would they be looking around Prince George?"

Abigail readjusted her glasses. "I've been thinking about that. It *might* be because of me."

When they all focused their attention on her, her cheeks turned red. "An article about me was published when I got my scholarship. Because it's a … *niche* field of study, the university thought it would be a cute publicity piece. If Silas and Supai were already looking for the Stone, asking the nerd who's made Arthurian artifacts the focus of her academic study would be a good place to start." She let out a sigh, casting her gaze to the ground.

The wolf paced back and forth in Nathan's mind, its claws anxiously scratching at him. The Lupatus Stone could free him from the curse, rid him of the years of fighting with conflicting instincts inside of him. The possibility left him breathless.

And if the Stone could control other werewolves, no wonder Silas wanted it.

"Nathan?" Abigail whispered, causing him to flinch. She peeked at him over the rim of her glasses. "How do you know Silas?"

Oh no.

Jessica and Damien also watched him intently. Nathan swallowed painfully. "W-what did he tell you?"

She spoke to the notebook in her hands rather than him. "He said … he said you aren't who you say you are."

"It-it's not that simple." His voice cracked. Digging his fingers into his palms, Nathan used the pain to anchor him in the present. Memories of the past clung to his skin like soaked clothing, weighing him down.

"What does he do?" Jessica prodded, more a suggestion than a question.

Yeah … I can start there. "He's an antiques dealer — the scummy, black-market kind. He usually works out of the States. I don't know why he's here, but h-he—" Nathan forced the words out. "He was the one who attacked me in the woods, Abby."

Her eyes went wide, and one hand clutched her abdomen as if she had been punched. "They said … they said it was an animal bite."

Nathan nodded, trying to string the words together despite his spinning head. He knew he couldn't lie, but if he could provide truth without giving away his curse, maybe she could understand.

"H-he had dogs with him," Nathan explained, his mouth tacky. "I caught them on a hunt. You know how it was banned back then. He tried to shut me up, but I got away. That's when the ranger found me and brought me to the hospital. W-when the fire started, I-I managed to get out. It's mostly a blur."

When Nathan, his body torn between human and wolf forms, had regained consciousness after the fire, Silas had been there with him. He'd wanted Nathan to be his prodigy. When Nathan had refused, Silas had left him to die in the forest. Alone with the monster Silas had created inside of him.

"I was afraid … I was afraid he would hurt you if I came home." *Afraid that* I *would hurt you.* "So I ran away. I never … I never thought I could come back." He risked a quick peek at Abigail. She was frozen in place with moisture building in her eyes.

"But you've seen him since then?" Jessica asked in a soft voice.

He nodded, but it took him a minute to speak. "We've run into each other a few times over the years."

Nathan had slowly travelled north as he grew up, always via unconventional means since he didn't have any paperwork. Staying off the radar had also brought him into contact with Silas's community from time to time.

Each time, Silas had given Nathan a chance to join him, and each time, Nathan had lost the resulting fight when he refused. Silas would leave him, like a cat refusing to kill a mouse, and his condescending chuckle would echo in Nathan's head for days after.

Nathan had thought living in the middle of the woods would save him from future encounters with Silas. For three years, he'd been alone — just him and the wolf that hated him.

"Has he mentioned the Lupatus Stone before?" asked Damien.

"Our *conversations* don't usually last long, but the words are familiar, so he must have talked about it."

Jessica placed her hands on her hips. "The question now is how do we find it before he does?"

It took all Nathan's willpower to keep from looking at Abigail, though he sensed her stare burrowing into his skin. "He won't stay fooled for long," he warned.

"Maybe, maybe not," Abigail objected. "Silas didn't seem to know anything about the Stone. He was demanding I tell him how it works when the fire — the *fake* fire — started."

"If he doesn't know how to use it, it might take a while for him to figure out that it's never going to work," Damien said. "Hopefully."

"Which means we can get ahead of him." With a determined nod, Jessica said, "Abigail, could you show us your research?"

Finally, Abigail dragged her gaze away from Nathan; relief made his knees wobble. His heart pounded against his ribs, and he wished he could rip it out and stomp it into the ground to make the guilt stop.

Carefully pulling out the notebook, Abigail opened it a few pages in and held it out for the rest of them to see. The pages were covered in small, intricate cursive, which were nothing more than illegible scribbles to Nathan.

"The first half of my notes detail the supposed historical timeline of Camelot, and when the myths occurred. I'm trying to show how the legends can bring insight to what life was like during the Anglo-Saxon conflict," Abigail explained as she flipped through a few pages. The notes became less structured, shifting from structured note-taking to a collection of thoughts.

"Then I found this book in the library." Her forehead tensed as she stopped on a page with a few lines of writing circled in the centre. "It contained a collection of legends I had never heard of before, and which aren't found in any other text. This is what I have about the Lupatus Stone, including the riddle that reveals the Stone's resting place." She cleared her throat. "Not a location, specifically, but the *description* of the Stone's hiding place."

"What is it?" Jessica asked, her tone lifting. She joined Abigail's side, her forehead creasing as she skimmed the page. "That's interesting."

When Abigail turned to her in surprise, the witch's chin dipped, and she looked away. "I can speak a few languages," Jessica confessed.

"How many?" Damien asked.

"Five."

Damien whistled, and Jessica sent him a shy smirk.

"So what does it say?" Damien asked, nodding to the notebook.

"*Ubi umbrae solem vorantque terra ad caelum clamat, hic gigas illam potestatem ex defectu natam servat*," Abigail read. "'Where the shadows swallow the sun, and the earth roars at the sky, here the giant guards the power born from weakness.'"

Nathan groaned. He hated riddles as much as he hated puzzles. "What's that supposed to mean?"

"That, I don't know for sure. And I don't know where the answer to the riddle is. I haven't had time to read through the whole chapter." She closed the notebook with a snap of the pages.

"Do you think we would find more pieces to the puzzle if we checked out that book?" Jessica pressed.

Abigail's expression lit up with renewed eagerness. "Absolutely!"

"Well, then. I guess we're going to another library." Jessica shot Damien a wicked grin. He didn't look keen.

"A *normal* library?" he asked.

Jessica giggled. "Can you show us this book, Abigail?"

"Hold on," Nathan cut in, holding out his hands. He pushed off the wall and turned to face Abigail. "If you start looking for the Stone, Silas is sure to come after you again. I can't let you do that."

"Can't *let* me?" Abigail's eyes narrowed. "I had to become an adult a long time ago, and I will make my own choices. You don't get to make decisions for me."

He flinched as if she had physically hit him.

"Besides, the safest place I can be is with Jessica, right? It would be stupid for me to go off alone now." Turning her back to him, Abigail gestured to the exit of the alley. "I'll show you to the library," she offered and set a brisk pace in the direction she had indicated.

Jessica gave Nathan a sympathetic look before quickly catching up to Abigail, Damien close behind her.

Nathan tried to move, but his feet were stuck in place. Abigail had no reason to trust him. It wasn't like he could jump back into her life and be her brother again. That trust had died in the fire all those years ago.

"You coming?"

He looked up with a jerk. Damien lingered at the end of the walkway, watching Nathan with a stone-like expression.

As much as he wished he could turn the other way, the chance that the Stone could free him of his curse was too good to ignore. If he could be free from the wolf, if he didn't have to worry about losing control or hurting Abigail, then he could tell her what really happened that night. And he had to protect her from Silas; Nathan had no doubt he would target Abby just to torment Nathan.

"Yeah," Nathan muttered, mostly to himself. "I'm coming."

CHAPTER 10

Nathan

The smell of thousands of pages wrapped in layers of cardboard, dust, and leather enveloped Nathan as they stepped into the library. He couldn't remember the last time he had been around so many books. It made his palms clammy. Having only an elementary school education, he felt like the books were judging him. They knew he didn't belong. He lingered back as the others stepped into the fluorescent lighting.

"It's empty," Abigail murmured. "This time of year, students should be working on their final projects. That's strange."

"Strange is never a good thing," Jessica muttered.

"At least it's not alive," countered Damien.

"Are you scared?" Jessica teased.

He smirked, unfazed by her taunting. "As long as there aren't books flying at my head this time."

Abigail turned to the witch. "A living library?"

"We visited an elven library in Toronto when we were trying to find a way to stop Supai from being summoned."

"She means we broke in," Damien corrected with a side-eyed look.

Jessica scoffed, narrowing her eyes. "We weren't *stealing*, remember?"

He grimaced. "I remember the walls moving like an upset stomach."

Abigail's eyes stretched wide. At this rate of discovery, Nathan feared her eyes would become permanently round. "That's amazing. Do you think there'd be a living building here?"

After a drawn-out, dubious look, Jessica shrugged. "Anything's possible, I guess. But it's not something I recommend seeking out, if that's what you're thinking."

Obviously disappointed, Abigail led them past the two welcome counters and into the aisles of books. "The history section is back here."

The rows of bookshelves were lined up like dominoes in front of them. Slipping into the first row, Nathan watched the titles passing by as if they were clouds. All of them were foreign to him. He'd always pictured libraries as rooms full of wooden features, but these shelves were metal and added a sharp tang to the room's scent. Flares of perfume and cologne from previous visitors sprang up from all directions.

"Having fun?" Damien murmured, looking at Nathan over his shoulder.

Nathan scowled. "Not with your commentary."

The soldier shrugged, turning his attention forward again. Nathan stopped looking at the shelves and focused on the back wall of the room instead.

Abigail stopped them in front of an intersection of shelves and gestured to three of the rows in front of them. Each row extended the width of a basketball court.

"This is all history?" Nathan asked, eyeing the collection uneasily.

"Everything pre-1800s is in these three rows," Abigail explained. "The Dark Ages stuff is down there" — she pointed to the shelf on the right — "which is where we should start, but every time I've come looking for this book, it's been shelved in a different place. We'll have to hunt it down."

Jessica ran one hand through her ponytail as the other tapped her hip. "What did it look like?"

"It's got a thick spine, with a hard green cover and gold writing. It's written in an old language that's a combination of Latin and Celtic, so the title looks a bit gibberish," Abigail explained. "I'll start down here. Jessica, maybe you can take that aisle?"

"Abby," Damien cut in. "Could I see your notebook?"

Hesitantly, she placed the notebook in his hands, her eyebrows drawing together. "Do you read Latin too?"

"No," he replied, undeterred. "I'm just curious." He thumbed through the pages while Abigail and Jessica turned their attention to the search.

Nathan was about to join them when Damien whispered. "Wait." He closed the notebook quietly and handed it to Nathan. "What do you think?"

Scoffing, Nathan leaned away from the book as if were a rat. "I can't read it either."

"You don't need to. Smell it."

Nathan blinked, staring at the notebook silently. His cheeks burned. *Why didn't I think of that?* "It might not work."

Damien flashed him a smug look as he held out the book.

Nathan pushed it back toward Damien. He didn't need it—Abigail's scent was already imprinted in his mind. If she had handled the book recently, it should hold a lingering trace of her smell. He turned his nose to the air and inhaled deeply, sifting through the scents.

Abigail's presence was very clear, so he searched for a softer trail of her honey scent. Three rows over, he caught a faint whiff. He glanced at the sign hanging above the row of books, which read 'Mythology and Folklore.'

The arrangement of brown and green hardcover books created a skyline effect across the shelves. *Grimm's done well for himself,* Nathan thought, noting the name that marked most of the books on the top shelf.

He was surprised to recognize the titles of old fairy tales. *Snow White and the Seven Dwarves, The Frog Prince,* and *Sleeping Beauty* were all familiar, though he had only seen the animated movies. Their parents, often busy in their mechanic shop, always made a point to have a family movie night when they were free. Abigail had hated *Sleeping Beauty*. She'd been seven when they'd watched it, and complained the whole time about how boring the princess was. Nathan hadn't cared for those movies, but movie night had been special, a time when all four of them were able to sit down together. He remembered liking the part in *Sleeping Beauty* when the evil fairy turned into a dragon.

As Nathan went deeper, the English titles melted away, giving rise to a variety of languages he didn't know. Not that he needed to read them — his nose did all the work.

Stopping at the spot where the smell was most concentrated, Nathan pulled out green books one at a time, comparing them with sniffs. He lingered on the largest hardcover with gold writing. The scent was faint, but the book matched Abby's description. He frowned at the title. "Definitely gibberish."

Tucking the book under his arm, he retraced his steps.

"I think I found it," he said, his voice carrying easily to the others.

They rejoined him quickly, and Abigail smiled wide when she saw the book. "That was so fast," she said with admiration, holding out her hands for the book, which Nathan handed over gladly.

Abigail balanced the spine in one hand as she opened to the table of contents. The book was as thick as a dictionary and the green had faded around the edges. The elegant gold cursive across the front still glittered under the unpleasant fluorescent lights above them.

Abby pulled each yellowed page aside with care, releasing the muted smell of aged dust with every turn of the page. She paused, running her palm down one of the pages with a wistful smile on her face.

"I've never seen a language like that," Jessica admitted.

"I can't say I'm fluent," Abigail replied. "Honestly, it's a lot of guessing, but I think it comes from the same period we theorize Camelot existed. Given the timeline, the people would have spoken native Celtic dialects influenced by the Roman occupation."

She paused, looking around at their faces. "Sorry," she said with a nervous chuckle. "I get excited when it comes to this kind of stuff."

Jessica smiled. "I find it fascinating too," she said encouragingly. "What's this book about?"

Abigail flipped another page. "From what I've read so far, it records the quests that knights embarked on in search of different treasures, detailing the trials they had to pass along the way. The pictures help with figuring out the story."

The group circled Abigail, all looking down at the open book. In the centre of the page was a drawing of a man covered head to toe in fur, with the head of a wolf and claws for fingers.

"Definitely a werewolf," Nathan muttered.

"And you can translate it?" asked Jessica.

"I can make educated guesses. With some time," Abigail explained.

Biting on her lower lip, Jessica glanced at Damien. "Maybe I can come up with a translation spell."

"Do you know a translation spell?" he asked, raising an eyebrow.

"No, but I could probably make one." She tilted her head. "Does that surprise you?"

A small smile slipped across his lips. "You constantly surprise me."

Jessica's smile creased in her cheeks, and she was quick to turn her focus back to the book. "How much have you read so far, Abigail?"

"About a third. I started this chapter a few days ago, but, um … I skipped to the end to see what the treasure was. That's why I have the clue to the Lupatus Stone's hiding place, but I don't know how to get there. If we start back here …"

Nathan's focus shifted away from the conversation as a disturbing smell tickled his nostrils. It was as faint as the smell of freshwater but was growing rapidly stronger. His skin turned cold as he recognized the scent of smoke.

"Guys."

Jessica's forehead tensed. She slowly scanned the space around them.

Another wave of the smoky smell wafted through the air. Nathan whirled around, ready for a fight, and … saw a woman standing patiently behind them, instead. Her black hair was locked in a tight bun on the top of her head. The brown skin across her arched cheekbones and around her pointed chin sagged slightly but was otherwise flawless, making it hard to discern her age. She was as short as Abigail. Nathan had a good foot on her at least. Her eyes, a strange amber colour, stared at them unblinkingly.

She appeared harmless in her pink pastel shift dress and dark blue cardigan, but the smell of smoke was definitely emanating from her, and her steely gaze made the hairs on the back of Nathan's neck stand on end.

"Can we help you?" Jessica asked, taking a protective step forward.

The woman raised a dark eyebrow, scanning Jessica slowly. Then she looked at Abigail. "That book was not meant to be shelved. I will need to take it back, please."

With a disappointed sigh, Abigail closed the book with a soft thump. Before she could hand it over, Jessica put out an arm to block her.

"I'm sorry, could you tell us your name?" Jessica asked politely.

A twinkle of amusement flickered in the woman's eyes. "Theodora."

"Theodora." Jessica lowered her arm but kept her position in front of Abigail. "How long have you worked here?"

A slight smile curled on Theodora's thin lips. "Many, many years. I built this collection." The way she tilted her head reminded Nathan of a curious wolf. "Are you a student?"

"My friend is." Jessica nodded at Abigail without taking her focus off the woman. "She was showing us around."

What is she doing? Nathan leaned toward Jessica's ear. "Jessica, she's not—"

Jessica shoved her hand out to stop him, and Nathan quickly retreated from her palm. *Does she know this woman isn't human?*

Theodora's smoky smell lacked the warm undertone usually found in humans. Even Jessica, with her odd fizzy undercurrent, had the fleshy quality of human mixed in with her fresh-rain smell. Nathan suspected Theodora's human form was fake. He rolled his shoulders, preparing for a fight.

"Nathan, why don't you and Abigail go put the book back," Jessica suggested, keeping her eyes on Theodora.

Nathan quickly picked up on her true meaning. *Run?* He was happy with that plan.

"Wait, shouldn't we—" Abigail tried to say, but Nathan took her by her shoulders and steered her away from the woman.

"You heard the witch," he said under his breath. "Let's get out of here."

Behind him, Theodora let out a soft chuckle. "I see," she said softly. "You aren't normal students."

The temperature in the library spiked as if they had suddenly stepped into a sauna. The ground rumbled, sending vibrations up Nathan's legs. Abigail yelped and lost her balance, falling backward into Nathan's torso. He crouched low, keeping his grip on Abigail's upper arms to hold her upright as he glanced back at the others.

Theodora stood, an immovable statue, among the quaking floor and shaking bookshelves. Jessica and Damien were riding the waves with their knees bent and hands spread out for balance. The folklore and mythology section to Nathan's right toppled, and the bookshelves fell down the length of the library like dominoes.

Abigail gripped onto Nathan's forearm with her free hand, cringing from the chaos while Nathan swatted away falling books with his free hand. Even with the threat of a bookshelf falling on him, Nathan couldn't take his attention off Theodora.

Theodora's expression remained unfazed. Her skin slowly shifted from brown to blue as reptilian scales coated her body. Her hair faded like mist and was replaced with a row of green, triangular scales that ran down the back of her elongated neck. The human form melted away, leaving behind two stout arms with three-toed hands tipped with large white talons. Her nose stretched forward into a rectangular snout, like an alligator's. Once the earth stopped quaking, its rumbling distress was soothed by the soft sweep of a long tail across the ground behind Theodora.

Nathan stammered meaningless syllables, too shocked to form words.

"A dragon," Abigail said breathlessly, her lips parted in awe.

That Theodora was a dragon should have been the most shocking part of her big reveal, but for some reason,

Nathan's mind got stuck on the fact that her height hadn't changed. *Shouldn't a dragon be giant?*

Jessica was the first to recover from the shock. She shoved her palm forcefully toward the mess behind Nathan and Abigail. A bookshelf that was leaning precariously against its fallen neighbour flew back, crashing into the far wall and clearing a path through the rubble.

"Run!" she shouted.

Nathan didn't hesitate. He scooped up the book Abigail had dropped during the earthquake with one hand, grabbed his sister's hand with the other, and pulled her toward the door.

"Th-at's a dragon. An actual dragon!" Abigail shouted as she stumbled along behind him.

"Exactly why we are running!" he retorted. He rounded the mess of toppled bookshelves and rushed toward the door.

Nathan was nearly close enough to reach the handle when Theodora slid in front of him, blocking his path. He skidded to a halt, managing to regain his balance and jump back before her snake-like tongue could touch him.

Theodora scented the air again, standing like a Komodo dragon on its hind legs, with an oddly disappointed look in her eye. *That book is not permitted to leave the library.* Her jaw hung open as she spoke, but Nathan heard her voice echoing between his ears as if she had spoken directly into his mind.

Putting himself between the dragon and Abigail, Nathan ushered his sister back to join Damien and Jessica in the centre of the library.

"We can't leave without the book," Jessica said.

That sounded like a stupid idea to Nathan. "What else are we supposed to do?"

He flinched when Abigail grabbed the book out of his hands. "I'll read as much as I can about the Lupatus Stone quest. You keep the dragon busy."

Jessica and Nathan shared a look of shock, but before they could object, Abigail jumped behind one of the fallen bookshelves for cover.

"You heard the historian," Damien said. "Let's go." He turned toward Theodora.

Jessica gawked as she joined him. "Are you crazy?"

Before Nathan could throw himself into the fray, Abigail called out, "What are you doing?"

He turned, surprised to see her concerned expression. "It's a *dragon*, Nathan. We can't fight that! Let them handle it."

"Ah … but … yeah. Okay." His shoulders drooped. "Hurry up and read; I'll watch your back."

She nodded her determination and buried her nose in the book.

Holding the sentry position in front of the bookshelf, Nathan kept a close eye on the fight. His body buzzed with the desire to jump in, but he couldn't do anything if Abigail was watching. If he attacked with his full strength and speed, she would realize he wasn't human—and he wasn't good at holding back. The wolf snarled as heat rushed through his body, invigorating his quivering muscles. He clenched his jaw to keep himself in place, his nostrils flaring as he watched from the sidelines.

Theodora, despite her height, was faster and stronger than Jessica and Damien. She jumped toward the witch and drove her fist into Jessica's stomach before darting over to swipe at Damien with her talons, all while maintaining a blasé reptilian expression. *I insist you return the book immediately*, she scolded before jumping high above Jessica's head and slamming her tail across the witch's shoulders. Jessica fell to her knees, her outstretched hands keeping her from being flattened.

Damien, to his credit, clearly recognized he was outmatched. He held back, keeping distance between himself and Jessica, forcing Theodora to move farther to attack him. While she was busy with Jessica, he grabbed one of the books from the floor and threw it at the dragon with a loud grunt. The makeshift projectile caught Theodora on the side of the head, knocking her sideways, briefly stunning her. Then she narrowed her eyes at Damien.

"What are you doing?" Jessica shouted, her eyes widening in horror as Damien picked up another book.

He hefted the thick hardcover above his head. "I'm utilizing my resources." Once again, he heaved the book at the dragon. Theodora snaked her body to the side, easily avoiding the attack.

Damien dropped the next book so he could block a tail strike with his forearms.

"They're pieces of history, Damien!" Jessica argued. Yet she picked up a book and, after a moment's hesitation, threw it at the back of Theodora's head.

It struck with a loud thud. A growl bubbled up from deep in the dragon's belly, rumbling across the room like an encroaching storm. *I will not tolerate disrespect for my collection*, Theodora warned, her voice raspy. She spun and struck Damien with her tail, sending him rolling across the floor, before turning back to Jessica.

"I don't feel good about this," Jessica complained as she lifted another book, a smaller novel. "But since magic doesn't work directly on you, I have to find more indirect means." The book in her hands glowed purple and its surface bubbled like it was boiling.

Poison? The acidic stench reminded Nathan of rotting lemons, causing his stomach to clench.

Theodora dipped her snout as she bent her hind legs, preparing to spring.

Jessica threw the book like a ninja star. It flew at a startling speed, faster than a human should have been able to throw it. Nathan's enhanced eyesight followed the book as it shot toward Theodora's chest.

The dragon leapt into the air, dodging the toxic tome. Unable to stop her momentum, she crashed into the ceiling, and her body dropped limply onto one of the bookshelves with a bang, denting the metal.

Jessica raised her hands and dozens of books rose into the air. They circled Theodora, creating a vortex of paper around the dragon.

Nathan's fists shook at his sides, and his nails dug into his palms. As Theodora pulled her reptilian body up, Damien approached Nathan. "We could use your help," he said in a low voice.

"Can't Jessica handle it?"

Before Damien could respond, a sharp swear word pulled their attention back to Jessica. The dragon had forced her way through the vortex. Jessica ducked beneath Theodora's tail and hooked her foot around the dragon's ankle, yanking it backward so she fell onto her front claws. Jessica leapt onto Theodora's back, gripping onto the spines of her neck.

"Stay *down*," Jessica demanded through gritted teeth. A faint red glow surrounded the witch's body, and the dragon buckled as if Jessica had suddenly gotten heavier.

Nathan's eyebrows pulled together, divided between impressed and concerned. "Jessica can be pretty scary, huh?"

"Yeah," Damien replied, his voice full of pride. "I know she could handle it, but apparently magic doesn't work directly on dragons, so physical force is the most effective tactic. That makes you a better choice to fight her."

"I would love to," Nathan said through clenched teeth. "But I *can't*." He wanted nothing more than to test how he matched up against the dragon, especially seeing how Jessica held her own, but he couldn't do anything with Abigail watching.

"Abigail, how are you doing?" Damien asked

"Need more time," she said without looking up.

"Focus on the book," he ordered, turning back to Nathan. "I'll cover you."

Looking doubtfully at Damien but keenly aware of Jessica's grunts of pain, it didn't take long for Nathan to concede. Cracking his knuckles, he pulled his lips back with a feral smile and charged.

Theodora threw Jessica off her back and was about to lunge when Nathan jumped between them, catching the dragon's hands. Her eyebrows knitted, adding extra wrinkles between the scales on her forehead. She tried to close her fingers around Nathan's, her talons scraping the backs of his hands as he resisted. A sharp pain pulsed deep in the wrist that Jessica had injured, but he held strong. Any show of weakness could allow the dragon the opportunity to skewer him.

Interesting, Theodora's voice mumbled in Nathan's head.

Growling in reply, Nathan twisted his heel and pitched his weight to the side, using the momentum to throw the dragon over his shoulder, slamming her to the ground. "Stay out of my head."

Theodora stared up at him from the ground, blinking a translucent eyelid. *I will not part with any of my collection,* she warned him. *Merlin himself gifted that book to me.*

"I don't care about some old wizard."

The dragon spun and struck the backs of his knees with her tail. He fell onto his hands and knees with a loud grunt, and the dragon jumped onto his back.

Her scales scratched his neck as she wrapped one of her arms around him and dug her talons into his bicep with the other. Nathan wasn't sure if she had pierced skin, but he wasn't going to wait long enough to give her the chance.

No one is meant to have the Stone. The relic should die—

Theodora lost her words along with her breath as Nathan reared up and fell backward, crushing her beneath his weight. Her grip loosened around his neck, allowing him to pull away.

Nathan leapt to his feet, readying himself for another attack. If he'd had the option, he would have run happily back to his den. But Silas was already too dangerous, even without the Stone, and the treasure was the key to a possible cure. With Abigail caught up in hunting for the Stone, there was no way Nathan could turn his back now.

Theodora took her time getting to her feet, her claws scraping the laminate floor as she struggled to find her balance.

Nathan glanced over his shoulder at Jessica. "Hurry it up, will you?"

After shooting him an incredulous look, Jessica withdrew to the back of the library where Damien and Abigail were. Nathan positioned himself in the dragon's path, guarding the others.

"Abigail!" Jessica shouted, "How are you doing?"

"I-I need more time."

Smoke spilled from Theodora's nostrils. *Enough. You are not permitted to read it either,* she said. Her teeth glistened and dark-grey smoke started to pour out of her mouth, as dense a tar as it crawled across the floor toward them.

"We're out of time," Jessica snapped. "Leave the book, Abigail."

"But—"

Jessica grabbed the book from her hands, held it up to show Theodora, and then tossed it to the side, ignoring Abigail's cry of alarm. "See," she told the dragon. "We're not taking the book. We good now?"

No. Theodora whipped her tail, striking Nathan in the ribs. A sharp pain laced through his abdomen, causing the rest of his body to shake from the aftershock, and giving Theodora an opening to slip past him and charge toward the others.

Nathan's heart jumped into his throat. He reached out to try and grab the dragon's tail before she could get too far.

Jessica threw out her hands, and a large green cloud poured from her palms. The fog swept across the floor, swallowing Theodora's smoke, and crawled up the walls

"Oh god!" Abigail cried out, covering her nose.

Nathan quickly covered his nose with both his hands, but it was too late. He gagged as the horrid taste of rotten eggs and skunk-spray coated his tongue. Theodora coughed beside him, the deep sound shaking his ribs, and she fell to the ground as the green vapour enveloped Nathan's vision. The visceral twisting in his stomach stole his strength, forcing him down to a knee as he kept his mouth closed despite the painful urge to cough.

Someone grabbed his wrist, hauling him up. Blindly following the pull on his arm, Nathan squeezed his watering eyes shut and ran through the putrid smog.

CHAPTER 11

Jessica

Jessica released a heavy sigh, sending a cloud of fog into the air. They made it back to the parking lot without any more obstacles. Nathan and Abigail rested on the small snow-rimmed field next to the trucks, but Jessica couldn't shake the tension from her shoulders.

Damien moved to stand at her side. His eyebrow lifted, revealing a subtle, amused expression behind his stoic façade. "I said no more flying books."

Jessica laughed unexpectedly, followed by a quick snort.

His grin quickly faded as he took a step closer, looking intensely at her face. "You okay?"

"Yeah," she said, despite the ache in her stomach from where the dragon had struck with her tail. "Why wouldn't I—" She stopped when he reached for her face. Every muscle tightened as she held herself in place, and her heart thumped loudly in her ears as Damien cupped the side of her chin. His thumb rubbed across her cheekbone, and when he pulled his hand back, his finger came away with a smear of blood.

The tension in his face eased. "Just a papercut," he said with a wink. "I was worried it was deeper."

"See," Jessica replied, her voice coming out breathy. "It's nothing."

"You took on a dragon. You honestly expect me to believe you're not *at all* hurt?"

"It's fine. Just some soreness." It was difficult to form words when he was looking at her so intently.

"Jess, honestly—"

A small groan interrupted Damien. He glanced over, and Jessica followed his gaze. Nathan was lying on his back with his eyes closed and his chest heaving. Abigail crouched next to him, watching him.

Jessica cringed. The stink bomb wasn't her proudest moment, but it had been the most effective distraction at the time. Other than the stench, it was harmless. Nathan would be fine after some time in the fresh air.

"Jess."

Damien's deep voice drew her attention back to him. He reached out and brushed her fingers with his hand. "Be honest with me."

"It's only bruising, Damien, honestly." It wasn't like he was any better than she was. Theodora had knocked him clear across the room.

Damien's expression softened, and a twinkle in his eyes promised mischief. "I could take your mind off the pain," he suggested, his voice low as his eyes dipped briefly to her lips.

Her lungs squeezed out their remaining air as alarm bells sounded in her mind. *Is he suggesting …?*

They hadn't kissed since the gala—the same night he held a knife to her back and betrayed her to help his brother summon Supai. It had been a week since then, and they still hadn't talked about it. She felt a magnetic draw to Damien, but instead of embracing the pull in her chest, her mind skipped to panic.

Damien waited, watching her, his expression growing concerned as she hesitated.

"I'm alright," she said, her voice quiet. She took his hand and squeezed it, hoping that he could understand the words caught in her throat. There was a craving in her gut, one that continued to grow stronger, and the intensity of those feelings scared her. She pulled away to join the siblings before the heat in her cheeks got any worse.

Standing at Nathan's side opposite Abigail, Jessica looked down at the werewolf. "Sorry," she murmured, giving him a sympathetic look. "Dragons are impervious to direct magic, but they're highly sensitive. It was the best distraction I could think of."

Abigail glanced warily from Nathan to Jessica and back to her brother. "It wasn't *that* bad."

The werewolf frowned, lines deeply creasing his cheeks. "You weren't in the *middle* of the smoke."

Jessica winced. This would be much easier if Abigail already knew her brother was a werewolf. Then she could be sympathetic to his suffering.

"He'll be fine," she assured Abigail. It would be better that they changed the subject. Jessica straightened, her back protesting from a lack of proper sleep and the dragon fight. "What did you learn from the book?"

Abby shot to her feet. "The chapter outlined the entire quest! But it was hard to focus with all the commotion—" She dipped her chin sheepishly as the others gave her a disapproving look. "I didn't get all the details, but I got the clue that will get us started."

Damien stepped forward, standing near Nathan's head. "Does that mean it's a scavenger hunt?"

Abigail nodded, gesturing excitedly as she spoke. "Quests are made up of a series of trials, usually meant to test the knight's strength and virtue. There are four trials on the quest for the Lupatus Stone, I think. Had I had time to read the whole chapter, we would know every detail." She sighed, her gaze drifting off. "I wish we could have kept the book."

"I think you're underestimating how hard it is to fight a dragon," Jessica scolded, crossing her arms over her chest.

Abigail pushed up her glasses, her cheeks turning red. "Sorry. Wishful thinking."

Jessica waved away the apology. She wasn't offended—if anything, Abigail's passion for the story made Jessica nostalgic. It took her back to when she was a kid, and Nonna would tell her the legends of different species to educate her about the magical world. Those stories had become Jessica's normal, but Abigail still had that unfiltered look of amazement that, admittedly, she envied.

"You could have ripped out the page," Nathan grumbled. Abigail gasped in mortification, while Jessica shook her head. The three of them stepped back, giving Nathan room. As he sat up, he rolled his eyes. "It was just a suggestion."

"That would have been reason enough for Theodora to come after us," Jessica reminded him. "I'm sorry, Abigail, but I think the book is probably gone for good." She was struck by a pang of guilt as Abigail's face fell.

"The dragon may still come after us, now that she knows Abby's read it," Damien said, his words tightening the air around them. "What is the first trial?"

Abigail opened her mouth to answer, but then stopped and drew back.

Sharing a wary look with Damien, Jessica's brows knitted. "Abby?"

"It's just …" She wet her lips, mustering some courage before meeting Jessica's gaze. "If I tell you, do you promise you'll let me come with you?"

Oh no, Jessica silently pleaded with Damien. *Tell her she can't come.* He would be so much better at this conversation than she.

Damien raised an eyebrow but didn't speak.

Pursing her lips, Jessica tried to give him a serious scowl, but he was unmoved. *You are no help.*

"Look, this is incredibly dangerous, and we don't know what we're getting into. It will be safer if you give us the information and leave it—"

"Don't patronize me because I'm human," Abby interjected, surprising Jessica into silence. "I have spent my whole life studying these stories, wishing that they could be real. Now that I know that magic exists, I can't walk away! This is *my* research. I want to see it with my own eyes."

"Are you kidding me?" Nathan pulled himself to his feet with a groan and put his hands on his hips, towering over Abby with his ridiculous height. "Silas is after the Stone. You can't—"

"Can't let him get to the Stone first? Absolutely." Abigail squared off with her brother, matching his stance and surpassing his conviction. "We have a head start. We can stay ahead of him. And if we run into him again, Jessica can beat him up."

Jessica raised her hands defensively. "Wait, hold on a—"

"Why are you being so stubborn?" Nathan said, a growl in his voice. "If it's a werewolf treasure, it's probably in the middle of the woods. How do you expect to keep up?"

Abigail's nostrils flared as she narrowed her eyes at her brother. "I can keep up," she assured him. "I go hiking every weekend. Several-hour-long hikes, too. Just because

I don't look like an athlete doesn't mean you can assume what I am or am not capable of!"

Nathan recoiled as if he had been struck, and Abigail held her head higher as she turned toward Jessica and Damien again. "I know these legends, and the languages they're written in, the best. There will be multiple trials along the way, and you will need my knowledge."

Damien looked at Jess. "She has a point."

Grinding her teeth together, Jessica stared at Abigail. The girl held her gaze without wavering. Finally, Jessica sighed. *Why do humans think they're invincible at the worst times?*

"Whether or not you can keep up, this is going to be dangerous."

"I'm not stupid," Abigail argued. "If there's a fight, I'll get out of the way. But I want to make sure Silas doesn't get the Stone. While I'll admit I can't do it without you, I'm also not going to sit back and trust you'll get it done."

Nathan's jaw went slack, and he stared at his sister as if she were an alien.

Jessica blinked, her eyebrows lifting. *I never would have guessed she'd have such a backbone.*

"If Abby's going, so am I," Nathan said, louder than was necessary. He ignored Abigail's furious stare, his ice-blue glare clashing with Jessica. "I know these woods better than anyone."

"He's right," Damien agreed, ignoring Nathan's skeptical look.

Rolling her eyes, Jessica crossed her arms over her chest. "I never said any of you couldn't come. I just don't think it's a good idea." How did she always manage to surround herself with crazy and strong-willed people? She didn't like the idea of dragging another human along with her—at least Damien had the training to defend himself—but without Abby's knowledge of the quest, they would end up wandering aimlessly through the woods.

"But there's one condition," she warned, focusing on Abigail. "You have to listen to *everything* we say. If we tell you to run, you run. No questions asked. Got it?"

"Absolutely."

Despite her suspicions of Abigail's quick acceptance of the rules, Jessica let it go. "So what is the first trial?"

Abigail's smile was so infectious that Jessica struggled to keep a straight face when she launched into an explanation. "The first trial is one of perseverance, and it starts where the blood of the land moves like a snake, the key held by something of Mother Earth. I'm certain that 'blood of the land' means a river or stream, but the rest is confusing."

There was a long pause as the words sank in. Jessica bit the inside of her cheek. She had never enjoyed puzzles.

"Could you be more specific than 'something'?" Damien asked. His focus made Jessica smile. He was as fascinated by the quest as Abigail, in his own quiet way.

Abby rubbed her palms together as she spoke, unable to stand still. "The tricky thing about language is that it's not a straight conversion from one to the other. One word in Latin could take on a few different possible meanings in English. Add the Celtic layers that I'm unfamiliar with and it becomes guesswork. The word used in the text roughly means a … *thing* produced by Mother Earth — but that could mean a piece of the earth, like a rock, or maybe one of the creatures believed to have been birthed by the earth." She chuckled to herself as if at a joke only she knew. "Under different circumstances, this would be a fun riddle."

"Okay, so the potential rock we need to find is resting by the river? Where's the nearest river?" Jessica asked.

They all turned to Nathan, whose expression Jessica couldn't quite understand.

"North of here, the river twists back and forth. Kinda like a snake," he mumbled. His heavy tone made Jessica wary, but they didn't have time to unpack Nathan's problems.

She turned to Damien. "Any chance your compass works for normal directions?"

"Nope."

Interesting. Since they'd left Toronto, she had been trying to coerce more information about the magical device from him, but Damien wasn't keen on giving up the details. Instead he had turned it into a game that, despite protesting the juvenile idea, she was determined to win.

"You have a compass that doesn't work?" Nathan asked.

To Jessica's surprise, Damien pulled the golden contraption from his pocket. Nathan's skeptical glower came as no surprise — it looked like a regular pocket watch until the case was opened, revealing the compass face. When Damien popped the cover, Jessica shivered as its energy rippled over her.

"It points to magical creatures," Damien explained.

Nathan flinched at the same time as Jessica realized the danger. The needle focused on Jessica when the case opened, but then the needle shivered and flinched in Nathan's direction. When it was about to shift focus to the werewolf, Damien snapped the lid shut and stashed it into his pocket.

Nathan let out a heavy sigh. Jessica shook her head at Damien and the roguish gleam in his eye. *He's as bad as an imp.*

Most people wouldn't see Damien's mischievous side at first glance — his stone-like composure rarely cracked. But Jessica knew what it meant to see the dangerous twinkle in his eye, and how his eyebrows twitched ever so slightly when he was amused or intrigued. He had clearly taken an interest in provoking the werewolf. His compass antic left poor Nathan looking like he had seen a ghost.

"I have a location spell that will point us north," Jessica said, eyeing the pocket the compass had vanished into. She would love even just five minutes to examine it. "In the meantime, we should find a place to crash for the night." The cold had begun to cling to her skin, and soon the light would evaporate completely.

Abigail hugged herself tightly, casting her gaze to the ground. "That's a good point."

"We're going to find a motel," Damien said, watching Abigail closely. "You could come to stay with us."

"No, that's alright, thanks. I'd rather have my own bed."

Jessica shared a concerned look with Damien. After all the girl had been through, being alone wasn't a good idea.

"Maybe we could sleep on your couch?" Jessica suggested. She wasn't keen on the idea, but there was a chance Silas might come back for her. "You should have some protection."

"Nathan could do it," Damien suggested. Abigail and Nathan looked at him with wide-eyed stares.

"Jess is right, you need protection. Nathan's capable, right?" Damien stared down the werewolf.

Nathan swallowed nervously, his nostrils flaring as his attention flickered between Damien and the ground. Finally, he dipped his chin, glancing at Abigail. "If that's okay with you?"

Abigail hugged herself, looking Nathan up and down. An ache beat in Jessica's chest. She knew how it felt to see oneself as a monster. The siblings clearly wanted to connect, but Abigail wanted answers Nathan was still too afraid to give her.

"Yeah, okay," Abigail said. She gave Nathan a polite smile as he lifted his chin, though caution still lingered on her features. "But you're sleeping on the couch."

He nodded.

"We'll meet back at this parking lot at sunrise," Damien said. He turned his gaze on her. "Shall we go?" One of his eyebrows raised.

Fruitlessly attempting to ignore the fluttering in her lungs, Jessica nodded and followed Damien to their truck, listening to the shuffling feet of Nathan and Abigail as the siblings headed for Nathan's beat-up red truck.

Watching them drive off did nothing to settle Jessica's nerves. That truck could be more dangerous than the werewolf driving it. *I guess we'll see if they survive until morning.* She couldn't even fathom being in Abigail's situation—a sibling you thought was dead reappearing in your life. What would happen if Connor magically came back? Her stomach twisted at the thought of Damien's deceased brother returning, and she shook her head to rid her mind of the thought, not ready to bring it up.

Damien went straight to the driver's side of their rented truck. They hadn't discussed it before, but he always drove. It didn't bother Jessica—it meant she could look out the window and take the time to think. Besides, if she pressed the issue, she was confident he would hand over the keys. Grudgingly, but he would. Thinking about it brought a shy smile to her lips.

As they drove down the hill leading away from the university, Jessica tucked her legs to the side and stared out at the city lights winking past the window, looking for a motel sign.

Damien reached over and flattened her hand against her knee to stop her incessant finger tapping. He left his hand gently on hers. "You're worried about them?"

She snorted. "How do you know what I'm thinking?"

"I don't," he said, squeezing her hand before pulling away. "That's why I'm asking."

Her fingers were cold without him, so she pulled her hands into her lap. "I'm thinking about a lot of things. Too many questions," she admitted, watching Damien's profile closely. "Why are you picking on Nathan?"

Damien's expression remained neutral. "Is that what you think I'm doing?"

"You're provoking him."

Damien's lips twitched. "He doesn't like me. I don't know why, but he's made that clear. If he's focusing on hating me, he's less likely to fixate on hating himself."

Jessica leaned her cheek into her fist as she propped her elbow up on the car door. "You noticed that too, huh?"

Just over a year ago, before she'd moved to Toronto, Jessica had lived with a pack of werewolves. Normal as it was for them to want to solve every problem with their fists, it was clear Nathan and his wolf were out of sync. "If a werewolf is required to find the Lupatus Stone, having Nathan along could be useful. On the other hand—"

"He's a liability."

"Exactly."

"It's nothing you can't handle," Damien reminded her.

Cheeks warming, Jessica leaned back into her seat. "I'm not worried about the physical risk, but I am concerned about having him and Abigail together. It feels like we've gotten ourselves stuck in the middle of soap opera."

"We'll have to wait and see how they get on tonight."

"I guess."

Damien glanced at her from the corner of his eye, raising his eyebrow.

Jessica sighed. "I was also thinking about this werewolf Silas. Doesn't it seem weird that someone as arrogant as Supai would enlist help?"

Nodding, Damien slowed the truck, pulling into the parking lot of a small two-storey motel. The green awnings didn't quite match the peeling white exterior.

"And how did Supai learn about the Lupatus Stone?" she went on, her worries beginning to flood out of her mouth. "Maybe the magical realm is more connected to our world than we thought, which is a dangerous possibility. Or maybe Silas was the one who told him about it. Then there's Supai loaning Silas the demons, but we haven't seen him yet. And the last corpse demon that escaped with him. And what about—"

Damien turned off the truck and reached over, taking her hand in his again. Jessica's heart palpitated as she was trapped by his warm gaze. Her lips were tempted to smile, even though she didn't have a reason for that other than him holding her hand. *Ridiculous.*

"What's the priority?" he asked, rubbing his thumb across her knuckles.

"Get the Stone."

"Then we focus on that." His small smile eased the knot in her stomach and made her muscles feel gooey. "We already know what to expect from Supai, and you have a strategy for fighting the demons. Until we see them, there's nothing we can do about it."

"That doesn't make me feel much better," she complained lightly.

"We can make a plan and get supplies tomorrow."

"Yeah … okay." She matched his grin, the warmth from his hand spreading to the rest of her body. They stayed like that for a moment, staring at each other, her hand wrapped in his.

Jessica was acutely aware of every inch of her skin. Were her legs always so long? Why did she feel like a zit had popped up on her cheek?

What do I do now? She had the inexplicable urge to move, but she couldn't tell if she wanted to pull away or pull him closer.

Damien released her hand and sat back in his seat. "So what should we do about … you know?"

"What?"

Damien gestured to the motel. He gave her a sheepish look. "Our … sleeping arrangements?"

A fire lit up in Jessica's belly. "Oh. Um. Uh." They had only spent one night together, and it had been on the way up to Prince George, sleeping in the car. Jessica sat up straight, staring at the motel door. She felt like she was sitting on the edge of a cliff.

You've fought demons, werewolves, harpies, and leprechauns, and you've faced down a freaking god. Being honest with Damien should be easy.

Wringing her hands in her lap, Jessica sucked in a steadying breath. "I'd rather get two rooms," she admitted. Clenching her jaw, she braved a look at Damien.

"Works for me," he said, his expression giving away no hint of his true feelings. He pulled the keys from the ignition and opened the door. "I won't have to listen to you snore."

Jessica's jaw dropped as Damien left the car wearing that taunting smirk. "Hold on a minute," Jessica said, scrambling to catch up with him. "I do not snore!"

CHAPTER 12

Nathan

How did I get here? Nathan stared up at the beige ceiling of Abigail's living room, wishing he were looking at treetops instead. Yesterday, he had slept on his dingy mattress, surrounded by the quiet, familiar sounds of the forest. Now he lay rigidly on a leather couch, his ankles dangling off one of the arms, unable to sleep. The comfort of the cushions made him uncomfortable.

The rustling from Abigail's bedroom had stopped three hours ago, so he assumed she was asleep. *Good.* She must have been exhausted.

The only evidence of her attackers' presence was the broken back door, which Nathan was facing to keep an eye on, and a small bloodstain in the middle of the living room floor. Nathan's throat tightened when he remembered the man's eyes stretching in panic before the life disappeared from them. Abigail had stared at the stain silently for a minute and then retired upstairs without a word to Nathan.

I'm not going to sit back and trust you'll get it done.

Her bold words echoed through his mind. This was not the sister he remembered. The Abby from his childhood would have cowered from Jessica's threat. He'd smelled her nervous sweat and heard her quickening heartbeat, but her conviction had been as palpable as her determined gaze. She was stronger than he was by far.

The sound of shuffling drew his attention toward the second floor. He watched the stairs between him and the kitchen, his muscles tensing as the footsteps got louder. When Abigail stepped into the living room, she looked in his direction and gasped.

Crap. Nathan shut his eyes, wishing he had been smart enough to pretend to be asleep.

"Sorry," she whispered. "Did I wake you?"

"Nah," he assured her, reluctantly turning his head. "I don't sleep well."

"Oh." She rubbed her arms like she was cold. "Neither do I."

Unsure how to reply, Nathan stared at her as the silence thickened, filling the room like sludge.

"I'll be a few minutes," Abigail said finally, nodding toward the kitchen. "I'm just making hot chocolate."

Nostalgia wrapped Nathan in a warm embrace. "Like mom used to do," he murmured. He sank deeper into the couch, wishing he could disappear into the cushions.

"Yeah," Abigail said quietly. "When we had nightmares."

Nathan tried to ignore the painful quiet, focusing intensely on the rise and fall of his chest.

"Do you want one?"

"What?" He looked at her in surprise. "Oh, no, that's okay. I'm good." He stared at the ceiling, watching her movement from his peripheral vision. Abigail nodded and shuffled into the kitchen. The light came on, followed by the sound of a metal pot being placed on the stove.

Nathan couldn't remember the last time he'd had hot chocolate. His throat tightened as he tried to picture his mom's face and failed. He couldn't remember his dad's features either. Time had blurred the images.

He remembered other details vividly though. His mom had had the same curls as Abigail, but a dark chocolate brown, unlike Abigail's sandy brown. He and Abby had inherited their hair colour from their dad. Their parents always had oil stains on their clothes because they ran a mechanic shop. No one had known where Abigail got her bookish smarts from, except their dad had enjoyed trivia and used to read quiz books with her before bed. Nathan didn't like reading—he'd run around the backyard until his mom would finally yell at him to come inside. He was always outside, no matter the time of year. They'd never scolded him for the mud he tracked in; Mom had simply made him clean up his own messes.

He was so lost in his memory, his senses consumed with the ghostly smell of machine oil and his mother's rose perfume, that he didn't notice Abigail's presence until she was standing next to the coffee table. He sat up and swung his legs around to sit properly on the couch. She placed a mug in front of him before taking a step back, holding her cup up to her nose. She wasn't wearing her glasses, and Nathan got a good look at the dark circles under her eyes that had been hidden by makeup before.

She nodded at the cup on the table. "It might help you feel better," she said quietly.

Nathan looked down at the cup, watching the steam wafting up from it in fascination. *For me?*

"If you don't want it, you can pour it down the sink," she said, taking another step away.

Nathan reached for the cup, lifting it carefully for fear it might break if he moved the wrong way. "Thanks," he whispered, too stunned to drink it. If the warmth hadn't been pressing into his palms, he would have thought he was dreaming.

Abigail stared down at her cup. Swallowing his nerves, Nathan cleared his throat. "Are you alright?"

Shifting her weight, she lifted her gaze to his. "I'm sorry for getting mad at you earlier. I meant what I said but … I wish I hadn't said it the way I did."

The words pressed into the emotional bruise on his heart, but he deserved it. "I respect that." He gave her a soft smile. "You shouldn't apologize. It's been a messed-up day. But …" He lost his nerve, looking down at his hands as he wet his lips. "I shouldn't have said you weren't capable of hiking through the woods."

To his relief, she gave him a meek smile. "Thanks."

"I don't want you to get hurt," he explained, the words escaping before he could think about what he was saying. "I know the monster Silas is, and I couldn't keep you safe from him or his idiots. If you come on this quest, then … then—"

"Nathan," Abigail said firmly. She rubbed her mug as she spoke, her focus shifting between him and the floor. "You took on three thugs possessed by demons all by yourself and … and you still came after me." Her nervous swallow filled the quiet of the room. "This is … a lot to take in. After Mom and Dad died and you …"

She hesitated, releasing a stressed breath from her nostrils. "Life wasn't all bad, but it was hard being alone. I changed foster families four times until, finally, someone kept me, but none of it was ever home. Books were all I had to rely on, and now that knowledge might be useful. I've dreamt my whole life of an adventure like this."

She met his gaze, her eyes glistening. "It's nice you want to keep me safe and all, but, well, you don't know me, so please don't tell me what to do. And I don't know you either," she added quickly. "We don't owe each other anything."

Nathan nodded, his head hanging low. The smell of chocolate tickled his nose but brought minimal comfort. She was right—of course she was right. That didn't make it hurt any less.

"Maybe this could be a chance to, you know, get to know each other again."

A jolt of hope surged through Nathan's body, helping him to lift his head a little higher while his heart kicked into overdrive. "Yeah," he said in a wispy voice. "I'd like that."

She sighed and turned her attention to her drink. Nathan lifted his mug to his lips. The thick bittersweet chocolate coated his mouth and the warmth spread down his throat. He watched over the rim of the mug as Abigail's forehead crinkled like she was trying to solve a puzzle. Her lips parted, her chest rising like she was about to say more, and Nathan panicked.

"You should get some sleep," he blurted, cutting her off before she could ask any questions that he was too afraid to answer. "It'll be a long day tomorrow."

She met his gaze, the questioning expression lingering. "Alright," Abigail said finally, the words heavy. "Sleep well."

There was so much more Nathan wanted to say, but he had no idea how to translate his swirling emotions into tangible words. He stared at her back until she retreated upstairs. Once her door closed, he leaned back into the sofa and rested the cup of hot chocolate on his knee. He stared at the liquid until it grew cold, his attention consumed by the thoughts swarming inside his head like angry bees. Nathan wasn't sure when he had last had a good night's sleep, but he knew he wasn't going to get one tonight.

CHAPTER 13

Nathan

By the time the sun cracked the horizon and they were in the truck on the way to meet Jessica and Damien, neither Abigail nor Nathan had spoken a word. Nathan had never been so irritated with silence before. He couldn't shake the feeling that he was *supposed* to say something, and by the time they made it to the university, his chest was so tight it felt like his lungs could barely fit.

Abigail was quick to get out of the truck and join the others, who were sharing a quiet conversation in the snowy parking lot.

Jessica smiled politely when she spotted Abigail. "How are you doing?"

"Ready to go," Abigail replied. She still had her ratty purple jacket, but she had layered a fleece underneath it, was wearing a better pair of hiking boots, and had packed extra layers in her bag. She knew what she was doing. Nathan still wore his jeans, sneakers, and sweater from the day before.

Damien turned at Nathan. "Any trouble?"

Shaking his head, Nathan eyed the backpacks in the bed of the truck. "You got supplies?" He'd assumed Jessica would magically conjure whatever they needed.

"Just some basics," Jessica explained. "I try to minimize my magic use when I can."

"*Why?*" Nathan and Abigail said simultaneously, with equal disbelief.

"Because if I use it carelessly, I tire myself out," Jessica explained, "and that could be even more dangerous."

"And what about you? You got some special soldier gear on you too?" Nathan asked sarcastically, gesturing at Damien.

"I have what I need." His expression didn't move an inch.

Jessica clapped her hands, causing Nathan to flinch. "Alright, let's go."

Abigail turned to Nathan. "Should we go back to your … um, cave first? So you can get your things?"

"Oh. Um, yeah. We could do that," Nathan said, rubbing the back of his neck. He hadn't considered returning to the den — he didn't need anything but the clothes on his back, except maybe a jacket for the evenings. Normally, he changed into wolf form if he was sleeping outside, but he wouldn't be able to do that with Abigail around.

"Which way is it?" Damien asked.

"About an hour east of here."

Jessica waved the idea away. "Damien's got extra clothes. You can borrow some of his things. We don't have time to waste going there and back."

Nathan shrugged his acceptance. Abigail gave him a confused look but didn't press the issue.

"How are we going to find our way if Damien's compass doesn't work?" she asked Jessica.

In response, the witch rubbed her palms together, and a golden light grew between them, as if she were creating a lightbulb. "By the guiding light of Polaris." When she drew her hands apart, the golden light swirled together and formed the shape of a compass the size of a small dinner plate.

It appeared solid, but when Nathan leaned forward to examine the instrument she had conjured from nothing, he could see Jessica through it.

"Wow," Abigail gasped, stepping closer to peer at the magic.

"It's a navigation spell," Jessica explained. "We can follow this north."

"Can I ... can I touch it?"

Jessica nodded, and Abby reached out to touch the compass. Her hand passed right through it. "Wow! This is incredible."

The translucent needle twitched to life. It lazily turned a full circle around the face of the compass, and then settled on north.

A flicker of admiration pulled a gentle smile to Nathan's lips. "That's pretty handy."

Jessica closed her palm into a fist and the compass burst into a small shower of gold. After wiping off her hands, Jessica placed them on her hips and addressed the group. "We found a public trail in the area that should give us a good start. It's about two hours away."

"Could I … could I go with you?" Abigail asked. "I'd like to ask you some questions about magic."

"Um, sure," Jessica replied politely, giving Nathan a wary look over Abigail's shoulder.

He didn't mind. Admittedly, he was relieved to have the space to give his brain some time to think straight. "I'll follow behind," he said.

Damien cast a suspicious look at the old pick-up. "Will that thing make the drive?"

"I bet I could beat you there."

"If you knew where we were going," Jessica chided.

With a sheepish look, Nathan nodded his silent agreement that they would lead the convoy. He watched Jessica and Damien lead Abigail to their black truck. His sister didn't waste a second before starting the interrogation.

"Have you always known you were a witch?"

"Yes," Jessica said, leaning away as Abigail inched closer.

"Is it genetic?"

"As far as I know."

"Are there limitations other than getting tired?"

Jessica's jaw dropped slightly. "You want me to *tell* you my weaknesses?"

Nathan zoned out their conversation as he retreated to his truck, his lungs finally filling with some ease. It was momentary. Soon, he would be spending twenty-four hours with a dangerous witch, an irritating soldier, and the sister who had thought he was dead for the last seven years.

Gritting his teeth, he slid into his truck and started the engine. It took three tries, but he wasn't in a rush. For the first time in his life, he was running toward trouble—but this trouble was possibly the only way to cure the last seven years of torment. His throat tightened. *This'll be fun.*

Two hours later, Nathan's hands clenched the steering wheel as Damien's truck pulled off the highway into the small parking lot that marked the entrance to the public trail. Grudgingly, he pulled up next to them and slipped out of his truck. He left it unlocked, as usual, and leaned against the door while the others exited the other vehicle.

Jessica's expression was a strange mix of amused and exhausted when she crawled out of the passenger seat. Abigail hopped out of the back a moment later with twice the energy she'd had when they'd left.

While Abigail continued her questions, Nathan helped Damien unload the backpacks from the bed of the truck, keeping one ear on Abigail.

"Do witches and werewolves get along?" she was saying.

Nathan bristled, turning his attention sharply to their conversation.

"What do you mean?" Jessica's forehead creased, crouching in front of her bag.

"I've read that some species are natural enemies, like vampires and werewolves. Do witches have any rivalries like that? Is there an instinctual drive that makes you want to fight Silas?"

Pausing her work, Jessica straightened and faced Abigail. "You ask questions I never expected a human to ask."

As a bright blush bloomed across Abby's cheeks, Jessica turned back to her bag, checking the contents as she spoke. "Anyway, that's not completely true. Those rivalries usually happen between species that are naturally territorial, like werewolf packs and vampire covens. Witches don't have natural enemies; we'll make them with any species as we go along."

Damien coughed.

"Well, there are witch hunters," the witch corrected, looking at Damien from the corner of her eye. "But they're everyone's enemies."

"Witch hunters?" Abby asked.

Nathan scrunched his nose. "Isn't that something you should be worried about?"

"The name is misleading," Damien cut in. "Witch hunters are humans that fight any magical creatures who threaten the peace."

"You won't have to worry about them," Jessica assured Abby with a smile. "Even they're not *natural* enemies. They're raised or trained to think the way they do. Similarly, once a werewolf makes up their mind, they're among the most stubborn creatures I've ever met. You usually have to fight them before you can get a word in." She stood and hoisted her bag onto her back.

Sounds about right.

"More stubborn than you?" Damien asked. He slung his backpack on and turned toward the trail before he could see Jessica sneering playfully at him.

Abigail giggled and reached for her backpack.

Nathan cleared his throat. "I could … carry that for you?" When she frowned at him, he held up his hands defensively. "I don't mean you can't," he added quickly. "It's just, I got nothing to carry."

Abigail pressed her lips together. Nathan prepared for the backlash but, instead, her expression softened. "Sure. Thanks." She handed him the bag. Surprised by how light it was, Nathan smiled with relief and put it on.

Damien strolled in front of them and Nathan behind. The path started flat, the snow melted from the consistent passage of people, though it clung to the banks on either side of the trail. Nathan eyed the sky warily. The area usually had a coating of snow by this time of year, however thin it was. They were overdue for a storm.

"How did you learn so much about the magical world, Jessica?" Abigail asked, taking up an easy pace next to the witch.

With a shrug, Jessica readjusted her bag. "From my grandmother, who raised me, and life experience, mostly. For example, I lived with werewolves down in Seattle for about seven months before I moved to Toronto."

Damien raised an eyebrow at her. "How does that story go?"

Nathan heard a distinct spike in Jessica's heart rate. "I was chasing a harpy that was stalking campers and accidentally ran into their territory. We got into a fight, but once I proved I could hold my own, they invited me to stay."

"They attacked you?" Abigail asked in a loud whisper. Her curly hair bounced as she skipped a step to keep up with Jessica's steady gait.

Nathan found himself upping his pace to close the distance between them, his ears closely trained on Jessica's words. Other than Silas, he hadn't encountered any other werewolves. Everything he knew about his abilities, he had discovered through trial and error.

"I've got a set of scars on my ribs from one of the lieutenants," admitted Jessica, speaking of the memory with fondness. "Malcolm was tough, but since I bloodied him just as much, I guess I impressed him."

Nathan tilted his head curiously. The tips of Jessica's ears were turning red.

Abigail let out a whistle, which sent a chill down Nathan's spine like someone had run their nails across a chalkboard. He was thankful she couldn't see him cringe.

"You know," Jessica said, glancing back at Nathan with an apologetic look, "that's a great way to disarm a werewolf."

Abigail's excitement shifted into a serious focus. "How so?"

"They're like enhanced humans," Jessica explained. "They're stronger and faster, more durable, et cetera. But their senses of sight, hearing, and smell are also heightened."

Damien stopped on the trail, halting their march. "If Silas shows up again, scream as loud as you can."

Nathan winced. It was good advice, but his stomach dropped at the possibility of Abigail using that skill against him.

Abigail's eyebrows knitted together. "How far do you think we can get before he tracks us down? If his sense of smell is so good."

Jessica and Damien exchanged a nervous glance, but Nathan spoke without thinking. "The car will help. Gasoline is an intense smell and will cut off our scent trail. It should take him a while to figure out where we are."

Expression brightening, Abigail turned her refreshed determination to the trees next to them. "Are we turning off here?"

Damien nodded. He had stepped to the side of the trail to check both directions for bystanders before leading the charge up an incline into an uncharted area of the woods. Jessica went next, rubbing her palms together to summon the tracking spell, followed by Abigail. Nathan brought up the rear, squeezing his eyes shut for a moment to mentally prepare for a human pace.

His summoned patience didn't last long. They hiked straight up for over two hours, and his cheeks burned in frustration at the excruciatingly slow pace the others set. He was used to the freedom of moving at his own speed and having to slow down to keep up with the others was making the wolf restless.

Filling his lungs with the crisp smell of pine trees, Nathan focused on their surroundings. The sun had cracked through the clouds, and it poured down between the gaps in the leaves, scattering light across the ground. Aside from their footsteps, he could hear the rustling of creatures escaping their path. The forest was always noisy, filled with the echoes of animal footsteps, the scratches of small claws or talons across bark, and the whispering of winds snaking through the leaves. He could pick up on the faint scuttling sound of the bugs, puttering through sodden logs that lay across the limp foliage. Their footsteps crunched into the thin layer of snow, which had become icy since the last snowfall a few days ago. It wasn't enough to slow them down, but the moisture quickly soaked into Nathan's sneakers, adding a squishy bass drum to the orchestra of the forest.

The wolf itched to go off the trail, to explore and take in the wood's nuances, but Nathan pulled the urge back. If he veered too far off their route, the others would be suspicious. With a frustrated huff, the wolf slunk to the back of his mind, its presence a constant quiet rumbling in Nathan's head. He had spent years fighting with the wolf; ignoring it completely was never possible.

By the end of the third hour, the pace had slowed even more. Though no one looked overtly tired, the others' breathing sounded like gales of wind to Nathan, and the scent of sweat was giving him a headache.

"Can we rest for a minute?" he called up to the front of their troop.

Damien stopped, turning halfway back to the rest of them. He had been checking over his shoulder frequently throughout the hike, but now he paused to evaluate them. "Good idea." He slid off his backpack and looked at Jessica pointedly.

She pressed her lips together before conceding with a sigh and extinguishing the tracking spell. "Fifteen minutes?"

"Sure," Abigail said. She placed her hands on her hips, rocking back and forth between her feet, and forced in a deep inhale. The curls around her forehead were a shade darker now, coated in sweat. "The bushwhacking does make it more challenging."

As they rested, Nathan shifted himself to higher ground so he could get upwind of their body odour. Surveying the area, he noticed Jessica's head was on a constant swivel.

"You worried about something?" he asked.

"The demons," she replied casually.

Abigail tensed. "Demons?" She pushed her glasses up her nose. "It's not like they can sneak up on us. Right?"

She glanced nervously at Damien, who gave her a grim shake of his head.

"The demons you experienced had possessed the men who attacked you," explained Jessica. "Demons in their natural form look very different. The ones that Supai has been using are living shadows."

"Living shadows?" Nathan cut in, gesturing as he spoke. "Like, smoky body, red eyes, and weird claws instead of fingers?"

Jessica turned her head sharply. "You saw them?"

He nodded, shifting under her intense stare. "That was why I ran in front of your car yesterday. I got jumped by a few of them in the woods." He sneered as he remembered their frustrating, cowardly tactics.

With a grimace, Jessica bit her lower lip. "It would be nice to know when they're coming, but it's impossible to find them unless I'm actively using a tracking spell. The best we can do is look for hints of their presence, such as shadows that look like they're moving on their own."

"What about Damien's compass?" Abigail pointed to the soldier.

"Limited range," he replied. "And if they've melted into the shadows, it doesn't pick them up."

"Really?" Jessica asked, her voice pitching like she had solved a big puzzle.

Grinning, Damien waggled his finger at her. "That's all you're getting."

While Jessica tried to press for more details, Nathan lifted his nose to the air, flaring his nostrils as he searched for the void of scent he had experienced the last time he met the demons. There was nothing out of the ordinary; because of the breeze they were walking into, he was only privy to the scents that waited for them ahead. There was no telling what could be following behind.

"Let's get going," Nathan said. "It looks like there's a plateau up ahead."

Abigail gave him an amused smile. "I appreciate your optimism."

He smiled back sheepishly, focusing on the ground. Too bad he couldn't tell her he could see the bend in the earth up ahead, the way the foliage stopped topping each other, and the flattened terrain.

"I'll lead," he offered, but Jessica stepped in front of him.

"If you lead, you'll leave us in the dust," Jessica said with a smirk. She marched forward before he could think of a retort.

With a grumble, Nathan brought up the rear, trapped right back where he had started.

This is going to be a long day.

CHAPTER 14

Jessica

From the small peak where they stood, Jessica stared down the hill with a sense of dread sitting heavily in her stomach. The river was visible through the trees at the bottom of a ravine. The fastest route would be straight down fifty feet of steep incline.

"Everyone move slowly. I don't want to have to levitate anyone down." If they stepped on any loose ground, it would be a dangerous ride. She took the first few careful steps, looking for rocks and roots to support her weight. All they had to do was make it into the ravine, and then they could get some water and take a break.

Damien was close by her side. "Does it take a lot out of you to levitate?"

"It's not a difficult spell, as long as you stay still," she admitted, pausing so she could catch his expression. "The bigger concern is that it will leave you *really* gassy, and no one wants to deal with that."

He choked on a short laugh, shaking his head. "You're not joking, are you?"

Jessica's lips quirked. "I wish I were." All spells left a signature behind, whether ambient magic or a particular effect. The metallic aftertaste of transportation spells was a good example. Levitation spells caused varying levels of gaseousness.

She looked back at the siblings. Nathan's brow was tightly furrowed as he watched Abigail traverse the landscape. Jessica admired her focus. She had exhausted Jessica with her endless questions about magic, but when needed, Abigail held her tongue and focused on the task at hand, her composure solid. So unlike Nathan, whose hands kept flinching at his sides.

At one point, Abby stumbled, and Nathan reached out to catch her. Abigail caught herself and shoved her palm out to stop Nathan from intervening. "I'm fine."

He grimaced and stepped back, crossing his arms over his chest as he gazed regretfully into the forest.

It was only a matter of time until Abigail figured out Nathan was a werewolf. Jessica dreaded the trouble that revelation was going to bring. Sighing, she turned her attention ahead and focused on getting to the bottom of the ravine.

The last hurdle was a six-foot drop off a ledge to the rocks below. Jessica and Damien managed it fine, and Nathan followed with ease, almost looking bored. Abigail hesitated, staring down at the jump pensively. She toed a pebble off the ledge, her nose scrunching in disdain when it crackled against the stones below.

"I can levitate you if you want," Jessica offered, hoping the tease might entice Abigail forward.

"No, that's fine," she replied quickly. "I'll manage." She swallowed nervously as she sat on the ledge.

"Is this when you admit you're afraid of heights?" Damien asked casually. Everyone turned to him with a jerk.

Abigail scowled. "I'm not afraid," she corrected. "I'm vertically challenged, and not inclined to jumping off ledges like *some* people." The skin between her eyes wrinkled as she scooted her butt closer to the edge.

While Abby was focused on the ground, Damien nudged Nathan with his elbow. "What?"

"Offer to help her."

Nathan frowned. "She gets mad at me when I do that."

"I said to *offer,* not to do it," Damien said, motioning his head to Abigail.

"And I said—" Nathan stopped himself as the words sank in. "Oh."

With a stressed exhale, he positioned himself below Abigail. Being the towering giant that he was, he would be able to touch her knees if he reached up.

"I'm here if you need it, Abby," Nathan told her, his voice hesitant.

Abigail swallowed again, looking between Nathan and the ground below. "Um …"

Surprise took over his face for a moment. "Can I … help you?"

There was a long pause before Abigail finally said in a quiet voice, "Yeah. Okay."

Nathan reached up. "Put your hands on my forearms, and I'll catch your waist to slow the fall."

Pushing herself as close to the edge as she could without falling, Abigail reached out for her brother. Nathan positioned his hands on her knees, ready to catch her waist, and she braced herself on his forearms.

"Make sure you bend your knees when you land."

"I know how to jump, Nathan," Abigail retorted, but Jessica noticed her fingers digging into his forearms.

"Any day now, squirt."

She let out an abrupt laugh. Then she took a deep breath and tipped off the ledge. Nathan grabbed her waist, easing the fall, and they both dropped to the ground in a crouch. Abigail's weight pitched forward, throwing her into Nathan's torso; he shot one heel back to keep upright.

"Sorry!" Abigail said, scrambling to detangle herself from Nathan.

"It's okay."

Straightening, Abigail brushed the dirt from her back. "Thanks for the help," she murmured, fixing her glasses.

"No worries." Nathan blushed, turning away.

"Well, we're here," Jessica announced. "Let's get some water."

The small, loose rocks of the ravine were slippery from melted snow and river spray, but the area was otherwise flat—a nice reprieve for the burning in Jessica's thighs. The canyon was expansive, with mountains stretching all around them to bracket the river. While most of the rocks close to the river's edge had been worn down to small pebbles, one large boulder the size of a shipping container stood to one side. They stopped next to the large stone and Jessica turned in a slow circle. "Could this be the place?"

Abigail frowned, also scouring the landscape. Jessica knew it was coming, but she still hated to hear Abigail say, "I'm not sure."

The historian sighed and took off her glasses, pulling the hem of her shirt from underneath her jacket to wipe off the lenses. "The first trial, the Trial of Perseverance, is supposed to be next to the snaking river, and it will be revealed by something produced by the earth. Seeing as the river bends up there"—she pointed ahead, where the eight-metre-wide river curved around a corner—"this seems like a good place to start."

After repositioning her glasses on her nose, Abigail paused. "Maybe there are instructions carved onto one of the rocks."

"You want us to search every rock?" Nathan asked with exasperation.

"It was just a suggestion."

Jessica let out a heavy sigh. She'd been afraid this would happen. "Let's have lunch. We're not going to get anywhere without a proper plan."

They dropped their bags on the rocky beach. Nathan and Abigail made their way to the water to get a drink, but Jessica caught Damien before he could follow. "Any chance you've thought of a plan?"

He hesitated a moment, then turned his gaze toward the siblings. "First, we see if Abigail can think of anything that might give us more direction. Maybe there's another legend that speaks about a trial by a river that she could cross reference."

Though his calm tone swept over her, settling her nerves, Jessica's nagging thoughts wouldn't leave her alone. "What if that doesn't help?"

"Then we split up and start searching. It's likely a subtle clue that can only be found if you know what you're looking for, or maybe a creature like Abby suggested earlier. That would be my bet, at least."

"But this clue could be anywhere along the river," she complained. The expansive stretch of riverbank they had landed on was half a kilometre long and continued deep into the mountains.

Damien sighed. "I'm not sure what more to tell you, Jess. Until we have more information, there's only so much we can do."

"Yeah, but—" She stopped and bit her lower lip. Taking in a chilly inhale, she let it out with careful control. They had a plan; that was better than nothing. "Thanks," she said quietly. "I'm glad one of us is thinking."

With a nod, Damien lowered his voice. "We could send Nathan to scout the area."

They looked toward the river, where Nathan lifted his head and glanced warily back at them. Sometimes super-sensitive werewolf hearing had its advantages. As long as they talked from this distance, Abigail would never hear them.

Jessica nodded, catching on to Damien's idea. "If this quest was designed for werewolves, a werewolf may have a better chance at finding the clue."

She kept her eyes on Nathan, who glanced warily at his sister before standing to his full height. Abigail was right behind him, her water bottle now full of river water.

"Nathan," Jessica said once the siblings were within human earshot. "Would you mind scouting the area? You seem the least tired."

"Yeah. Sure." His tone was heavy, but as he turned toward the forest, Jessica saw his expression lift, relief filling his eyes.

"I'll fill ours, too," Damien said, taking their water bottles to the river's edge.

While Damien refilled their water, Jessica sat down on the pebbles and stretched out her tight hamstrings. A moment later, Abigail copied her. Though they sat in silence, Jessica could hear the steady pulse of blood in her ears. She hated moments like this, when the polite thing to do would be to make small talk but she didn't have anything she cared to say.

Glancing at Abigail, she noticed the girl's gaze followed Nathan as he walked back to the treeline. "He'll be fine Abigail, don't—"

"Do you think he's hiding something?"

Jessica stiffened. "What makes you say that?"

Abigail shrugged, crossing her legs. "Just a hunch. He seems so different."

"It's been seven years, hasn't it?"

"Feels like it was yesterday." Abigail stared down at her feet, fiddling with her laces.

Shifting uncomfortably, Jessica searched for Damien. He had his back to her, hunched over the river as he splashed water on his face. *Hurry up*, Jessica pleaded silently. The silence pressuring her to say something. "Were you two … close?" she asked hesitantly, reluctant to see what door she might be opening.

Abby nodded without looking up. "We've always been opposites. Nathan bounced off the walls while I preferred staying inside with crafts. We fought a lot, but he was my best friend. Back then. Yesterday, when I first realized it could be him, it was like seeing a ghost. Losing all of my family, in one night …" She stopped, wetting her lips.

Jessica's shoulders softened. "You don't have to talk about it."

With a faint shake of her head, Abby met her gaze. "The first few years were hard," she admitted. "It's like a bruise that never heals. Until, you know …" She gestured in Nathan's general direction. "Apparently, he was alive all this time and never bothered to find me."

Pulling her knees to her chest with a loose grip on her wrist, Jessica picked up the bitterness in Abby's voice. "It makes sense you'd be angry."

"I guess I can understand if he was afraid of Silas coming after him, but … how could he think he couldn't come home? That we couldn't handle it together?" Her voice cracked. Abby closed her eyes for a moment, only lifting her head when she could continue in an even tone. "There's something he's not telling me."

"Do you *want* him back in your life?" After what Abigail had gone through, Jessica wouldn't blame her for wanting to distance herself from Nathan.

Expression hardening, Abby averted her gaze. "I don't know. I've done fine on my own."

"Honestly, I can't understand what you're feeling," Jessica admitted, giving Abigail a sympathetic look. "I don't have siblings, and I didn't know my parents. But this … this has to be hard on him, too." She glanced over her shoulder. Nathan had stopped at the trees, his nose turned up to the woods. "He probably needs some space to process it all."

Abigail sighed, leaning back on her hands. "I guess." Then she gave Jessica an apologetic look. "I'm sorry for dumping all that on you." She glanced in Damien's direction. "And I'm sorry you two won't get much alone time with us tagging along."

"What?" Jessica saw Damien was returning. "Oh no, that's not … I mean we're chasing demons, we're not—" She waved her hand around, as if trying to fish words out of the air.

Abigail pressed her lips together firmly, suppressing a chuckle. "Whatever you say, Jess. But you've got to admit …" Her voice trailed off as her attention was drawn over Jessica's shoulder. "Oh no."

Turning sharply, Jess spotted a party of three strolling up the riverbank toward them. She jumped to her feet, fingers ready at her sides. Silas sauntered closer with a chuffed grin; Supai, walking beside him, wore one equally smug. Between them was the corpse demon who had escaped Toronto with Supai. Her arms swung at her sides, limp as the stringy hair that framed her face.

"That's Mariel," Damien said in a harsh tone, joining Jessica.

She looked at him warily. He had never mentioned the woman's name before. It made the sight of her body being used as a demon suit all the more sickening.

"How did they catch us so fast?" Abigail asked, scrambling up and shifting behind Jessica and Damien. "Who's the other man? And who's Mariel?"

"The man with the tan brown skin is Supai, the Incan god we told you about," Jessica said through clenched teeth.

"Mariel is the corpse demon," Damien added. "She … she used to be a friend." His voice sounded like it was scraping across his throat as he spoke.

Jessica's fingers itched to hit Supai more than ever. She grasped Damien's hand instead, squeezing it tightly to remind him he wasn't alone. He squeezed back, his eyes focused on the encroaching threat.

"Well, well," Silas said. He stopped several metres away from them, his hands sliding into his pants pockets. He had traded his business attire for a tracksuit with sleek black pants and a dark blue jacket zipped up to the neck.

Instead of the black suit Supai had worn when they last saw him in Toronto, he was now dressed in a black tunic and cotton pants, though the same golden sandals were on his feet and the same jewellery adorned his ankles and wrists. "This certainly is an interesting coincidence," the god mused. A chill ran down Jessica's spine as his black eyes narrowed on her. "Do you remember what I told you last time we met, *witch?*"

'Next time, I won't leave you breathing.'

Stomach twisting, Jessica kept her hands ready at her sides. She remembered all too well how staring into Supai's smoky gaze felt like her soul was being pulled from her body. Both could be deadly if she got too close, and she also had to worry about the demon lurking behind them. Jessica forced down a painful swallow.

"This is the same witch you were telling me about?" Silas asked Supai.

"Yeah, hi there. I'm the one who tried to set you on fire yesterday."

The corner of Silas's lips tugged up into a snarl. "Yes, I saw you at the university. You were the one behind the fire *illusion?*" He made a show of looking her up and down. "I expected more."

Jessica scoffed. "It scared you pretty easily."

Supai put a hand on Silas's shoulder before the werewolf could retort. "Don't be baited by her sharp tongue."

"Yes, Silas, you should listen to him. He knows what he's talking about. He's lost to me once already," Jessica snipped, her heart drumming against her ribs.

She was satisfied to see the vein in Supai's temple throb. While he might pretend to be level-headed in front of his new ally, the crack in his composure, proof that her words had gotten to him, didn't escape her.

Damien pressed his arm into hers. "Stop provoking them," he muttered, keeping his voice low so Silas wouldn't hear them. "It's two against three."

He had a point. It was only her and Damien against a werewolf, a god of death, and a corpse demon. Abigail couldn't fight. Jessica worked hard to keep her mouth shut as Damien took a small step forward.

"Get to the point. What do you—" Damien bit off his words and cursed under his breath as Nathan sprinted out of the woods in a direct line for Silas.

"Nathan, stop!" Jessica shouted. Running in alone was idiotic, especially if he didn't want his sister seeing proof that he wasn't human. When he didn't slow down, Jessica threw out her hand, magic pulsing down her fingers. Nathan's eyes bulged, and his body decelerated.

Nathan's energy pushed back as he continued to trudge across the rocks. Jessica shoved her shoulder forward to push more magic into holding Nathan back. Her bicep quickly began quivering under the strain.

"Nathan!" Jessica ordered. "Hold on!"

Supai threw out his hands and a gale of wind bulldozed toward them. With her focus on Nathan, Jessica couldn't protect herself in time, and the wind knocked her backward. She rolled across the rocks, the stones pounding her body before she managed to grab hold of some rocks to stop her roll. Tossing her ponytail out of her face with a jerk of her head, Jessica quickly clambered to her feet.

Damien had managed to stay standing, shielding Abigail. Nathan had also been knocked off his feet and was slowly pulling himself to his knees.

Supai grinned, making Jessica's blood boil. "You know all too well, *witch,* that fighting me would be pointless."

"Yes, Nathan," Silas added, rocking back on his heels as the breeze ruffled his spiked hair. "I'm a werewolf, remember? How could you *possibly* take me on?" He tilted his head, smiling like he had already won a fight.

Baring his teeth, Nathan's clenched fists shook at his sides. He held his position and his murderous glare focused on Silas, who chuckled.

"You're a slippery bunch, I'll give you that much credit. A fake Stone, *tsk tsk tsk.*" Silas turned his grin to Abigail. "You're a clever human. I'll bet you know where to find the real Stone, don't you?"

Abigail let out a small growl under her breath.

"If you're afraid of a fight, you should say so," Damien quipped.

The god raised a thick eyebrow, looking down his nose at Damien. "You put on a good façade, hunter. I would have thought you'd be more shaken by seeing a friend in this state." He gestured to the demon with a malicious smile.

Watching Damien's profile nervously, Jessica caught the flex of his jaw, but otherwise, he held his composure. "My friend is dead. Your monster is wearing her body." Damien took a brave step forward, his hands casually at his sides. Jessica knew he was preparing to draw the knife strapped across his lower back.

Silas bent forward as laughter shook his body. Supai's malevolent smile stretched wider, but before he could answer, Silas said, "Look at you, trying to act brave. What advantage do you have? While your little witch is busy with our demon, you, a human, think you can take on a god? And that would leave Nathan to fight *me*." Silas drew out the word with great amusement. Nathan was going increasingly red in the face. "You know how well *that's* gone in the past."

Nathan's body vibrated, and Jessica could see the muscles protruding in his neck. How much willpower was it taking for him not to take on Silas's blatant challenge?

"Rather than fighting a hopeless battle you have no chance of winning," Supai added, taking a slight step ahead of Silas, "give us the girl, and we'll let you live. For now."

Silas glowered at Supai. "That wasn't the agreement. Who says we can't do both?"

"I do," he replied with force, not dignifying Silas's comment with a look.

"What do we do?" Abigail whispered as she pressed her back against the large boulder. Its shadow engulfed her. "We can't run."

"There's always another way out," Jessica muttered.

Across the beach, Nathan took a step toward Jessica and their group.

Silas caught the movement instantly and pointed a finger at Nathan. "Don't you move," he warned, his smile near-giddy. "If you do, I'll take that as instigation."

If Nathan could get closer to them, Jessica could use a transportation spell for their escape. It wouldn't work if they weren't next to each other. "We could split up. If we pretend Abigail knows the way, I can go with her. We can lead them off."

"No," Damien stated. "They won't take that deal if it involves you. I'll keep Supai busy while you get Abigail a safe distance away, and then—"

"You don't need so much time to think about it," Silas interrupted. He began crossing the beach toward them, his eyes narrowing on Abigail. "Get over here, girl."

Supai hung back, a deeply set frown marring his features.

Groaning loudly, Abigail tilted her head against the rock and stared at the sky as if she might find the answer to their problem in the dark-grey clouds. "If only I could have read faster, we'd be halfway to the Lupatus Stone by now."

Jessica was about to tell her how ridiculous and unhelpful that complaint was when the ground beneath them began to rumble. Holding her hands out to balance herself against the shaking, Jessica scanned the landscape. The rocks around her bounced as if made of rubber.

Abigail gasped and shoved herself away from the rock, falling right into Jessica. Turning around, Jessica's eyes widened as the giant boulder quivered.

"Get back!" Damien shouted. They scampered out of the stone's shadow, tripping and stubbing their toes. Silas and Supai retreated a few steps. From the looks on their faces, they didn't know what was happening either.

The boulder shuddered; its spherical shape distorted as some of the weight shifted toward the ground. Two stone hands pulled themselves away from the core, sending loose pebbles clattering to the rocky beach. The hands, attached to stone arms still secured to the rock, slammed their palms onto the ground one after the other, and the earth shock violently. Jessica bent her knees to absorb the shock.

The arms kept the rock steady while two legs unfolded from beneath the boulder and caused a similar vibration when they planted themselves onto the ground. Finally, a small rock popped out of the top of the larger boulder. Two eyebrow-shaped carvings shadowed its black eyes. The small rock turned from one side to the other, scanning the space.

Abigail's jaw dropped as the stone giant pushed itself up to standing. At its full height, it was as tall as two shipping containers stacked on top of each other.

The giant narrowed its gaze at Jessica, and then the stone split lengthwise beneath the eyes and the creature roared. The wind of it brushed Jessica's hair off her shoulders.

"Jessica, what is that?" Abigail's eyes stretched wide as she gawked at the rock giant.

Before Jessica could explain, Supai's tar-like voice rose behind them. She glanced over her shoulder to see him retracing his steps across the beach. "Leave them," he ordered Silas, whose expression had gone slack at the sight of the giant. "If they don't die here, we'll use them to lead us to the Stone."

Shaking his head and coming to his senses, Silas turned and jogged after the god. "Don't give me orders."

"Then do what I say the first time." They swiftly retreated into the thick of the forest.

Jessica didn't have time to chase after them — not that she was keen on confronting either of them yet. Or ever. She had much *larger* things to worry about.

They had found their first trial.

CHAPTER 15

Nathan

Silas had been there, within reach, and Nathan had been powerless to do anything. He was lucky Jessica had stopped him, though in the moment, he'd wanted to scream at her for it. Admittedly, he was relieved to see Silas retreating, even if it left them to face the roaring rock giant now looming over Nathan's sister alone. He sprinted across the beach toward her.

Jessica shoved Abigail backward into Damien's ready arms. He ushered the girl away, leaving the witch to stand alone against the massive creature. She barely came up to its knee.

The wolf's instincts took over, its strength and protective drive consuming Nathan's focus. He didn't have a plan—he rarely did. Once he was close enough, he lunged and slammed his fist into the giant's thigh.

The rocks gave way like flesh under Nathan's attack, and the giant stumbled sideways.

Nathan channelled his victorious momentum into another strike at the creature's shin. Pain rippled up his knuckles as his fist connected to stone and he cried out in alarm. Cradling his hand, he hopped three large steps backward to distance himself from the giant. When he examined his fist, he was shocked to see the back of his hand turning purple.

"What gives?" he shouted at the giant, who scowled down at him.

"Elemental giants can change the texture of their skin!" Jessica explained.

Now she tells me.

The giant threw back its head and roared. Nathan covered his ears, his body curling inward as the sound bounced through his eardrums. The ache passed quickly, and when he blinked his eyes open, the creature had raised both fists into the air, one above Jessica's head and one above his. They leapt out of the way as the giant's hands came crashing down, cracking the stones on the beach and sending pebbles shooting out like water spray.

When it realized it had missed, the giant stomped across the beach, chasing Jessica and Nathan toward the treeline. Each step made the rocks jump and pine needles rain down from the trees along the edge of the bank. The ground shook like it might rupture. Abigail screamed in the distance, and Nathan caught a glimpse of Damien using his broad frame to shield her from the chaos.

Shaking out his sore hand, Nathan ran at the giant again, dodging to the side as the creature tried to thrust its big rock hand at Nathan's face. He grabbed the giant's leg, but his arms barely made it halfway around the creature's shin. A horrible shiver raked his body as his nails scraped against the stone. He found a gap in the rocks and used it to get a better grip.

The creature shifted its weight onto its other foot and hopped up and down, trying to shake Nathan off as an aggravated sound rumbled from its chest.

Reaching up, Nathan dragged his body up the giant's leg. His feet slipped as the monster spun, and Nathan's teeth slammed together when it stomped its foot. Curse words flew through the air, mixing with the giant's angry grunts. Shifting his fingers into claws, Nathan stabbed his hand in between the folds of the giant's rocky skin, trying to carve out a handhold. The creature roared and thrust its legs violently. Nathan bit his tongue as his forehead slammed against the giant's shin. He tasted blood, but he wasn't sure if it was his or the giant's.

Nathan made it to the giant's knee and, when it paused its rampage, he checked his progress. His stomach dropped. He'd thought he could climb the giant's body and target its eyes or throat, which would likely be the most sensitive part of its body, but it would take him forever to scale the creature at this rate. The giant stared down at him, rocks sliding halfway over its black eyes like it was glaring at him.

The feeling's mutual.

The giant raised its fat palm, aiming at Nathan's head.

Desperately pulling back so he could jump off, Nathan found he had wedged the fingers of one hand too deeply into the creases between the rocks. He pulled sharply, but the fingers stuck, and a sharp pain lanced through his shoulder. Giant hands rushed toward Nathan's face, ready to squash him like a bug.

A boulder flew through the air and struck the giant in the shoulder. The rock exploded on impact, sending the giant reeling back on its heels as a shower of small stone fragments pelted Nathan in the head.

"Nathan, what are you doing?" Jessica shouted somewhere behind him.

"Keeping it busy!" he snapped back. "Hurry up and do something!"

The witch heaved a frustrated sigh. "Fine! Just don't let go!"

Couldn't if I wanted to. Letting go now seemed like a foolproof way to get squashed underfoot.

The giant stopped hopping and wheezed out of whatever part of the stone was its nose. It looked down at Nathan, obviously annoyed.

In his peripheral vision, Nathan saw Jessica running toward the giant's side. She jumped into the air and threw up one arm. A pillar of rock shot up like a geyser. She landed on its flat top and, without slowing, used the rising platform to gain height against the giant. Her shadow passed over Nathan's head as she soared through the air and landed on the giant's shoulder.

"Radetay uroay onguestay nday haresay uroay ordsway!" she shouted. "Please, stop!"

Shockingly, the giant listened. It straightened, and with the sound of stones grinding against each other, turned to look at Jessica with surprise.

Jessica's shoulders relaxed. "We mean you no harm," she said. "Please tell me why you're attacking."

There was a long pause. Nathan's blood pounding in his ears through the silence. He wasn't sure what he expected a giant's voice to sound like, but the grumbling that emerged from the giant's throat was not it. There was a rhythmic pattern to the grunts, and Jessica made an *mmhmm* sound like she could understand it.

"Is that why you're here?"

The giant responded with two grunts.

"Well, personally, I would rather talk than fight. I'm sure my friend will let go if you agree to that."

After a long, thoughtful pause, the giant gurgled in reply. Nathan wasn't sure what Jessica meant, but beneath his hands, the giant's skin gave under his grip, shifting back to a fleshy consistency. *This must be its relaxed state.* It probably looked like a rock for camouflage, while being able to change its skin to defend itself.

Taking the giant's calmness as a sign of good faith, Nathan unwedged his fingers and jumped off the giant's leg, shuffling backward until he had a clear view of Jessica. She had settled down on the giant's shoulder and was nodding intently in response to its grunting.

Nathan retreated further, meeting up with Damien and Abigail to observe the seemingly pleasant conversation between Jessica and the giant.

"Are you alright?" Abby's face had paled. "I can't believe it attacked you!"

"It's a good thing you're fast and could dodge all its rampaging," Damien added with forced articulation.

After letting Damien's words sink in, Nathan nodded stiffly. From their perspective, Nathan had gotten caught on the wrong side of the giant and had been trying to get away from it.

"I got lucky, I guess," Nathan managed, though his mouth had dried up. *Too lucky.* He cursed at the wolf for taking over and at himself for losing control.

Abigail stared at him, unblinking, and Nathan could smell the cold sweat wafting off of her.

He softened his gaze. "I'm fine, Abby. I've dealt with dangerous things before. You know. Living in the woods."

"Okay," she said in a quiet voice before returning her focus to Jessica. "How did she manage to calm it down?"

"She must have found a way to talk to it," Damien guessed.

After several minutes of quiet conversation, Jessica stood on the giant's shoulder. It lifted an open palm for her to step onto and lowered her gently to the ground.

"Thank you," Jessica said. She gave the giant a little wave as it turned away from them and marched back to the indent in the beach where it had previously been resting.

With a sigh, the steam of its breath rising into the air like the puff from a steam engine, it curled into a boulder once again and went still. They stared silently at the giant, waiting to see if it would jump up again.

Jessica joined their small gathering. "Everyone alright?"

"Are you?" Abigail asked in amazement.

Jessica shrugged, a crooked smile on her lips. "Yeah, I'm fine. That wasn't how I expected that to go." Her eyes lingered on Nathan for a moment, and he noticed the muscles of her jaw flex.

Nathan's cheeks flushed as he averted his gaze.

"How did you do that?" Abigail asked, splitting her focus between Jessica and the sleeping giant.

"I used a language spell that allowed us to understand each other. Honestly, I was hoping to use it to find a weakness but turned out it was friendly." She made a small *hmm* noise and glanced over her shoulder like she couldn't quite believe the events herself.

"Its purpose is to test the persistence of those seeking the Stone. The task is to defeat the giant or tire it out, but since we were the first to try and *talk* to it, it was pretty happy to let us pass. The clue to the next trial will be revealed when the giant goes dormant again."

"I guess no witches have tried to find the Lupatus Stone before," Abigail murmured. "Where does the clue appear?"

Jessica motioned to the boulder. "On its body."

They trekked back to the stone, approaching with cautious steps once they were within arm's reach. Abigail's hand shook as she gingerly placed her fingers on its surface. "Amazing," she said, her face lighting up. "It feels like regular stone. Hard to believe it was moving a second ago."

The stone shuddered, and Abigail pulled her hands back with a jerk. Cracks in the rock glowed an iridescent blue, trailing across the surface. They swirled and changed direction until the letter *A* formed.

Peering closer, Nathan realized it wasn't cracks glowing, but magical letters painting themselves across the surface.

"Wow!" Abigail pushed her brother until he stepped aside so she could stand in front of the letters as they formed and held steady. Nathan didn't understand the words, but his sister squealed excitedly.

"What does it say?" Jessica jostled Nathan's other side to get a better view. With a grumble, he retreated, resigning himself to the sidelines with Damien.

"'Follow the path to the edge,'" recited Abigail, "'and listen for the Beast's roar. Judgment of your soul'—no, *heart*—'will decide your future.'"

"What 'path'?" Jessica asked.

Abigail scrunched her nose at the letters.

To Nathan's surprise, Damien beat them both to the explanation. "It's telling us to follow the river."

"What makes you say that?" Jessica asked.

Damien shrugged, but his eyes were bright. "Rivers are nature's pathways. Indigenous peoples around the world have used them for centuries."

Abigail was smiling. "The edge will be the end of the river. Maybe a waterfall."

"Which could also be 'the Beast's roar,'" Damien added, cracking a smug grin.

Nathan's heart sank. He was useless with puzzles and this whole journey was one riddle after another. From the pout on Jessica's face, he guessed she felt the same. *At least she has her powers.*

Jessica grabbed her backpack and set it on a small rock so she could brush off the dirt it had accumulated during the chaos. "We should get moving. I doubt Silas and Supai went far. From now on, we have to assume we're being watched."

Everyone stiffened. Nathan lifted his nose to the air and inhaled deeply, hoping to catch Silas's scent. If he knew where the werewolf was, maybe he could go off and fight him, ending this before Silas ruined his life once again. Nathan's heart spasmed at the idea.

"While we walk," Abigail said, enunciating each word precisely, "I think you need to explain some things."

Jessica paused to look at Abigail, who shifted her shoulders down her back to keep her posture firm. "For starters, what is a corpse demon?"

"Something worse than possessed," Nathan muttered. That woman looked like a zombie with red eyes, different from the black eyes of the possessed men the day before. Supai also had those black eyes — which reminded Nathan of something the god had said.

"The god called you a *hunter*. What does that mean?" He narrowed his eyes at Damien.

Jessica and Damien stared at each other in silent conversation. Damien was the first to move, running a hand through his curls. "We should tell them."

"Are you sure?"

"Yes," Nathan demanded, unfazed by Jessica's obvious disapproval.

The witch sighed, her hesitation making the hair on Nathan's arms stand up. She shot Damien one last nervous look before saying, "Supai murdered witch hunters and used demons to possess their corpses. The process caused the two to fuse, creating a demon inside a human body. They can't turn to smoke, but they're stronger and more durable than regular demons, making them nearly impossible to destroy."

Abigail's eyes widened in horror as she looked at Damien. "You said that woman used to be your friend."

"What?" Nathan dropped his arms, hands clenching at his sides.

Damien met his glare head-on. "I'm a witch hunter."

With his muscles tightening, the wolf reared up in Nathan's mind, teeth bared, wanting to lunge at the threat.

Jessica put herself between Nathan and Damien, shoving Nathan in the chest to push him away. "Back. Off."

Nathan shuddered. A surge of energy rippled down his spine, forcing him to pause.

"If not for Damien, I would be dead," Jessica said with unwavering conviction. "If you have a problem with him, you have a problem with me."

As his lungs struggled to keep up with his racing heartbeat, Nathan forced himself to take two steps back. A small, weak voice in his head knew he was acting irrationally, but the protest was squashed by the wolf's more powerful impulses. The wolf was as furious with Nathan as it was with Damien. Its instincts saw Damien as a threat and urged Nathan to fight, but his human thoughts desperately fought against those feelings.

I hate this, he thought as his shoulders sank.

"This could be a good thing, Nathan," Abigail told him, shocking him with her confident tone. "We're up against a werewolf and a demon god. Having someone on our side who can hunt magical creatures is a *good* thing."

"You can trust him," Jessica assured them.

Nathan nodded as he stared at his feet.

Damien gestured toward the river. "Let's go. We want to get as far as we can before it gets dark."

They all agreed silently. After locating their other bags they headed out in the direction Damien had chosen, though everyone walked with a heaviness in their step. Jessica lingered behind, watching Nathan closely. He slowed his already dragging pace until they were out of earshot of the others.

"What were you thinking, attacking the giant like that?" she whispered as they walked side by side. "You rushed in without even thinking. We were lucky it chased us toward the trees rather than running toward Damien and Abigail. You can't be that reckless."

Every word was a punch to his gut. "I can't change what I am," he argued weakly.

"I'm not asking you to. And neither is she," Jessica said, gesturing at Abigail, who was conversing quietly with Damien. "I think she wants her brother back, but how can she trust you again when she doesn't know who you really are? Not that you seem to know the answer to that question. You and your wolf clearly have some issues to sort out."

He kept his eyes focused straight ahead while blood rushed to his head at the thought of his reckless behaviour.

"I'm trying to help."

"I didn't ask for help." Nathan's urge to run was an incurable hunger gnawing away at his stomach, but there was nowhere to go. "I don't want your help or advice."

Jessica stared at him silently, her expression tight, like she wasn't sure what to do with him. *As if I have a clue.*

Finally, she turned away from him and headed toward the others. Then she stopped, pinning him with a fierce gaze. "You're going to have to face this eventually."

Nathan bit the inside of his cheek to keep from saying something stupid, until Jessica had joined the others. Then he let out a heavy sigh, his muscles trying to drag him to the ground as fatigue and regret overwhelmed him.

"Come on, Nathan!"

He flinched at Damien's call, realizing he had dropped far enough back that Damien had to project his voice to reach him. Abigail was bracketed by the others, but she looked over her shoulder before returning her focus to the path ahead.

Nathan gave a half-hearted wave, acknowledging he was following, and then shoved his hands into his pockets and kicked a rock that had the misfortune of getting in his way. He hated that Jessica was right. He could be a danger to Abigail and the others in his current state. *Get the Stone.* Once the wolf was gone, Nathan wouldn't be a burden anymore. He just had to make sure he didn't hurt anyone before then.

CHAPTER 16

Jessica

What little warmth had been present throughout the day had quickly abandoned the skies, leaving a chill in its wake that caused the hair on Jessica's arms to stand on end. The forest was dense with the fresh smell of oncoming rain. Keeping a distrustful eye on the darkness, Jessica dropped her backpack and stretched her arms overhead.

Their campsite for the night was a cramped clearing among the trees, providing level terrain and a thick canopy that would help protect them if there was a major snowfall. Once the debris had been cleared, Damien deemed it suitable for sleeping.

"Alright, let's set up the tent," Jessica said, cracking her knuckles and squaring off against her bag.

Abigail stared at the backpack curiously. "How did you fit a tent in there?"

"I didn't say I wouldn't use *any* magic," Jessica replied with a smirk. Squatting in front of the backpack, she gripped it firmly with one hand while wiggling the fingers of the other over the opening. "*Massimo assoluto.*" The sides of the bag stretched out, squeezed in, and then settled back to their normal shape.

Jessica reached into the backpack up to her shoulder and rummaged through its contents. *Come on, tents*, she coaxed, trying to find the handle of the tents' duffle bag inside the magically enhanced depths. The spell was great for packing, but the results were terribly disorganized.

"I think this is it," she said as she grasped onto a strip of canvas. With a firm tug, she pulled the duffle bag free, which was no small feat considering it was three times the size of the backpack she was yanking it out of, and tossed it to the ground victoriously. "There should be two tents in there."

Damien unpacked the tents, while Abigail stood frozen with her jaw hanging open. "How … but … was that …?"

"It's an endless bag spell. I can store as many inanimate things as I want in there without feeling the weight."

Giggling, Abigail took the tent poles from Damien. "That's amazing."

"I have a tarp in here somewhere," Jessica added, reaching back into the backpack. "We can lay that down beneath the tents to protect us from the snow." They would need as much protection from the cold as possible.

Once Jessica had pulled out the tarp and handed it to Damien, she scanned the campsite for anything else they might need. Her attention landed on Nathan, who was sulking off to the side. Her expression softening, Jessica let out a light whistle.

The werewolf flinched, sending a tense look her way.

"Could you go get some firewood? We're going to need it soon." Jessica hoped that would give him the space he needed to sort out whatever was going on in his head.

To her surprise, his forehead creased deeply, and he shifted his weight between his feet. "The wood will be soaked."

"That's fine, I can dry it out." *Take a hint.* "See what you can find. Take your time."

After a silent stare down, Nathan's expression eased and he nodded, turning back to the forest.

"That was weird," she muttered, watching Nathan disappear into the trees. "I thought he'd jump at the chance to get some space."

"He's probably wary of leaving Abigail unprotected," Damien said, keeping his voice low as he checked Abigail's position. She was focused on the second tent on the other side of their small clearing.

Jessica crossed her arms. "That's ridiculous. We are perfectly capable of protecting her."

Damien shrugged, his gaze lingering on the gap in the trees where Nathan had disappeared. Without responding, he turned to the tent they were setting up.

She watched his profile as he secured the tent poles into the ground and the shelter took shape. "Do they remind you …" She bit her lower lip to stop the insensitive question as her curiosity got the better of her.

Rising to his full height, his expression softened. "I can empathize," Damien answered anyway. "Losing close family is always painful."

"Sorry," she murmured, hating how the brightness in his eyes dimmed at the memory of his parents. No doubt the memories stirred thoughts about Connor as well. "Do you want to talk about it?"

"There's nothing to talk about." Damien went to help Abigail finish setting up the second tent, leaving Jessica with her awkward feelings.

Crossing her arms, worry lines deepened across her forehead. It hardly seemed fair for Damien to bottle things up when he constantly nagged her into sharing her emotions. Watching him interact with Abigail, seemingly at ease, she wondered if maybe he was genuinely okay.

As they finished with the tent, Abigail scanned the campsite. "Where's Nathan?"

"He went for firewood. Don't worry, he'll be back before it gets dark."

But as the faint orange and pink hues of sunset winked at them through the trees, even Jessica began to worry. He'd been gone for over an hour.

Abby huffed.

Brushing off his pants, Damien stood and zipped up his jacket. "I'll go look for him."

"That's a bad idea," Jessica said, giving him a bewildered look. The idea of Nathan and Damien being alone together made her muscles tense.

"I agree," Abigail said, sharing a worried look with Jessica.

"We'll be fine," Damien said, winking. Before anyone could protest further, he was gone.

With a loud huff of her own, Jessica leaned back on her hands. "*Men.*"

Abigail sighed, mimicking Jessica's stance as they both stared at the empty spot where the fire was meant to be. "Agreed."

CHAPTER 17

Nathan

Nathan didn't realize how dark it was getting until streaks of dying light cut through the trees. He cursed the sun for setting so quickly and turned to hike back the way he had come.

How far did I go? This forest was unfamiliar to him. As soon as he had the space, he had fallen into a sprint without thinking. The wolf complained because he hadn't shifted, and despite the exercise, he still felt as wound up as a twisted towel.

"Later," he promised the wolf, rubbing the heel of his hand into the skin above his heart. Once the others were asleep, he would go for a run in his wolf form. They both needed the release that would only come from using his full power. With a sense of satisfaction, the wolf receded, its presence surprisingly quiet.

Nathan stopped and stood in silence, listening to the calm in his mind with a sense of awe. It was unfamiliar and strangely peaceful.

Though suspicious of the wolf's stillness, Nathan pushed on. Branches crunched beneath his feet. The smell of fresh pine filled his lungs, along with the dense scent of the soil buried beneath debris and snow. Whispers filled his ears, this time from the gentle breeze that shifted through the leaves, rather than the taunting thoughts of guilt that usually plagued him.

The memory of Jessica's words tumbled through his mind. *You don't even know who you are.* He wished he hadn't snapped at her, but how was he supposed to carry a conversation when she rattled his brain like that?

When he reached the plateau that would lead to the campsite, he remembered he was supposed to be gathering firewood. Grumbling, he bent down, grabbing whatever decent sticks were in reach. "This is dumb," he muttered to himself, looking at his sad collection of twigs. Maybe he should break off some branches instead.

A scent caught his nose and Nathan tensed, turning to the trees at his back. A moment later, Damien emerged.

"You should be watching them."

"Abigail is safe with Jess," Damien replied calmly.

Nathan was confident of that; he just didn't want Damien around *him*. "Then go watch her back." He waved the other man away.

"We were getting worried about you."

Nathan paused, instinctively filled with mistrust. "'We'?"

Instead of replying, the witch hunter focused on the ground and picked up a fallen branch the length of his arm. After considering it for a second, he tucked it under his arm and continued his search.

Nathan narrowed his eyes, watching Damien suspiciously. "I don't need your help." He would be happy to beat the hunter into the ground to prove it.

"I know."

"Then why are you helping?"

"Because I want to." Damien stopped and met Nathan's glare with one of his own. "You got a problem with that?"

"Yes," Nathan muttered, though he couldn't articulate why.

When Damien didn't stop, Nathan gave up on the idea of fighting him and filled his arms with sticks instead. When he and the witch hunter had their arms full, they turned back toward the campsite.

Nathan listened intently to the sounds of Damien's movements, waiting for anything that might be suspicious. The reveal that Damien was a witch hunter didn't satisfy Nathan's nagging sense that there was something *other* about the man. Maybe it was his scent, though there was nothing out of the ordinary about that.

"You remind me of my brother."

Night had fully set now, but Nathan could see Damien's tense expression through the dark.

"How so?"

"You're emotional, hot-headed, overprotective," Damien explained, his tone light. "Connor was like that. Not that there's anything wrong with—"

"I didn't think so," Nathan lied.

"But it's also dangerous. Connor used to think he had to solve the world's problems on his own. Actually ... maybe we had that in common."

The honest confession made Nathan's skin tighten. "'*Used* to'?"

Damien nodded. "I prefer doing things on my own, but we were supposed to have each other. Instead, Connor acted as if he was completely alone. That was our difference, I guess."

"How is that a difference?"

"On your own and alone aren't always the same thing."

"You lost me," Nathan complained. *Can't you just leave?*

Damien shifted his twigs, freeing one hand so he could scratch the back of his head while he paused. "You have someone to turn to now. You can choose to be on your own, but you're not alone anymore."

Nathan shifted his weight restlessly. "As far as Abigail's concerned, I've been dead for the last seven years."

"And nothing can change that, but you're here now." Shaking his head, Damien glanced down the trail toward the campsite. "What I mean is, this could be your start."

Following his line of sight, Nathan made out the shape of the tents in the darkness. "Why are you telling me this?" he asked, but Damien was already moving on, heading toward the campsite.

Strange, Nathan thought, the tension in his body easing as he watched Damien. His heart softened as warmth seeped in. From the heaviness in Damien's tone, Connor must have been important to him—or at least there was more to the story that he wasn't sharing.

Nathan stopped himself, shaking his head furiously to rid himself of the sentimental feelings. He couldn't let his guard down, even if he did understand the witch hunter a smidgen better. He knew from the start that Damien was a protector by the way he interacted with Jessica. Nathan got the distinctive sense that Damien's brother was someone the hunter had failed to save.

Filling his lungs with fresh air, hoping some bravery would come with it, Nathan followed Damien toward the tents.

CHAPTER 18

Nathan

Nathan felt lighter the next morning. He had spent half the night running in his wolf form, and the memory of the snow squishing between his toes and the wind caressing his fur gave him a boost of energy. He needed any help he could get after so little sleep. The sky remained grey, and clouds hung above them like a heavy blanket. It wasn't dark enough to suggest snowfall, but that could change in a second.

Damien was the first to emerge from the tents. He nodded at Nathan and went straight to work collapsing his tent. Nathan watched him curiously, still puzzled by the unsolicited advice the night before.

Abigail, on the other hand, rubbed her face aggressively as she pulled herself out of the tent she and Jessica shared. She jumped when she noticed Nathan already standing by the remains of the campfire. "You're already up?"

He shrugged. It was better than telling her he hadn't slept at all, or that he'd most of spent the night lying on the dirt outside the tents. "Did you sleep?" he asked. The bags under her eyes were darker than the day before.

Stretching her hands above her head, reaching for the sky, and letting go with a heavy sigh, Abigail replied, "Not really. There's a lot on my mind."

"Are you … okay?"

"Hmm?" She looked up at him, then glanced away, wrapping her arms around herself. "Yeah. Fine."

A groan escaped the tent, followed closely by a grumpy-looking Jessica. "I hate sleeping on the ground," she muttered, stretching her neck. "Bedrolls suck."

Damien chuckled, earning a glaring look. He smirked, and she rolled her eyes in response. Nathan watched the exchange with one eyebrow raised. *Why is Jessica able to trust Damien so easily?*

"They're close, huh?" Abigail whispered, also watching as Jessica stomped over to Damien and poked his ribs, scolding him for laughing at her.

Nathan nodded. "I don't get it," he whispered back. "She gets mad at him, and he *smiles*."

"It's all about intention," Abigail said with a giggle, sharing a smile with him before turning back to the tent to collect her things.

Nathan lifted his head higher and joined in the cleanup.

It didn't take long for them to get moving again. They hiked through the woods with the river, its dark blue water choppy and unsettled, always in their peripheral vision. Even if Silas wasn't tracking them, walking along the exposed riverbank was more dangerous than navigating the woods, where the thick trees could provide places to hide and cover from the weather.

This time, the witch took the lead, with Damien and Abby close behind. They traversed a path through the chaotic mix of sodden branches, broken twigs, and scattered rocks that peppered the snow. The forest was active with small scratching sounds and a random rhythm of birds cawing. As the trees thickened, so did the mosaic of smells that surrounded them. Every scent was brightened by the freshness of the dense moisture that hung in the air and soaked into the earth.

Though the sun remained hidden by the thick clouds, Nathan guessed it was about midday when the river curved into a patch of woods. As they broke through the treeline, they found the river had narrowed to meet a small waterfall, about two storeys high. The rumble of the water crashing into the waves below filled the air with a steady drumbeat.

Abigail stepped closer, her shoulders rising as she filled her lungs with the crisp, chilled air. "This is beautiful," she murmured, admiring the tumbling water.

Stepping around the few small boulders that marked the line between the trees and the river, she carefully navigated the border of algae-coated rocks to crouch next to the river and dip her fingers into the water. Shuddering, she retracted her hand with a big grin on her face. Nathan knelt next to her.

"Can you imagine going swimming in this?"

He shrugged; he often bathed in glacial waters. Cupping his hands, he brought a handful of the water to his lips, appreciating the chill as it slipped down his throat.

Hearing Abigail snort, he looked at her curiously. "What's so funny?"

"You're a very loud slurper."

Nathan couldn't think of a good rebuttal and huffed in response.

Abigail smirked, sitting back onto a rock next to the river and glancing at Jessica. "Could this be the waterfall from the riddle?"

Jessica ran a hand down her long ponytail, her forehead tense. "It's hard to say. What do you think?" she asked, turning the question to Damien.

He scanned the area. "It's possible. Either that or there's another waterfall higher up."

Jessica slid her backpack off her shoulders and placed it on a boulder so she could rummage through it. "Everyone fill up your water bottles. We don't want to—" A sudden shiver overtook her, and Jessica froze. "Woah."

"Jess?" Damien asked, concerned.

She reached for Damien's arm to steady herself, her shock morphing into worry, and the tension made Nathan's jaw clench. Her attention veered off to the trees surrounding them. "Something's coming. I've never—I've never sensed this kind of magic before."

Nathan tilted his nose toward the treetops, inhaling deeply, and fell into a coughing fit.

"Nathan?" Abigail asked.

"It's—" He caught Abigail's gaze. "Nothing," he said quickly. "I'm fine." He couldn't tell her that he'd scented the approaching figure through the trees. The mossy smell had a powerful undercurrent similar to Jessica's, only this one felt more like firecrackers going off in his nose. And it was coming closer.

Nathan stood, and Abigail followed his lead. He strained his hearing toward the woods across the river. The rhythm of crunching snow suggested it was a four-legged creature, but it was too loud to be a light-footed deer.

Abigail gasped, her hand flying up to cover her mouth as her glasses slipped from her face. Following her gaze, Nathan's breath caught in his throat.

Stepping out from behind a tree was a creature Nathan never could have imagined. Its serpent-shaped head dipped toward the water as it neared the river's edge. Soft yellow scales covered its face and continued down the serpentine neck that then melted into the body of a leopard the size of a horse. The black spots of its short fur matched the speckling of shadow caused by the light broken by the leaves overhead. The mismatched creature had the legs of a deer, which it tucked under its body as it settled next to the riverbank for a drink, even though the neck was long enough to reach without kneeling.

"Th-that's—"

"Spit it out, Abby," Nathan urged, keeping the creature in his peripheral vision as he watched Abigail's features twitch. He took her shoulder to try and turn her back toward Jessica and Damien, but she was frozen in place.

She clutched her hands together, lips parted as she shook her head. "It's … it's real. It's actually real."

"Abiga—"

"It's the Questing Beast."

Nathan glanced at Jessica and Damien, finding them as stunned as his sister. When the Beast stopped drinking, its brown eyes tilted up to look at Nathan and Abigail. Surprisingly, the irises reminded Nathan more of his wolf form than of a snake's eye.

Its gaze shifted between Nathan and Abigail as it slowly raised its head.

"What is the Questing Beast?" Nathan asked, finally succeeding in tugging Abigail behind him.

"It's a creature of Arthurian legend. This … this is *very* bad," she explained, though her mesmerized expression suggested awe more than fear.

"'Listen for the Beast's roar,'" Damien murmured, and Nathan nodded in agreement. There was no way this could be a coincidence.

"This must be the next trial, the Trial of Heart. The book said the knight would be judged for their virtue." Abigail gulped audibly. "That's all I was able to learn about this task. I didn't see anything about the Beast."

A lion's tail swished behind the creature before it stood fully. Its neck towered over the river as it watched them. Nathan shoved his sister toward Jessica and squared his shoulders to the monster, his fists balled at his sides.

"Nathan, what are you doing?" Abigail hissed as she stumbled. Jessica caught her flailing hand and pulled her back to a safe distance.

"You can't fight it," the witch warned him, her tone doubtful.

"I know that," Nathan said through gritted teeth. Abigail was watching, and for once, he wasn't all that keen on fighting. The power he sensed emanating from the creature unnerved him. It was as if the firecracker texture of its scent had soaked through his body, making his insides quiver. But if Jessica had tamed a giant by listening, maybe he could do the same. Or maybe he could intimidate the creature into backing off, at least.

The Questing Beast opened its mouth and unleashed a horrendous howl. Nathan covered his ears and cringed as the sound filled the forest and thousands of needles stabbed his eardrums. It sounded like a hundred hounds baying at once. His knees buckled as he curled his body inward.

As the howl tapered off, Nathan heard Abigail's strained tone behind him. Her voice sounded distant. "That's how the Beast got its name," she groaned. "Because the howl sounds like an army of dogs on a hunting quest."

With the ringing in his ears fading, Nathan cautiously opened his eyes and came face to the face with the Beast.

It had waded into the water, stretching out its neck until Nathan's nose almost scraped against the Beast's snout.

"Don't move, Nathan," Abigail pleaded.

"How … can … I?" He held his body rigid as the Questing Beast's head dipped and tilted, examining Nathan from every angle.

"The Beast never attacked anyone in the stories," Abigail said, though Nathan wished she sounded more confident. "If you stay still, maybe it will move away."

Nathan's nostrils flared, filling with the mossy scent. There was an ancient quality to the stoic creature. Up close, there was a hint of clouding across its eyes.

"You better back off," Nathan warned it, pulling his head as far back as he could without physically retreating. Giving up any ground could be considered a sign of weakness, and Nathan was the last line of defence between the monster and his sister. His heart thundered against his ribcage. *If I can't fight, what good am I?* The uselessness caused a nauseated twist in his gut. There had to be a different way.

The creature's head plunged toward him.

Nathan gasped, throwing out his hands defensively. He caught the muscular neck of the creature but was unable to stop its head from bending down and nuzzling the side of Nathan's face.

He froze, jaw tense, as the Questing Beast butted its nose against the side of his face again, prompting him to return the gesture.

Huh.

"Are you … are you okay?" Jessica asked. He sensed the familiar pressure of her magic on his neck, ready to pull him back if he needed it.

"Yeah, fine," Nathan said, his voice breathy in disbelief as the creature rubbed its nose across his chin and its scales scratched his jaw. "It's … friendly?"

Curious, Nathan loosened his grip on the creature's neck and stroked his hand down the scales. A soft baying sound slipped from the Questing Beast's throat, almost like it was purring.

Jessica pulled her magic away, leaving Nathan's shoulders free to soften as the Questing Beast rested its chin there, its head twice the size of Nathan's.

"Its eyes are closed," Damien pointed out with a surprised laugh.

"Who knew," Jessica agreed, and Nathan heard the smile in her tone. "Nathan is a Beast whisperer."

As he stroked the scales of the Beast's neck, the weight of its head got heavier. "Alright, that's enough," he said, patting it softly. "Please stop now."

Lifting its head, the creature rose to its full height. "You're a weird-looking thing," he muttered as he craned his neck. Animals typically wanted to fight him or run away. He had never before met a creature that wanted to *snuggle.*

"Wow," Abigail whispered, approaching cautiously. Her attention was so fixed on the Beast, she didn't even notice her glasses were crooked. Before Nathan could say anything to stop her, she was standing next to him.

The creature tilted its head curiously at her. With a trembling hand, Abigail reached out. Her fingers were a whisper away from the scales on the creature's neck when it flinched.

Nathan covered her hand with his and turned it, so her palm was facing up. "Give it a minute," he said softly. He met the creature's brown eyes, silently coaxing it forward as he stretched Abigail's hand as far as it could go.

Looking between Nathan's face and the outstretched hand, the Beast lowered its snout tentatively. Its nostrils flared as it sniffed Abigail. After a long, considering pause, the creature lowered its head until its chin gently rested in her palm.

Watching carefully in case the creature changed its mind, Nathan released Abigail's hand and let her stroke the underside of the Beast's chin. She grinned, and her eyes misted behind her glasses as she scratched its cheek, eliciting the same purring noise.

Without warning, the Beast reared its head. A growl slipped over its jowls as it eyed their small gathering.

"Wh-what's going on?" Abigail asked.

Nathan took a step forward and placed his hands on the Beast's neck.

"Hey," Nathan said, trying to calm it. Its muscles were tense beneath his palms.

The creature didn't seem to hear him. Its head darted back and forth as its gaze scoured the landscape. When it began to move forward, Nathan shoved it back, stepping into the frigid water. "Calm down."

The Beast's growl vibrated down its throat, and Nathan's arms burned as he used his full strength to keep it at bay.

"It's staring at me," Abigail said, clutching the straps of her backpack.

"Come on, big guy, calm down. That's my sister. She's no threat."

But the creature's fury was focused on Abigail. It shoved a knee forward, trying to push through Nathan. He couldn't stop the Beast's head, on its long neck, from lunging over his shoulder and driving its open jaw toward Abigail.

"No!" Nathan tried to grab at the Beast's throat, even as he knew he wasn't going to make it in time.

Abigail threw up her hands in a feeble attempt to defend herself as the creature sank its fangs into the shadow at her feet. A loud hiss split the air as the Beast raised its head and pulled a wriggling shadow demon from the ground in front of Abigail.

Nathan's jaw dropped as the Questing Beast raised the demon into the air, whipping its head back and forth as if trying to tear off a piece of the shadow. The demon screeched, and with one final jerk, the Beast tore its arm off. As the shadowy body fell to the ground, it dissolved into ash, as did the arm still clutched between the Questing Beast's jaws.

There was a long silence as everyone stared at the demon to be sure it was gone. Then the Beast dipped its head and looked at Nathan with a slight tilt, as if to say, *What did you think I was doing?*

Relief flooded him, and Nathan stroked a gentle hand down the creature's neck. "Thank you," he whispered. He could only sense the shadow demons when he detected the strange void of smells their presence created. If they remained as shadows against the earth, they didn't disrupt the natural smells of the forest. But if the Beast had been able to detect the shadows even in their incorporeal form, did that mean he might also have that ability?

Jessica shouted, "Nathan, behind the Beast!"

Two more shadow demons stood on the opposite riverbank. At the same time, Abigail gasped and cried out in pain.

Three more demons had materialized behind them, and one had grabbed Abigail by the hair.

"Nathan!" she cried, choking on his name as the demon wrapped its other clawed hand around her neck.

"Abby!" He turned to help, but the Questing Beast crashed into him, knocking him to his knees.

The other demons had jumped onto the Beast's back. It reared up with a loud howl, and the agonizing sound kept Nathan on his knees as he tried to cover his ears. A thin stream of blood trickled down the creature's neck where one of the demons was holding on.

Nathan forced himself up, even as his muscles quivered from the lingering pain of the howl. Through the ringing in his ears, he heard Jessica order, "Nathan, help the Beast. We need it for the quest! I'll help Abigail."

The blood pounding in his ears added a bass drum to the shrill ringing taking its time to fade. Warily, he turned.

The Questing Beast was thrashing in the river. Water sprayed out and struck Nathan in the face as he fought his way closer. The water was only up to his knees, but with the Beast sending it flying in all directions, Nathan might as well have been swimming.

With a growl of his own, he reached up at the split second the Beast had all four hooves on the ground and grabbed one of the demons by its leg. Since it was holding onto the Beast, it was in its physical form, and Nathan was able to get a firm grip on the demon's ankle and rip it off the Beast's back. He used his other hand to grab it by the neck as he stared into its beady red eyes.

"You're not taking her," he said through bared teeth.

The demon's toothless smile stretched further, heating Nathan's fury. He squeezed until the demons' eyes stretched wide before crushing its neck. The demon crumbled to dust in his hand.

Killing shadow demons wasn't that hard. Catching them was the challenge. The remaining demon had learned from the death of its friend and had pulled up its feet so it was crouching on the Beast's back, out of Nathan's reach.

Nathan had to jump out of the way to avoid getting hit by the hooves as the Beast kicked out, trying to buck the demon off.

"Hold still!"

Nathan cursed as the Beast continued its rampage and looked back at the riverbank to see how the others were faring.

Jessica and Damien had thrown their bags aside and were each battling their own demon. The shadowy figures were dancing around to avoid attacks, blocking them from chasing after the third shadow, which was dragging a struggling Abigail toward the woods. Nathan's heart spasmed. The wolf tried to push Nathan back toward the Beast, its instincts urging him to focus on *their* fight, but Nathan shredded that thought as he caught the horrified look on Abigail's face.

"Screw this."

The Beast wasn't going to let Nathan help; it could handle itself. He charged toward his sister, leaving the Beast behind.

Jessica lit a fire in her palm and looked toward Damien. They nodded simultaneously, and Damien tried to force himself past his demon. The shadow turned to follow the hunter, exposing its back to Jessica, who threw a basketball-sized ball of fire at it.

Nathan got onto solid ground as the demon burned to ash, freeing Damien to go after the one holding Abigail. No way was Nathan trusting the hunter to save his sister.

As he charged forward, slowed by the dragging weight of his soaked clothing, he caught Jessica's eyes. She shot him a furious look. Raising her hands to deal with the demon still in her way, Jessica's back was to the water. From his position, Nathan saw the demon that had been riding the Questing Beast leap off the creature and charge toward Jessica.

Before Nathan could warn her, the demon landed on Jessica's back. She screamed and fell to her stomach, giving her demon the chance to pile on her as well. Their bodies consumed hers in shadows.

"Jessica!" Damien shouted.

Nathan turned, nearly twisting his ankle as he changed direction, heading for Jessica. *Your fault, your fault, your fault.* He ran forward, his hand outstretched to grab the cloud of darkness that smothered her.

The vibrating huddle of demons froze, and beneath them, Jessica screamed, "Enough!"

Golden light burst out from underneath the demons, ripping through their bodies. The force barrelled into Nathan and knocked him sideways, onto his stomach. Damien crouched low, ducking his head as the magical light rushed across the riverbank, a tidal wave crashing into Abigail and her captor. The demons exploded into a cloud of ash, knocking Abigail onto her back.

As the light faded away, the forest fell quiet again, silent except for the sound of their collective heavy breathing and the rumbling of the waterfall in the background.

"Abigail!" Nathan scrambled to his feet and sprinted to her side. She was already sitting up, holding her head in one hand.

"What was that?" She blinked several times before shifting the hand holding her head to rub against her heart. "I felt it through my chest."

"That was an exorcism," Nathan said quietly, finally daring to look back at the others.

Jessica was also sitting up, breathing heavily. Damien knelt at her side. Even from a distance, Nathan could see the gold shining in her eyes. She looked up with a jerk, her gaze meeting his, and Nathan's throat seized.

Her enraged expression made his mouth go dry; the golden glow of her eyes made Jessica appear almost godly. Her anger pulsed against him in waves, its burning energy searing into his heart.

I'm screwed.

CHAPTER 19

Jessica

Even though she knew the demons were gone, Jessica couldn't get her heartbeat under control. Her lungs were trying desperately to keep up. Every muscle in her body felt like it had fallen asleep and was waking up again; the tingling sensation coated her entire skin as her magic coursed through her.

"You controlled the magic," Damien said. The words were reassuring, but Jessica's arms were still quivering as the rush of power faded. The strength that had surged through her body had been overwhelming, and it terrified her.

"But it could have been anything." Her panic had taken over and she had acted on instinct. Exorcism magic was harmless to those not possessed, but what if she had chosen a fire spell in the adrenaline of the moment? It would have been devastating.

"You didn't," Damien said firmly. Before she could object, he shifted in front of her knees, grabbed her hands, and pulled her to her feet. He held her steady as she found her balance. "Trust yourself."

With Damien holding her, she finally felt some of the panic ease. "Working on it," she muttered. When Damien let go of her hands, they were still shaking.

Her body had gone on autopilot when the demon slammed her into the ground. She couldn't feel the scrapes covering her arms, left behind by their claws as they had tried to smother her. When she remembered the shadows and the horrid hissing in her ears, the shake in her hands intensified. Instead of giving the fear more fuel, she focused on the other emotions warring in her mind.

She stomped toward Nathan.

He was helping Abigail to her feet, but as soon as he saw her coming, he stiffened. Considering he had nearly a foot on her, it was difficult to think she could possibly intimidate him, but the guilt written across his face was, admittedly, satisfying.

Jessica tempered her anger for a moment to check on Abigail, who had some scratches but nothing serious. "Are you alright?"

Her nod was jerky. "I knew you'd save me."

Jessica hadn't expected that, and it almost made her feel better—until she looked back at Nathan.

"This is your fault." Her nostrils flared and anger heated her stomach as she struggled to keep her tone even. Shouting wouldn't solve anything, even if it was tempting. "All you had to do was keep the demons and the Beast busy. That was *it*."

Nathan flinched.

Jessica didn't feel sorry. "We were trusting you to watch our backs, Nathan. We trusted you, and all you had to do was trust us in return. We said we would take care of the demons. And we *were*."

His mouth opened, but Jessica cut him off. "Your recklessness puts us all in danger, including Abigail," she said as she pointed at his sister. "Do you understand that?"

After a long pause, Nathan nodded. His Adam's apple bobbed as she heard his audible swallow.

Jessica huffed, crossing her arms over her chest to hide her shaking hands in her armpits. The quivering had calmed down. At least she felt a bit better now.

"Maybe … maybe Nathan should leave," Abigail said in a quiet voice.

Jessica cursed in her mind. If he weren't a werewolf, she would absolutely agree. But they needed him and his abilities to pass the trials just as much as they needed Abigail's knowledge to find them. Nathan's eyes went wide as he stared at the ground, unable to look at his sister.

"I mean," Abby added quickly, placing a hesitant hand on Nathan's arm, "you're putting yourself in unnecessary danger. You've seen that they can keep me safe, right? You shouldn't put yourself at risk."

Nathan's mouth opened and closed silently. His chest shuddered as he inhaled, and a pang of sympathy hit Jessica in the gut.

"I'm not giving up on him." She gave Abigail a reassuring smile, despite how weak it felt. Then she turned to Nathan, who stared at her in shock. "I'm not giving up on you," she repeated, surprised by how true the words were. She needed him for the quest, and that was where their connection should end. But the horror on his face as he realized what he had done exactly mirrored the way she felt when she thought of all the ways her magic could have gotten out of control.

"But from now on, if you don't think before you act, I am going to fight back. Do you understand?" She would build a magic cage and lock him in it if he proved to be a danger again.

Nathan nodded. "I'm sorry."

"Good." Jessica let out a heavy sigh. The tingling had faded and now her muscles were jelly. Exorcisms took a lot more out of her than she was willing to admit. It was magic that literally cost a small piece of her soul, which would regenerate with time, but was consequently very taxing the more she used it. That was why she tried fire instead wherever possible. If she told Damien the cost of exorcism magic, he would probably try to bar her from using it.

Damien placed a gentle hand on her shoulder. "We should get moving. There could be more."

Jessica nodded and turned toward the river. To her surprise, the Questing Beast was waiting for them. Her delighted relief quickly faded as she saw the trickle of blood running down its neck and a faded crimson stain in the water at its feet.

"Oh no," Abigail gasped, seemingly forgetting the tension in the air. She quickly headed for the river, but when she got close to the edge, the Beast stepped back and nodded at the opposite bank.

Damien, Nathan, and Jessica joined Abigail at the river's edge. Jessica watched the Beast curiously. "Are we supposed to follow it?"

With a nod, the Beast turned away from them and stepped onto the opposite shore. As it walked away, it began shrinking. Its neck and appendages retracted as its yellow hide turned into snow-white fur. The lion tail became bushy, and four more tails sprouted out to create a fan of fur at the creature's back. As its head shifted out into a ferret-like face, and its paws resembled a canine. The Beast's new shape reminded Jessica of a fox, until two long triangular rabbit-like ears rose out of its head. The ears flattened back before the creature slipped into the bushes and vanished.

"I'm guessing that's the path we take," Damien said. He had retrieved their bags, handing Jessica's to her before putting on his own.

"Alright, let's get going," Jessica said, and without hesitation, she stepped into the water to follow the Beast's path. The cold water stung her skin, and she sucked a sharp breath through her teeth.

Damien followed, shooting her a disapproving look. "I was going to offer to carry you."

She scoffed at the idea. "Why would I need to be carried?"

He shrugged. "I thought it would be nice."

Oh. Her cheeks flushed. "Well, snooze you lose."

Behind them, Abigail cringed with every step. Nathan was even further behind, still dragging his feet.

"Abby," Jessica said, changing the subject before Damien could say more. "Do you know what that weird fox form was?"

She lifted her drooping face, and a hopeful look took over. "There are a few conflicting descriptions of the Beast. One of the vaguest is a white fox-like creature. Maybe it's a shapeshifter."

"And why is the Questing Beast a bad thing?" Jessica asked.

"The Questing Beast was seen as an omen of doom. It appeared to Arthur right before the events that led to the fall of Camelot. Sir Pellinore nearly drove himself to death in his obsessive hunt for the creature."

"'Doom'?" Damien repeated.

"Because we didn't have enough stuff to deal with already," Jessica muttered, kicking her feet through the water.

They stepped out of the water one after another, and the frigid chill lingered on their skin thanks to their soaked clothing.

Jessica glanced back at Nathan, and her heart sank at his heavy expression. *Stupid feelings.* Glancing at Damien, she gestured to Abigail subtly with her eyes, hoping that he would get the memo. She smiled when, with one quick glance, he understood what she was asking.

Damien turned to the historian. "Abigail, could you tell me more about the Beast?"

"Really?" she asked, lifting her chin as she joined Damien.

"Yeah, I'm curious."

Together, they took the lead, and Abigail shook off the strain in her voice to recount tales of the Questing Beast.

Her shoulders tense, Jessica held back until Nathan had caught up with her.

He flinched when he realized she was waiting and angled his gaze away. "You wanna tell me off again?"

She pursed her lips. *I'm trying to be nice. Don't make it difficult* was what she wanted to say, but in an effort to be sympathetic, she held her tongue. "Actually, I have a question."

He tilted his head, narrowing his eyes slightly.

She gestured for him to join her on the path and waited until he fell in step with her before continuing. "This may sound odd, but can you describe what the Questing Beast smelled like?"

He blinked and then barked a sharp laugh. "That's the first time I've ever been asked that."

"I'm serious," she assured him.

Eyeing the others ahead, he hesitated. "Why do you want to know?"

Jessica shrugged. "Curiosity. It's important to learn as much as possible about every magical creature, to be prepared. And tracking is one of your strengths."

Nathan blinked again, his jaw slackening in surprise. He crossed his arms protectively. "I thought you were mad at me. Why are you complimenting me?"

A compassionate warmth spread through Jessica's chest. "When someone gets mad at you, it's because they care enough to tell you," she explained, keeping a gentle, honest tone. "If you didn't matter, I would walk away. I don't like to waste my time."

Nathan's pensive expression shifted to one of calm composure. He unfolded his arms and slid his hands into the pockets of his jeans as he gave her a shy look. "Thanks," he said quietly.

Jessica had forgotten how refreshing speaking to werewolves could be. They were characteristically blunt and honest, and they always said what they meant. It was the style of communication she felt the most comfortable with. "Do you detect the Beast's trail now?"

Shaking his head, Nathan stared up at the trees that shielded them overhead. "It smelled like moss. But with a sparkly texture similar to the one that you have."

"That I have?"

"Yeah." His cheeks turned red, like his blush was turned on by a switch. "It's hard to explain."

She watched him closely, and when he met her gaze and realized she wasn't giving up on the conversation, he scrunched his nose the same way Abigail did when she didn't like an idea.

"Your scent has this weird underlayer to it," he said, chewing on the words for a moment. "It's like … if the bubbles of a fizzy drink could be turned into a smell."

"That's what I *smell* like?"

"That and rain, with something floral mixed in."

Jessica giggled at the description and narrowly missed tripping over a rock. He wasn't the first to describe her smell, but his explanation was so … Nathan.

He eyed her suspiciously. "You're not weirded out by that?"

"Not at all," she assured him. "When you date a werewolf, you get used to things like that."

The words were out before she could catch herself.

Nathan stopped abruptly. "*What?*"

Her cheeks burning, Jessica focused on the trees ahead rather than his bewildered expression. "Yeah. The werewolf pack I lived with before … I was dating Malcolm at the time."

It took Nathan a few beats before he got his footing, and he had to jog to catch up with Jessica, who had powered on ahead, hoping she could leave that particular piece of information behind them.

"The same lieutenant that bloodied you up in the fight?"

"*Maybe.*"

"And now you're dating a witch hunter." He scoffed, a little too loudly. "And I thought I had issues."

Her cheeks reached a new temperature. "No one said we were dating."

"You're not?"

"No." At least, she didn't think they were. "We've got a mutual interest in stopping Supai. That's all." Staring at Damien's back, Jessica suddenly felt like he was really far away. She wiped her clammy palms on her jeans, blaming the exertion of climbing the hill for her increased heart rate. "I'd rather focus on your problems."

When she risked a glance at Nathan, she was surprised to see a thoughtful expression on his face. He looked at her from the corner of his eye. "Is that why you're not scared of me? 'Cause you're used to werewolves?"

"Probably."

He pressed his lips together but then shook his head. "No. It's because you're like me."

"Um—"

"How do you do it?" His voice held an edge of desperation. "Control it?"

Oh. He was referring to her power. "I can't say I'm always good at it," she admitted quietly, her mind threatening to slip back into darker memories. "But it's like I told you yesterday. You're not going to get anywhere unless you and your wolf get on the same page." Her heart dropped along with Nathan's expression. "I wish I could give you more, but that's the starting point. Especially for you."

"It's just …" He clenched his teeth, looking up the incline at his sister.

Jessica tried to smile at him, but it was forced. "She might surprise you. I'll be shocked if she hasn't already figured it out."

He ran a hand through his wavy hair with a heavy sigh. "She doesn't even want me here." His jaw tensed, holding back yet another secret. "And if I tell her what I am, I'll have to tell her the truth about that night, and … and I can't."

Jessica slowed her pace to distance themselves farther from Damien and Abigail, a look of concern spreading across her face. Normally, she wouldn't pry in someone else's business, but Nathan was too unpredictable to leave a mystery, especially when his history might tell them more about the enemy. "What *else* happened that night?"

Nathan's face paled. "It's … I—"

"Hey, guys!" Abigail waved at them from the top of the hill. "We found something!"

Jessica waved back. "I understand the past can be terrifying." Her heart rate picked up at the thought of her nightmares about losing control of her magic. "But it's a lot harder to carry that burden on your own."

"You keep saying that," he muttered in reply, "but I can hear your heartbeat freaking out. Do you take your own advice?"

Jessica couldn't think of a counterpoint. It was hardly fair for her to be giving advice when she didn't listen to it herself.

Nathan gave her a sad, knowing look and picked up his pace. Letting out a stressed sigh, Jessica kicked into a jog to catch up.

They found Abigail and Damien standing in front of a large stone at the crest of the hill. The slab of rock was taller than Nathan, its face smooth like a supersized writing tablet. Carved into its surface, at Jessica's eye level, were three lines of script in the same shimmering blue they had seen on the back of the rock giant.

"Another clue?" Jessica was relieved she could understand most of it this time.

"Yeah, and the letters change!"

"What do you mean?"

Damien pointed to one of the words in the second line of text. "Watch this."

Focusing on the letters, Jessica waited. Just as she was about to question their vision, the word shifted.

Abigail adjusted her glasses to take a closer look. "The first part says that the Trial of Perseverance and the Trial of Heart have passed. The mind must face its test. The letters were shifting around and used to say one of your party must conquer the task for you to pass, but now that you've arrived, it's changed to two."

"So only two of us are supposed to take the Trial of Intelligence?" Jessica asked.

"Which means it should be me and Jessica." Abigail looked around the group. "No offence, but that makes the most sense, right?"

Except Jessica didn't want to put Abigail in unnecessary danger, and the task was likely designed for a werewolf's mind, which meant Nathan was the best choice.

"Nathan and Jessica should go," Damien said. They all turned to him. Nathan and Abigail were skeptical, but Jessica was relieved. Damien was two steps ahead of her.

Damien slipped the backpack from his shoulders and placed it by the rock as if settling down for a break. "Jessica has the brains and the magic; Nathan has the strength. It may be an intelligence test, but since we don't know what the trial will look like, we need to cover all our bases."

Even though Damien was being logical, Jessica was flattered.

"You're strong, too, Damien," Abigail countered.

He smirked. "Believe it or not, I'm confident Nathan is stronger."

Abigail's eyes widened, and she waved her hands as if in a panic. "I-I didn't mean—"

"Glad to hear you admit it," Nathan muttered cheekily, earning him a scolding glare from his blushing sister.

Damien shrugged, and Jessica held her fist to her lips to stifle a laugh.

"I'll go," Nathan agreed, stopping Abigail before she could protest. She swallowed whatever she was going to say.

Jessica dropped her backpack and cracked her knuckles. "Alright," she conceded. "How do you think we start?" With Nathan beside her, she squared her shoulders to the stone. Abigail and Damien stepped aside.

Crossing his arms over his chest and shaking his head, Nathan let out a huff. "It's probably something stupid like *we accept the task*."

The blue iridescent letters shone brighter, and Jessica winced against the glare. The skin on the back of her neck tightened to the point of pain, all the hairs standing on end. Before she could warn Nathan about the magic she sensed surrounding them, the earth disappeared beneath her feet.

CHAPTER 20

Nathan

Nathan's heart flew into his throat. He twisted his body so he could see the ground as he fell, and then pulled in his knees so his feet were beneath him. He landed in a deep crouch, his knees nearly hitting his chin. Jessica, to his shock, landed flat on her stomach, her forearms catching the ground just in time to stop her head from hitting the dirt.

She groaned loudly as she pulled herself up to her knees, forcing air into her shocked lungs. When she had caught her breath, she brushed the debris off her elbows and looked at him quizzically. "Are you sure you're not part cat?"

He was tempted to roll his eyes but worry won out. "Are you okay? You landed pretty hard."

"I tried to stop myself," Jess complained. Pursing her lips, she flexed her fingers. Then she rolled her wrists. "I can't use magic at all."

"*What?*"

"It's fine," she said unconvincingly. "This must be part of the trial."

"But—"

"The more important thing is figuring out where we are."

He was about to protest when she held up a hand to stop him. There was a strained look in her eyes. "This is a trial for intelligence. We're supposed to solve our way out, not use magic."

Nathan shook his head, baffled. "You're surprisingly calm about this."

After a moment's hesitation, Jessica sighed. "I'd rather focus on the task at hand," she said, looking up at him as if it was a question.

Nathan nodded and offered her his hand. When they were both on their feet, they scanned their surroundings.

It looked like they hadn't moved. The stone was still in front of them, its letters dull and faded to grey. The dense, snow-capped forest surrounded them. Abigail and Damien were gone.

"Where are they?" Nathan asked, panic tightening his voice. He lifted his nose to the air and sniffed, his forehead creasing. "I can't smell or hear them."

Jessica turned in a slow circle. "They'll be fine." Her tone bordered on scolding. "Abigail has Damien."

"That's not very reassuring."

"He's a talented fighter," she assured him. "He's almost killed me numerous times."

"You're not helping," he said, clenching his jaw. "Why do you make it sound like that's good thing?"

Jessica waved away his concern. "Let's start by looking for an indicator."

"An indicator of what?"

"This can't be real," she said, gesturing to the forest. "Which means there should be a key that breaks the spell. It could be a symbol, a smell, an off-colour leaf. This is a test for werewolves, so it's probably something only you can find. See if anything stands out."

He grumbled as he turned to the trees and poked his head behind bushes. "This is ridiculous." The forest was the same—how was he supposed to find whatever was out of place?

After a few minutes of searching, Jessica called his name. "What about this?" she asked, holding up a large piece of fern.

He frowned, scrunching his nose. There was nothing unusual about the leaf that he could tell. "What about it?"

"Is this out of place?"

"Why would it be?"

She huffed. "Look at these markings." She held out the branch as he came in for a closer look. "This could be a pattern, right?"

He leaned closer. "Or it could be a squirrel's scratches."

She let out an irritable sigh and dropped the branch to the ground. "Well, it was positioned weirdly. I thought it could be an arrow."

"Or you're looking for puzzles that aren't there."

More than likely, they were looking for a needle in a haystack. They were like two mice caught in a trap — a witch without magic and a useless werewolf only good at fighting with nothing to hit.

"You look over there." She pointed to the forest left of the rock. "I'll take this side." Her voice was strong, but her sweat lingered in the air. Her heart rate hadn't calmed down since they had landed.

Wanting to find some common ground, something Jessica could take confidence in, Nathan asked, "What kind of magic do you think it is?"

Jessica kept scanning the brush, only slowing down to give him a shrug. "Could be an illusion. Or a hallucination." She shook her head at a particular group of leaves and wrapped her arms around herself. "It could also be a type of transportation spell, or an alternate reality, or—"

"Jessica—"

"I don't know for certain, Nathan," she retorted. "If I had my magic, I could probably sense it."

He internally cringed. The tightness in her voice made it clear the trial was getting to her more than she was letting on. "Maybe stop thinking about that so much?"

"Excuse me?"

"You said to focus on the task at hand," Nathan reminded her. "But I bet you're thinking about all the things you can't figure out, like you're reading off a grocery list."

"Okay, well …" Her expression softened. "I'm not the only one getting caught in their head. You've got all these amazing senses. Are you even trying?"

Nathan stilled, staring at the ground for a moment. Her kind words bounced off his thoughts of uselessness and fluttered to the ground like dying leaves. Whatever skills he had were because of the wolf, not him. An insistent growling erupted in the back of his mind—the wolf's protest was so visceral Nathan had to close his eyes to fight it off.

"Nathan?"

"I'm trying, I'm trying."

He lifted his nose to the air, filling his lungs with the scents of the forest. Nothing appeared out of place.

A spark of electricity ran up Nathan's spine, causing him to shiver. Jessica also flinched. There was a loud thud behind him, and the scent of blood and cologne hit him instantly. Nathan whirled around to see Silas picking himself up from a low crouch, his feet buried in the snow like he had fallen from a great height.

"You!" Nathan was too shocked to move, and his heart thundered against his ribcage as Silas leisurely brushed the dirt off his tracksuit. "What are you doing here?"

"Pleasure to see you too," Silas mused, running a hand through the top of his hair. "I was getting impatient waiting for you to find the treasure." He narrowed his eyes as he lowered his hands to his sides.

Nathan snarled, but Jessica cut him off. "What about Supai?"

Panic shook Nathan's body. He and Jessica were trapped in this illusion while Abigail and Damien were probably fending off the demon god by themselves.

To Nathan's surprise, Silas scoffed. "Our partnership has been officially terminated. I left him by the river. The foolish *god* thought he could order me around. I'm looking forward to seeing the look on his face when I rip him apart with the power I gain from the Lupatus Stone." Silas arched an articulate eyebrow, his gaze sharpening with laser focus. "Though I imagine he can't be too far behind."

Nathan's heart spasmed. "Did you hurt Abigail?" he demanded in a low voice. Silas would have run into Abigail and Damien to reach the stone marker and activate the trial. Nathan barely noticed Jessica had returned to his side.

A slow malicious smile stretched across his cheeks. "I bet you'd like to know."

Nathan was about to lunge when Jessica turned around and shoved him back with both hands. To Nathan's shock, she had the strength to stop him.

"If I don't have my magic, you're probably missing your power," she said in a rush. "The time you waste fighting him is time Supai has to find Abigail and Damien."

The panicked look in her eyes forced Nathan to pause. He still had his heightened senses but, as she'd suggested, his body felt eerily fragile. It was like his muscles had lost their density. Nathan tried to transform. Normally all it took was a thought, but as the wolf growled in the back of his mind, he realized that he couldn't feel the tense pull in his muscles or extreme electric sensation that initiated his shift. He couldn't change into his wolf form.

Nathan took a step back, a film of sweat coating his clammy skin. He couldn't beat Silas when he was at full strength — how could he stand a chance without his power?

"I can handle Silas," Jessica assured Nathan, her words earning a grumpy expression from Silas. "I know how to fight without magic. But this trial was designed for a werewolf. You are the only one who has the skills to find the key to release the spell. Silas knows that, and he's using your history to mess with your head so he has the advantage."

"But—" How did she expect him to focus when Silas was *right there?*

"Please," Jessica pleaded. "Trust me."

"You're going to let her order you around, Nathan?" Silas taunted. His stance shifted wider, his knees loose and ready to fight. "Time and time again, you prove your cowardice."

"You're just scared to fight me," Jessica shot back, squaring her shoulders.

Silas sneered. "Even without my ability to shift, I can—"

"I'm calling your bluff," Jessica interjected, and she sprinted at him.

Silas's eyes stretched wide and he threw up his forearms to block the fist Jessica swung at his face. Without slowing down, she pulled her punch and used the momentum to spin around into a high kick, driving the back of her heel into Silas's ribs. A groan escaped him. Jessica tried to retreat, but Silas closed in quickly and returned a jab to Jessica's obliques. She cringed and launched another assault.

Nathan told himself to move, but his feet were frozen in place. He couldn't leave Jessica to fight alone.

"You're leaving a girl to do your fighting, Nathan!" A growl linked Silas's words. He bared his teeth at the witch. "You are out of your league," he warned her in a low voice.

Jessica ignored him and pressed Silas back. "Nathan, get moving!" she shouted before ducking to avoid Silas's punch. She slipped beneath his guard and kneed him in the ribs. "I got this! Start looking!"

But I-I have to fight. Still, his body refused to move. Was this what it would feel like when he was cured of his curse?

The wolf snarled and its instincts surged forward. Nathan gasped, shocked by the aggressive shove against his mind. The wolf had never forcefully tried to take over before.

Instinct pulled him away from the fight between Jessica and Silas, urging him to focus on the woods.

Okay.

Jessica was right. They couldn't waste time. But as long as Nathan could sense Silas's presence, he couldn't concentrate. He couldn't do this on his own. *I need help.* He sighed, releasing his hold on the wolf.

But the wolf didn't take over. It melted into the forefront of Nathan's mind, its instincts mixing with human thought, sharing the space. Rather than vying for control, the wolf's confidence swelled inside of Nathan and softened the rough edges of his thoughts, giving his mind the breadth it needed to focus.

Nathan inhaled again, this time noting each smell carefully. The scent of the old pines was thicker than the young ones. It wasn't a stark difference, but he hadn't noticed it before. The grounding smell of the dirt mingled with the fresh scents of the plants, all of which carried a subtle, crisp undertone that reminded him of fresh water. Even in its smells, the forest was intertwined, interconnected in ways that went far beneath the surface.

He headed toward the stone that had launched them into the trial, thinking it might be a good starting point. He made it three steps before the wolf's instincts pulled him back, dragging his attention to the thicket to his left. Nathan tightened his fists, old habits telling him to resist. Then Jessica grunted behind him, the kind of pained noise that comes from taking a hit.

"Come on, Nathan!" Silas taunted, shouting at Nathan's back. "Now is your chance to prove—" He was cut off with a hiss. Nathan looked worriedly over his shoulder. Jessica had managed to kick the back of Silas's knee, forcing him momentarily to the ground.

"Focus, Nathan!" she shouted without looking at him. Silas was already on his feet and lunging at her.

"But …" He lost the word to a growl and forced himself to turn his back on the witch. *I'm not giving up on you.* At the time, Jessica's words had sounded empty to him, but now she was fighting for him, believing he could complete the trial on his own. The faster he found the stupid key, the less time she'd have to spend fighting his battles.

Nathan followed the intuitive pull to the left, his mind sorting through the kaleidoscope of scents. The wolf urged him into the dense brush, and his feet cracked twigs as he used his hands to push past an overgrown fern. The foliage grew thicker, trying to get in his way. A root twisted around his ankle, from his clumsiness or of its own accord, Nathan wasn't sure. He had to waste time detangling himself.

Suddenly, he caught a delicate floral scent, a dainty trail hidden among the dense tones of the dirt and snow-laden vegetation. It was faint, as small as a single pinprick across an entire body.

Nathan shoved his way through the foliage, desperation pushing his muscles as the scent wavered, nearly swallowed by the dense greenery around it. He found himself in front of a half-rotted log covered in fungi. The bark squished as he placed his hands down to lean over it.

Nestled among the weeds that sprouted through the snow on the other side of the log was a single purple flower, the size of a large coin.

You've gotta be kidding me.

The wolf's instincts calmed, settling back with a strong sense of satisfaction.

"Jessica!" he shouted over his shoulder.

The witch took a punch to her stomach with a grunt and caught hold of Silas's wrist. She curled her body forward, dragging Silas over her shoulder and slamming him down on his back. The werewolf groaned, giving her an opening. She sprinted toward Nathan, though her pace was disrupted by a slight limp on her left side. Her upper lip was split, her right jaw bruised, and she pressed one hand to her ribs, but despite the injuries, she had a fiercely determined look on her face. "You find something?"

Nathan nodded, looking back at the flower. Each heart-shaped petal had the gradient of purple, growing darker near the yellow centre, but one of them stood out. It was covered in brown dots like freckles. Four dots formed the shape of a box, with three outliers forming a straight line toward the tip of the petal. He didn't know much about flowers, but he thought the patterns were supposed to be uniform.

"What is it?" Jessica said panting heavily. Silas cursed behind them, the sound of dirt spraying out as he scrambled to his feet.

Nathan pointed to the flower. "There's, um. I mean, you said different, right? Well, this smells wrong."

Jessica looked over her shoulder and cursed. Nathan followed her gaze. Silas sprinted toward them, his teeth bared and his blue eyes as sharp as ice.

"Grab the flower!" Jessica ordered, turning back toward Silas.

"What? How do you know—"

"I don't, Nathan, but I trust your instincts. Just do it!"

"No!" Silas shouted, almost within reach.

Nathan grabbed hold of the flower's stem and ripped it from the ground.

Instantly, Nathan's vision blurred. The ground tilted and he toppled to the side, falling onto his back. Muscles melting into the ground, Nathan struggled to lift his head. It felt like a bowling ball had replaced his brain. He didn't have time to say anything to Jessica before his face involuntarily went slack. The spinning world vanished, and his vision went black as the sound of Silas's enraged howl faded away.

CHAPTER 21

Nathan

"Nathan?"

"They're coming around."

Nathan scowled. *Who is talking so loudly?*

"Yep, he's awake," Damien muttered. "Come on, Sleeping Beauty."

Despite the deep ache in his muscles, Nathan rolled to one side with a loud groan and used his forearm to shield his face as he opened his eyes. Once the twigs and dirt came into focus, he cautiously pushed himself up to sit cross-legged.

Nathan scrunched his face against the sharp pain in the back of his head. "What ... happened?"

"You vanished!" Abigail said, her voice shaky. "For an hour! Then you appeared again here on the ground."

Keeping his chin down, Nathan glanced up through his lashes and saw her crouching next to him, her expression tense.

"How do you feel?" she asked.

He took in a deep breath, and his body relaxed as familiar strength coursed through his muscles. "Sore," he admitted. "Are you okay? We saw Silas in the trial. Did he hurt you?"

Abigail shook her head. "He showed up and, when he realized you had started the trial, he decided to follow you. Damien tried to stop him but ... well, obviously that didn't work." She paused, her eyebrows pulling together. "Did he hurt *you*?"

"He tried but ... Jessica!" Nathan turned his attention to the side, where the witch was lying on her back, her eyes closed. Damien watched her with a worried gaze.

A lump of fear swelled in Nathan's throat. "Is she—"

Jessica moaned and blinked her eyes open. Nathan let out a heavy sigh. Relief washed over Damien's expression as he pulled her up to sitting. Jessica grimaced, holding a hand to her head.

"Are you alright?" Damien asked, strain in his voice.

"Mostly." She stretched her neck to the side, checking her range of movement. "I'm exhausted." The bruises and cuts had vanished from her body.

"What happened?" Damien demanded as he looked between Jessica and Nathan.

"Silas showed up," Jessica said. "But whatever spell was used on the trial prevented me from using magic and Silas from using his werewolf abilities. I fought him off, and Nathan discovered the key to breaking the spell." A proud but tired smile brightened her face. "Good job."

Nathan's mind sputtered. "It was just a flower," he mumbled, his cheeks turning red.

"*You* fought Silas?" Abigail asked Jessica, her eyes widening.

"Yeah." Jessica groaned as she rolled her left shoulder, pressing a steadying hand into her collarbone. "Looks like my injuries are gone, but my body *feels* like it's been in a fight. I thought his arrogance was for show, but he's really good."

Nathan knew that all too well. A ghostly ache blossomed in his jaw where Silas had struck him on numerous occasions. Nathan glanced nervously at the large stone with the inscription on it. "Do you think he'll be trapped in the trial forever?"

"I doubt it," Jessica said apologetically. "Since we entered the trial separately, there will probably be another key he can find to escape. We should get moving."

"We've completed three of the four trials," Abigail said. Unlike her previous contribution, she shared this knowledge with a grim expression. "The next is the Trial of Strength. It's the last step before acquiring the Stone, which means the trial will happen wherever the Stone is. And all we have is the riddle about the shadows swallowing the sun and the earth roaring to the sky."

An idea sprang up in Nathan's mind. He cleared his throat. "I, um, I might have a clue." Everyone turned to him, and the heat from his cheeks moved to his ears. "There was a weird pattern on the flower."

"What did it look like?" Abigail asked excitedly.

Nathan pushed himself onto his knees and used his finger to draw the dots into a patch of sodden dirt. "Like that."

"That's the Big Dipper," Damien said, his thick brows furrowed.

"Which means the next trial is to the north," Abigail suggested.

Nathan shrugged. "I guess that makes sense."

Abby was the first to grab her bag. "Let's get going."

"We'll go as far as we can while we still have light," Damien said, his tone calming Abigail's eagerness. "Then we'll continue in the morning."

All in agreement, Jessica offered to take the lead so she could scan for any demons on their path. Damien stayed close behind her, protesting that she shouldn't push herself so hard. That left Abigail and Nathan to bring up the rear.

Their walk quickly turned into a hike as north led them up the mountain again, and the sounds of the sloshing river faded. Their path zig-zagged as they picked the best route through the entangled foliage on the forest floor, weaving in between the trees that seemed to get thicker and taller this deep in the woods.

After their boots had reached a steady, crunching rhythm, Abigail glanced over her shoulder at Nathan. He lifted his eyebrows in question.

She shifted herself enough so they were nearly on the same plane. "Are you sure you're okay?"

"Um. Yeah?"

She frowned, watching him from the corner of her eye.

Nathan's jaw clenched, and his brain scrambled to guess what she could be thinking. He filled his lungs with the scent of the forest, focusing on the collage of smells instead of his thoughts.

"You do that a lot."

He coughed. "What?"

"Sniff," she said, with a slight smile. "You must really like the smells here, huh?"

He tensed under her watchful eye. "Oh, um, yeah. It's nice." The tips of his ears burned as his gaze shifted around the woods, trying to look anywhere except at her.

In his peripheral vision, he noticed Abigail close her eyes for a moment and lift her nose to the sky, inhaling deeply.

"It is relaxing." She waited a moment, finding the rhythm in her breathing to speak again. "Is that why you wanted to live in the mountains?"

Nathan shrugged, keeping the truth at bay. "It's easier. People don't like me much."

Frowning, Abigail paused. "People like you fine. I'd understand if you were *afraid* of people, but I'm curi—"

"I didn't say that," he said abruptly. The muscles in his thighs bunched, ready to run. The wolf growled, scolding him, smothering some of the panic.

Breathe, Nathan.

"I know," Abigail said hurriedly. "I'm trying to understand why you'd want to live in a *cave*."

"Why does it matter?" His defensive tone sounded harsh even to him.

Abigail's expression tensed, and he could hear her grinding her teeth. "You don't have to be rude. I'm just asking."

"Well, don't." His heart slammed into his ribs, running a race his brain couldn't keep up with.

Abby flinched and took a step away from him.

A deep ache punched Nathan in the gut. Saying anything more on the subject would only make the panic worse, and he didn't trust himself to control it. Talking about why he was living alone would bring up how he got there—and their past. *What if she asks about that night?*

The wolf became a snarling presence, but when it pushed for control again, Nathan pushed back. He wasn't ready to tell Abby the truth. He needed more time.

"It was my choice, Abby," Nathan said, "and it's … honestly, it's hard to talk about." The words scratched his throat. His eyes burned, the one small confession threatening to unleash a flood of tears. He clenched his fists to keep the guilt at bay, even though his heart was on a rampage. "I just … Can you … can we talk about something else right now?"

Abigail remained silent, watching him warily from higher on the incline as if he might suddenly jump at her. As if she was afraid of him.

Nathan's shoulders crawled up to his ears, and he wished he could shrink.

"Yeah," she said finally, her tone flat. She turned her attention back to the trees ahead. "Sorry I asked."

When the silence dragged on, Nathan hung his head and remorse burrowed into his stomach. He couldn't face the truth, not yet, but he wasn't going to run either. He had planned to get the Stone, free himself from the wolf, and then tell her the truth. But even now, he could feel the self-assuredness of the wolf, giving him strength as if propping him up. Nathan felt like his ribs were shrinking, squeezing his torso with the painful thought of what Abigail would do if she found out the truth about him. He might need the wolf when he finally told her.

"Would you tell me what you like about living in the mountains?"

Abby's gentle voice slipped in through the static in his mind. It didn't ease the throbbing, but he clung to her kind words.

"The fresh air," he said, lifting his chin. "And it's, um …" The right words evaded him.

"Quiet?"

"No," he scoffed, exhaling some of the tension. "The woods are pretty loud when you listen."

Abigail's eyebrows shot up. "Really?"

"Yeah." Nathan braved a slow step forward, motioning for her to keep walking. "Listen."

Abigail paused, her gaze lifting to the woods. After a moment, she smiled. "Thanks." Her soft word lingered in the air as she turned back toward their path.

Jessica and Damien had stopped to wait for them, and exchanged a look before continuing their march forward. Soon, the rhythm of their convoy evened out, a steady drumbeat accompanying the sounds of the surrounding forest.

Nathan let out a heavy sigh, suddenly exhausted. The desire to run was still strong, an irritating itch he couldn't scratch, but a lift of pride in his heart kept him moving. He wouldn't turn away. The wolf rumbled in his mind, the gentle vibration soothing his nerves. He listened for the wolf's voice and was met with a growl. To Nathan's surprise, it sounded pleased.

"Abby," Nathan said softly. "I'm, um."

"Hmm?" She glanced back at him.

His thoughts stumbled, the words mixing and fumbling in his mind before he got them straight again. "I'm glad to be here now."

Her expression softened, and she smiled. "Yeah. Me too."

Nathan felt like he was floating the rest of the hike.

By the time the group stumbled into a clearing flat enough to sleep in, the light had nearly evaporated. Through the thick canopy, heavy clouds covered the sky with a dark-grey haze, threatening snow. The cold stung Nathan's nose, noticeably sharper than the previous night.

"This will do," Jessica said. "We'll definitely need a fire."

"Good," Abigail said, scrunching her face and rubbing her arms as her shoulders rose to her ears.

Jessica placed a hand on Abby's sleeve. "You're still soaked?"

"This jacket is pretty old," she confessed.

With a shake of her head, Jessica raised her palm toward Abigail. After a brief hesitation, she flicked her wrist and droplets of water sprayed from Abigail in all directions.

Gasping, Abby patted her jacket down. "That's incredible. It's completely dry!"

Jessica smirked, causing Abby's cheeks to go bright red.

"Sorry," Abby said. "That was probably nothing for you."

"Actually, it's nice to have someone get so enthusiastic. Reminds me of the excitement of learning a new spell."

"Come on," Damien said with a small smirk of his own. "Let's get set up."

As Jessica pulled the tents out of her backpack, Nathan scanned the woods again. It was a good space, the trees spaced enough to fit two cars comfortably, but the clearing was sunken and would fill with snow if it fell.

Nathan froze as his nose caught a strange presence. There was a gap in the scents of the forest around them. His frown deepening, he pulled away from the group to walk to the edge of the clearing. It wasn't that there were no new smells — there was a void of scent somewhere in the woods, its emptiness blocking the wind that wafted gently toward Nathan.

"Nathan, you have to help too—" Abigail began to scold, but Nathan shushed her.

Abby scoffed. "Don't shush— *Mmh!*" She stopped as Jessica covered her mouth with her hand, attention also on high alert.

"Nathan?" Jessica whispered, slowly drawing her hand away from Abby.

She must sense it too. Multiple void spots were circling them.

"We're surrounded!" He jogged back to the others, all of whom were on their feet.

Abigail clutched her hands to her chest. "How do you know?"

Nathan didn't hear her. "There's at least eight," he told Jessica.

"Silas and Supai?"

He hesitated, inhaling the scents of the forest, and shook his head. "Not yet, anyway." Silas was dangerously good at hiding his presence, and Nathan wouldn't be surprised if the god could melt into the shadows like his demons. He could have sent them on ahead to find them.

Jessica nodded curtly, and by unspoken agreement she, Damien, and Nathan all turned their backs to each other, creating a protective circle around Abigail.

It didn't take long to detect the first hint of movement. A demon slunk out of the shadows in front of Nathan, followed closely by seven others. They surrounded the group like soldiers looking down from the small raised ledge that bordered the clearing.

Nathan curled his upper lip, and his fingers flexed as he prepared to shift his nails into claws.

Abigail whimpered behind him, and Nathan's skin turned cold. They couldn't fight and protect her at the same time. If one demon broke past any of them, Abigail was doomed.

Jessica must have had the same thought because, in a low, steely voice, she ordered, "Nathan, get Abby out of here."

He didn't have a chance to argue. All eight demons hissed and lunged forward.

Jessica threw out her hand and a tunnel of wind blasted through the trees, scattering the three demons to Nathan's right as he scooped up Abigail. He bolted after the tail of the wind. Abigail gripped his sweater as they ran, his shoulder smothering her startled gasp.

Nathan dodged the obstacles of the woods without slowing down. He kept running until he could no longer hear the scuffle behind him.

Skidding to a stop, kicking up a flurry of snow and dirt, he turned back the way he had come, his heavy breathing fogging up the air.

"Na-Nathan."

Nathan carefully lowered Abigail to her feet. She wobbled, clutching him as she steadied herself. Then she met his gaze and shoved him back.

"It'll be okay," he promised, scanning the woods. He sniffed but couldn't find anything that suggested they were followed. "Jessica and Damien will handle it."

Abigail kept shaking her head. "Y-you." She took another step back.

He frowned. "Abigail, what's wro—"

The fear on her face stopped him. They had just been attacked by demons, but she was looking at him as if he were the monster.

Nathan's expression fell slack as he realized his mistake. He had run too fast—his speed was inhuman. Maybe he could have lied his way out of smelling the demons, but how could he explain this?

"Abigail," he said carefully. He reached for her, but she flinched and pulled away. Nathan's heart dropped.

"You said … you said you were bitten by one of his *dogs*," she stammered, her unblinking gaze frozen on his face.

Tears welled up in Nathan's eyes, his jaw rigid and unable to speak as Abigail connected all the dots.

"You … in the mountains. And your wrist … it's been fine since we left. I thought the giant attacked you, but … then there was the Beast, and the demons, and you were fighting." She broke their eye contact and focused on the ground as if searching it for answers. "The cold—you're never bothered by the cold—and your eyes … they're like Silas's."

Tears blurred her eyes behind fogged glasses that were crooked on her nose as she looked up at him again, searching his eyes. The eyes that marked his curse.

"What did he do to you, Nathan?" Her voice was a whisper, but it shook Nathan like an earthquake.

He stumbled back, her question leaving his body numb to everything other than the pounding in his head. Even the wolf's strength was useless, drowned out by the panic.

"Nathan!"

Looking up with a jerk, he gaped at the raw fury on Abigail's face, her cheeks red and stained with tears. "Tell me!" she demanded. "What are you, Nathan?"

Nathan couldn't deal with this. Not now. He stepped back, shaking his head. He had to run.

"Stay here," he ordered, unable to look her in the eye. Leaving her shaking in the cold, alone, Nathan turned and sprinted back the way he had come.

His skin burned as if every pore was stretching open. The wolf pushed forward, and Nathan surrendered. He ran, kicking off his shoes as he pulled off his shirt and pants. Clothing either got tangled or shredded as his body reshaped itself, so it was best to be naked when it happened. He had years of practice undressing mid-run and he freed himself in record time, desperate to shed his human skin. The tingling spread across his body, quickly turning into an intense buzz as adrenaline coursed through his veins.

When he was younger, shifting into the wolf used to be agony. Now, after years of practice, pain mixed with exhilaration. Nathan's bones popped as his features rearranged, and his body twisted and contorted from head to toe. His teeth elongated to fangs, and his fingers shrunk into toe pads while his nails sharpened into claws. The feeling of hundreds of needles stabbing his skin signalled his fur sprouting across his body, a shade darker than the sandy-brown colour of his human hair. His perspective changed, dropping closer to the ground as he fell with ease into all fours. Nathan kept on sprinting, his paws pounding across the forest floor as he ran toward the sound of the hissing demons up ahead.

Nathan's vision sharpened as wolf and human ran together, the shared fear and rage sending a pulsing heat through his muscles. He wanted to rip apart the past that had turned him into this, and the closest he could get to that right now were those demons. As he neared the clearing, he saw Jessica and Damien surrounded by a dense black cloud as the demons used their smoky forms to swarm them.

Launching himself into the fight with his claws outstretched, Nathan aimed for the blur of smoke. He passed straight through the demons' bodies, his sudden appearance disrupting their swarm. The demons pulled their wispy bodies apart and separated into distinct snaking rivers of smoke, slithering in all directions. They pooled and solidified, once again standing like soldiers in a circle around the group.

As they became corporeal, Nathan used his speed to turn and tackle one to the ground before it could dissipate again. The caught demon screeched in shock; its cry cut off as Nathan clamped his jaw around its neck. The thickness of the flesh between his teeth suddenly dissolved into ash as the demon's body crumbled. Once he was sure the demon was gone and its ashes disappeared into the soil, he moved to the next.

Nathan tried to retreat into the back of his mind, to leave the fighting to the pure wolf instincts and hide behind its strength, but his consciousness was forced forward by a snarl that shook his body.

The wolf was stronger than the man. It had a will of steel, but it needed its human half to help it understand the world, and it wouldn't allow him to hide. With enemies and allies intermingled, the wolf could attack indiscriminately, knowing Jessica and Damien were probably able to handle any subsequent injuries. But with the human half guiding the fight, Nathan could move smarter.

Wolf instincts and human thought blurred together, working as one as they turned to the next demon.

The creature narrowed its beady red eyes, a low hissing sound pouring from its gaping mouth. Jessica was right behind it, confronting another demon.

Not that one. The demon was waiting for Nathan to attack, its eyes glinting with a challenge that was tempting to take, but if it shifted to smoke Nathan would fly through it and hit Jessica by mistake.

Quickly glancing left, Nathan saw Damien swinging his knife to ward off another demon. The hunter's face was steady as stone; even his heartbeat was level. The demon was taunting him, swooping within Damien's reach only to dissolve into smoke and shift to Damien's back to strike. The hunter was quick to turn, able to deter the demon with another swing of his knife, but he wasn't making any progress.

In a split second, Nathan had a strategy.

Nathan barked at Damien and charged toward him. The hunter glanced at Nathan in his peripherals and recognized the plan. He sprinted toward Nathan and they swapped places, Nathan tackling Damien's demon, which had paused in confusion, while the hunter distracted the one at Jessica's back. Catching the demon by surprise, Nathan clamped his jaws around its throat and crushed it, tasting ash on his tongue.

The strength that coursed through Nathan's body as he fought went far deeper than his muscles. His fur fit properly on his skin for the first time. He was powerful and knew the wolf felt the same. Nathan was two pieces of a puzzle finally clicking together as he ferociously ripped through demon after demon.

As the enemies' numbers dwindled to three, the wolf had to push Nathan to keep up their speed. He wanted the fight to continue, to not have to stop and think about what was awaiting him once it was over. Once the final demon was gone, he would have to face the truth of what he was

He would have to face Abigail.

CHAPTER 22

Jessica

Jessica had a newfound respect for Nathan. At first, she was furious he had left Abigail alone in the woods, but as the massive, golden-brown wolf broke up the demons that had been swarming them, she decided she would have to thank him. His surprise leap into the fray gave her the distraction she needed to conjure enough exorcism energy to blast the demon closest to her, dissolving it to dust. The fatigue from her fight with Silas made her muscles slow and her magic sluggish. She could only take one demon at a time and was grateful to have the werewolf on her side.

Nathan continued at his blinding speed, launching himself at demon after demon until he caught one at the right time and took it down as it was about to strike Damien. It burst into ash beneath his claws.

It was a fantastic strategy; the demons couldn't attack them without taking on their corporeal form, but when the next one tried, Nathan crushed it between his jaws. He moved with such ferocity and speed it was difficult to follow.

Throwing out her hands, Jessica used her magic to grab hold of one of the distracted demons. If she managed to capture enough of its smoke form, she could use raw magical energy to trap it.

As soon as she caught one, the demon took physical form and bashed against the invisible barrier she held it in. Thankfully, the shadow demons weren't as difficult to trap as corpse demons.

Clenching her jaw, her muscles burning with energy, Jessica lifted the demon and threw it across the clearing. "Nathan!"

He jumped into the air as she released her magical hold and sank his claws into the demon's abdomen. Falling forward as the demon dissolved into ash, he landed on another and crushed it into the ground as well.

One more.

Jessica was suddenly shoved aside. Damien had taken her place in front of a demon charging with its sharpened claws now aimed at the hunter's chest. Jessica's heels slipped as she tried to turn back, her legs scrambling to find purchase, but she wasn't going to make it in time.

Damien threw up his forearms to protect himself.

Nathan drove his shoulder into Damien's hip, knocking him out of the way in time for the demon to slice its claws into Nathan's flank. The wolf yelped and fell, while the demon towered over him, ready to strike again.

Jessica threw out her hands toward the demon, using the sizzling energy in the pit of her stomach to push her magic faster. A sphere of energy surrounded the creature, the barrier turning red as it grew hotter and hotter. Nathan scrambled across the ground in a desperate crawl to get away from the heat.

Within the sphere, the demon screeched, slamming its fists against the magical bubble. Jessica's nostrils flared, and she snapped her fingers. Contained within the magical barrier, the demon burst into flames and its screech died away. When the fire winked out and the sphere popped, ashes fluttered harmlessly to the ground.

Nathan bared his teeth at Jessica, followed by a sharp bark, making it clear he didn't approve of her fire magic. His shoulders were shaking, ears laid flat against his head.

"You're afraid of fire?" Jessica asked.

Nathan huffed, dipping his snout down shyly like he was avoiding the question. He started to shake out his fur but stopped and whimpered, lowering himself to his belly.

About to check on his injury, Jessica was distracted by Damien pulling himself onto his knees. Being human, any injury the witch hunter had would be more threatening than a werewolf with accelerated healing.

"Nathan, can you hold on a second?"

With his snout resting on his paws, Nathan rolled his eyes. Taking that as a *yes*, Jessica darted over to Damien and crouched down to scan his body, using her hands to check him for any threatening injuries.

"You're an idiot," she said sharply. She was the only one—other than Nathan, apparently—who could fight the demons, and Damien had been stupid enough to push her out of the way. Her hands touched his face gingerly, his stubble scratching her palm. Damien's strained expression softened as he watched her.

"That makes three to two life saves for me," he told her.

"I am so tempted to slap you." She shook her head, equally baffled by his actions and the smile he caused on her face. "What were you thinking?"

"Take the hit so you could position yourself better to take it out," he explained, far too calmly.

Jessica desperately wanted to argue against his logic, and when she found that she couldn't, she scoffed instead. "Did anything work?"

Grimly, Damien shook his head. "I strike, they change to smoke. They strike, I lose blood," he muttered, holding out his forearms. They were covered in scratches. None were deep enough to be of concern, but they would have to be treated to protect against infection.

With a heavy heart, Jessica gave him a sympathetic look. "Maybe only creatures of magic can beat them."

"I'll find a way."

His conviction nearly convinced her. *At what cost?* She hated to think how beat-up Damien would have to get before he figured it out.

Damien's attention drew past her, and Jessica remembered Nathan. She rushed back to the wolf. He had shifted to lie on his flank, legs extended to the side. His upper lip twitched as she got close.

"Don't move," she ordered, putting as much authority into her voice as she could muster. Gingerly, she used the tips of her fingers to push aside the blood-covered fur, trying to examine his ribs. There was no freshly flowing blood, which was good, but with the density of his fur, it was hard to treat him in his wolf form. But if he changed now, he would be naked, and Jessica doubted he would be comfortable with that, regardless of the injury.

Rubbing her palms together, Jessica pushed the residual heat of her adrenaline into her hands, and the green glow of healing pulsed out from her palms. She held the light over Nathan's ribs. His body tensed, jowls lifting for a moment before he let out a controlled exhale and relaxed into the sensation.

Satisfied that she'd remedied the worst of the damage, Jessica wiped her hands on her leggings. His accelerated healing would do the rest of the work. "We should get Abigail," she said, watching his face closely.

Nathan's gaze pulled away; fear already shone in his eyes.

"You both need to face this," she said quietly, the truth hanging between them.

Considering how fast Nathan had run, Jessica guessed Abigail had finally deduced what she probably suspected all along. Abby probably wasn't looking forward to this confrontation any more than Nathan was.

Warily, Nathan got to his feet, a shaky whine sneaking out of his throat.

He was gorgeous in his wolf form. Measuring from his shoulders, he was at least a metre tall; one of the larger wolves Jessica had seen. While Nathan's hair was light brown in human form, his wolf fur was golden-brown with highlights of bronze. The sides of his snout were white, gradually shifting into blond down his chest. His ice-blue eyes were alert and sharp, not missing a single movement in the forest, and contrasted sharply with the black creases that surrounded them.

Jessica looked over her shoulder at the hunter. "Damien, will you wait here?"

He stared at her for a moment before giving a reluctant nod.

Jessica let Nathan lead her through the woods toward where he had taken Abigail. The wolf dragged his paws, limping slightly on his injured side. The farther they got, the slower he walked, his ears perked and pointed forward.

Walking side by side with a wolf brought back memories. "Malcolm would like you," Jessica said thoughtfully. "Though he'd want to beat you into the ground a few times too."

Nathan peeked at her from the corner of his eye, his ears turning back.

"If you ever wanted some advice, you know, on how to be a werewolf," she said with an awkward chuckle, "I'd be happy to put you in touch. I know he'd be keen. He always enjoyed meddling in everyone's business."

Nathan's chest rumbled, attention shifting, but Jessica didn't detect an objection.

"And thanks for saving Damien," she added, earning a chuffed response. A blush warmed her cheeks. "He's useful."

Nathan scoffed and she replied with a scowl. "I could turn you into a kitten," she warned.

The threat didn't last long. The disturbed look that overwhelmed his face, his eyes bulging as his jaw clamped shut, made Jessica burst out in a brief laugh. It was incredible how expressive a wolf could be.

Once her chucking had subsided, she reached her hand out tentatively and stroked his back so the tips of his fur tickled her palm. "I'm guessing your clothes are nearby?" She almost didn't want him to shift back—his stress was clear, but he seemed more comfortable in his fur than he did in his skin. His breathing was controlled, his eyes were focused, and though she could feel the tension seeping off his body, he didn't look jumpy or ready to run. Yet.

Nathan nodded his head subtly and stopped, gesturing his snout to Jessica's left. She followed his point and spotted a discarded sneaker. If this was where he shifted, the rest of his clothes should be nearby.

"I'll leave you to it," she said. "I'll bring Abigail back this way." She kept her focus forward as she marched through the woods.

Her shoulders tensed as she walked, scanning the forest ahead in case more demons jumped out. The stillness was suspicious, and she had spent too many years dealing with the unexpected to relax.

Jessica heard Abigail before she saw her, the sound of her whimpering floating through the trees. She spotted the girl sitting on the exposed root of a tree, the toes of her boots shoved into the snow. Her forehead was resting on top of her knees that she held close to her chest with one hand. The other carelessly gripped one arm of her glasses. The glasses flinched as she sniffed loudly, collecting the composure she'd lost in her sobbing.

"Hey, Abigail," Jessica said softly. She crouched, waiting quietly for Abigail's breathing to even out.

With a last sniffle, Abigail lifted her head enough to use the back of her sleeve to wipe her nose. Her eyes were red.

Jessica kept her expression soft. She could never relate to what Abigail was going through, but she knew the kind of pain that caused tears like that.

"Are the demons gone?" Abigail asked in a raspy voice.

"Mmhmm." Lowering herself carefully to the ground, Jessica crossed her legs and rested her elbows on her knees, interlacing her fingers under her chin. Her heart fluttered, nerves unsettling her pulse as she tried to think of what to say.

They sat in silence while Abigail got her sniffling under control. She filled her lungs with a shaky inhale and let out a heavy sigh, finally lifting her head all the way and leaning it back against the tree. Using the heel of her hand to wipe the lingering tears off her red cheeks, Abigail positioned her glasses precariously back on her nose and stared at Jessica.

"You needed that, huh?" Jessica asked quietly. Abigail had done a good job of holding her head high and staying optimistic, but the shock of the last few days had to have taken their toll.

Abigail coughed out a surprised laugh. She rubbed her nose again, her chin a fraction higher. "Yeah." She sucked in a deep inhale, followed by a slow, controlled exhale. "Is everyone okay?"

Jessica's jaw tightened. "Nathan got a pretty nasty gash up his side." When Abigail's face stretched in panic, Jessica gestured for her to calm down. "He's fine, sorry! He'll be all healed in a few hours."

Her expression relaxing, Abigail eased the rest of her back into the tree. She searched Jessica's face, eventually dropping her gaze to the snow. "He's a werewolf, isn't he?"

Even though Jessica knew it was coming, she still winced at the truth. "I think it would be best if you two talked."

Shaking her head, Abigail turned her attention to the woods past Jessica's shoulder, her eyebrows knitting together and nostrils flaring. "I don't know how I'm supposed to feel right now," she said, her voice cracking.

Jessica shrugged. "Sounds to me like that's exactly how you should be feeling." Facing Abigail's frown head-on, Jessica offered her a small smile. "It's probably not going to feel good for a long time," she explained, trying to think about what she would wish to hear if she were in the girl's shoes. "But … do you feel *worse?*"

"No," Abigail said. "*So* much makes sense now. But I … but I need to hear it from him."

Pushing herself to her feet, Jessica offered her hands to Abigail. "I'm right by your side," she assured her, and she meant it. When they'd first started, she had been frustrated that Abigail was coming along. She'd thought the young woman would be a burden. But already she found herself missing Abby's bubbly energy.

Putting on a weak, brave smile, Abigail grasped both of Jessica's hands and allowed her to pull her up. After giving Abby's hands a squeeze, Jessica let her go and gestured back the way she had come.

Abigail nodded, tightly wrapping her arms around herself as they walked, focusing on her feet. "Alright," she whispered, the air fogging as she spoke. "Let's get this over with."

CHAPTER 23

Nathan

Nathan couldn't stop his hands from quivering, and he wrung them together as he paced. His brain was a soup of chaotic thoughts. Damien sat on one side of the sunken clearing, as still as a statue, but Nathan was so consumed by his anxiety he almost forgot the hunter was there.

When Nathan heard their footsteps, he froze. Turning to face the trees where Abigail and Jessica would emerge, he tried to steady himself, but every inch of his body was shaking at its own rhythm. His throat was so tight that the grounding inhale he tried to take threw him into a coughing fit instead.

Once the coughing had stopped and his stomach had relaxed, he straightened and saw Abigail staring at him, Jessica right behind her. They appeared out of thin air, only a few metres away. The distance felt like kilometres.

Nathan tried to speak, but was unable to make the words come out of hiding, so he kept his mouth shut instead.

Jessica joined Damien while Abigail stayed where she was and looked Nathan up and down. Her brows tightened. "Are you okay?"

Nodding, he gritted his teeth. He couldn't tell if the pounding in his head was from his pulse or his panic. *Is she worried, or being polite? Does she hate me yet?*

Abigail narrowed her eyes, her arms wrapped protectively around herself. "Jessica said you got hurt."

Nathan glowered at the witch, but all he got from her was a shrug. "Yeah," he admitted, "but I'm fine now."

"Show me."

"It's nothing."

"Show me," she said firmly. Her jacket creased under her hands as she squeezed herself tighter.

With a painful swallow, Nathan hung his head and lifted his shirt. The gash from his bottom rib to his hip on his left side was closed up thanks to Jessica, but the surface skin hadn't yet had time to heal. The swollen exterior of the wound glistened with a mixture of serous fluid and his sweat. He winced as he dropped his shirt again.

Abigail let out a heavy sigh. "Okay," she said quietly, reassuringly to herself. "Okay."

Nathan wanted to hug her and make all the pain go away just as much as he wanted to run in the opposite direction, but Abigail remained well out of reach. The fear that she could be afraid of him kept his feet locked in place as if cement had been poured up to his ankles.

"Nathan," Abigail said with a shaky breath. "I want you to tell me *everything*. What happened the night of the fire? What happened to you?"

Nathan struggled to find words while fear squeezed his throat like it was constricted by rubber bands. Shaking his head, he took a step back. "Y-you're going to hate me," he said in a hoarse, strained voice.

"No!" Abigail snapped before collecting herself. "No, Nathan. No more lying or running away. You can't do that to me again." The forest was silent around them, watching.

A wet breath rippled through Nathan as he sucked in all the air he could manage. Unable to meet her fierce stare as he spoke, he focused on her boot laces, clenching and unclenching his hands at his sides.

"I was exploring the woods," he said, starting with the part of the story she knew. "And I-I ran into Silas." An involuntary shudder overtook his body. "He had been waiting for me. He wanted me to stay; he said he had chosen me to be his prodigy."

Silas had smiled then, oozing confidence under a layer of malice that made Nathan's stomach twist with fear. Silas's smile was the first thing Nathan always relived in his nightmares. It was made worse by the memory of Silas explaining how he had come across Nathan in the woods while he was passing through, and then had stayed for weeks to observe the boy before he'd deemed him suitable. Nathan's memories of the hometown woods that had once been his natural playground, his happy place filled with hours of imagining himself an adventurer or famous explorer, had been destroyed by the sharp, blue-eyed glare of a predator hunting his prey.

"I refused and tried to leave, but he … he changed into a wolf and chased me through the woods."

Now, as an adult, Nathan knew Silas could have caught him in seconds. He had been toying with Nathan. Nathan's stomach twisted at the memory, as though someone were wringing it out like a wet towel.

"The wolf bite was from him. That's how … that's how you get cursed. How I got cursed." He dropped his head, the tears finally breaking free. They burned tracks down his cheeks as a wet sob shook his lungs. "I should have *died*, Abigail. I wish I had. Every day." He sniffed violently and rubbed his nose, forcing himself to stand up straight. He had to tell her the truth.

Her face was slack, her tears matching his own as they stared at each other through the dim light of the forest.

"The ranger found me." He forced the words out, using his anger to give them strength. "He took me to the hospital but,"—he swallowed—"but then I …"

Why is this so hard?

"You changed into a wolf?" Abby's quiet voice whispered.

Nodding slowly, Nathan wet his lips. "The rest of the memory is foggy," he admitted. "I remember the pain of the first transformation, and later, when I actually realised what I was, the fire was already everywhere. The next thing I remember after that is waking up in the woods. Silas had pulled me from the fire. He was so pissed."

The words tried to revolt, but Nathan forced them out past the stabbing pain in his heart. "He said the wolf must have lashed out. Mom and Dad and all those people, they're dead because of me. The wolf … I caused the fire."

The shallow strength that had been keeping him standing crumbled, and Nathan fell to his knees, shoulders slumping. Tears dripped into the open palms cupped on his lap.

"I ran because … because I didn't want to hurt you too. I couldn't come home, not when I was still stuck as a wolf and I-I could hurt you. I had to run. I—" He rubbed his face furiously with the heels of his hands.

The forest was filled with the sounds of his sobs and gasping breaths, swallowed by the darkness of the trees above as the night settled in to watch them.

Nathan lost track of time, but at some point, he realized he wasn't the only one crying. He looked up and noticed Abigail wiping tears off her cheeks, her eyes burning red, staring down at him with her nose scrunched and her lips trembling on the edge of a scowl.

"You … you started the fire?"

"I'm so sorry, Abigail," he said desperately, his body trembling. "I'm sorry, I don't—"

"I doubt that's possible," Jessica interrupted.

They turned to her, and she held up her hands in a careless shrug. "No opposable thumbs, no magic … just something to think about." Her blasé expression made the fire in Nathan's gut burn hotter. Even Damien's eyes had widened a fraction, staring at her from behind her shoulder.

"From what I've been told, the first shift is *excruciatingly* painful," Jessica added. "It can be disorientating and—"

"What do you mean, 'painful'?" Abigail asked firmly.

Expression softening, Jessica nodded. "The entire human form has to reshape itself. Bones shift and joints move into new places, while—"

"Enough!" Nathan snapped at Jessica, getting to his feet. "Stop trying to scare her."

Jessica's eyes narrowed. "That's not my point."

"Stay out of—"

"Was it that painful, Nathan?" Abigail's voice sharpened.

"Well … yeah …"

"What about the eyes?"

"It's part of the affliction," Jessica said. "The only werewolves I've seen with other colours were third- or fourth-generation, and usually because there was a human parent somewhere in the line. Rule of thumb, werewolves all have blue eyes like that." Her expression was unreadable as she met Nathan's gaze. "They would have changed during your first transformation."

Abigail shook her head, her curls rustling against her shoulders. She took off her glasses and rubbed her eyelids with her other hand, her body swaying.

"I'm sorry, Abigail. I was so afraid to tell you, so scared I'd hurt you. But now we can find the Stone. We can use it to get rid of the wolf, of this curse. We can go back to how things were."

Abigail looked at him in horror. "That doesn't change anything, Nathan," she said in a strained voice. "Even if the Stone could do that, it doesn't change what you did."

Nathan's hands shook as he took a dangerous step toward her, his heart's pleas urging him forward. "It's still me, Abigail," he said softly. "I'm still me."

"No, Nathan. You're not. You're not even human."

Nathan froze, his body numb. The cold of the night that wrapped around them couldn't touch him. The sounds of animals scratching and the whistling wind that had previously played a quiet background chorus were all silent. *Not even human.*

Abigail replaced her glasses and stared at him warily. "Even if you were, we're not the same people anymore."

Her words barely made it to his ears. *Not even human.*

"This is a lot to take in. It doesn't all make sense," she said, holding herself protectively.

Nathan took a step back. His chest was hollow, his heartbeat an echo. For once, he'd been right. He knew Abigail would hate him. Why shouldn't she? He didn't even like himself.

"You can't solve everything, Abby. This isn't one of your riddles."

She flinched, taken aback, before anger tightened her expression. "I'm trying to process this."

"There's nothing to process," he said bitterly. He continued backward, each step fuelling the anger. "Sometimes broken things can't be fixed."

She gaped at him. "Nathan, that's not what I meant!"

"I get it, Abigail, I get it." He could still make out her mortified expression through the tears in his eyes. That was exactly how someone should look at a monster. "I was dead as of a few days ago, right? And your life was *good*. You made a whole future for yourself, then I show up and look what happens. We all would've been better off if I'd stayed dead."

"Nathan, stop it!"

"Nathan, we can't do this without you," Jessica warned him. "Going after the Stone without a werewolf would—"

"You don't know that for sure," he reminded her, shaking his head. "Everything you've done so far you could've done without me."

"Except for dealing with the giant, winning over the Questing Beast, finding the key to the illusion, and detecting that we were surrounded by an army of demons." Jessica groaned in frustration. "Why is this so difficult to get through your thick head?"

He snarled. "Why do you care? This is none of your business!"

"Leave them out of it. This isn't their fault!" Abigail shouted.

Anger burned through his gut, streaking up his skin to the tips of his ears. In his fear and fury, Nathan reacted, snapping his teeth at Abigail. She lurched back, pulling her hands close to her chest.

The horror on her face turned Nathan's skin cold, and the heat rushing away left him dizzy. "See?" He gestured to her, his last remaining strength seeping away. "You're afraid of me. And you should be, Abigail. I'm not human anymore, right?"

"That's not fair," she argued. "That's not what I meant. Wait, Nathan!"

The words died away in Nathan's wake as he ran into the woods.

Nathan sprinted as far as his legs could carry him. He didn't care where he ended up—he just kept running. Intense heat consumed his body from his strained muscles, the anger in his gut, and the tears streaming down his cheeks. It all burned.

With his vision blurred, Nathan's toe caught on a root and he fell, slamming onto his stomach as dirt sprayed out in all directions.

While his heart thundered, ready to keep going, his body gave up. He dropped his forehead to the ground and surrendered to the storm of sobs. He balled up the dirty snow and dead leaves in his fists. The earth swallowed his tears as the darkness held him, and the sounds of the forest surrounded him as Nathan cried into the night.

CHAPTER 24

Jessica

Jessica hugged her arms protectively around herself as the sound of Nathan's footsteps faded. Abigail lowered herself to her knees with a choked sound, tears streaming down her face.

Shaking her head, Jessica opened her mouth to say more, but no words came. Her heartbeat was a dull thud in her chest.

Looking to Damien, she whispered, "What do we do?"

After a long pause, Damien's shoulders relaxed. "We do what we can." He crossed the clearing and crouched at Abigail's side, placing a hand on her back and speaking in a voice too quiet for Jessica to hear. A second later,

Abigail threw her arms around him, burying her face in his shoulder as she cried. The uninhibited tears startled Jessica, freezing her in place.

Jessica knew there was nothing she could do to help Abigail that Damien wasn't already doing, and the realization left a rotting feeling in the pit of her stomach.

We do what we can.

"I can set up the tent," she told herself. It didn't feel like helping, but Abigail would probably be exhausted soon and having somewhere to curl up and be alone for a moment might help her feel safe.

By the time Jessica was done, Abigail's crying had tapered off. She'd let go of Damien and hugged her knees into her chest. He shifted to sit next to her. Jessica set up a fire and sat across the flames from the two of them, watching Abigail warily.

"I'm sorry," Abby whispered, her voice scratchy. "I just met you and then … this."

Jessica and Damien shared a cautious look. Jessica tried to think of something to say. Instead, a list of spells came to mind: a sleeping spell, to help Abigail get some rest; a tracking spell, to go find Nathan and kick his butt for leaving. She knew of a time-reversing spell, but it was dangerous and certainly wouldn't fix any of the painful feelings. Would Abby want a memory-loss potion?

"You have nothing to apologize for," Damien said softly.

Abigail's body was quivering, but Jessica doubted it was from the cold. Her hands were balled into tight fists, and she used one to wipe her nose.

"How can this hurt so much?" She shook her head in disbelief. "We haven't seen each other in seven years. It shouldn't hurt this much."

"You have a big heart, Abigail."

"I said he wasn't *human*. I didn't mean it like he took it—I was thinking literally—but that look in his eyes." She groaned and rested her head on the tops of her knees. "I want to be angry with him. He said he wanted to keep me safe, but he keeps pushing me away."

"That's probably what he thinks he deserves," Jessica said quietly.

Damien and Abigail both looked up at her, the fire illuminating their faces and making the world around them black.

Jessica flinched. "Considering how he became a werewolf and what he said about the fire, all he's good for is hurting people."

Fury overtook Abigail's face and she lurched forward like she was about to tackle Jessica across the fire.

Jessica quickly threw up her hands to stop her. "I meant that's how he sees himself! And only he can change that image."

Jessica crossed her legs and rested her hand on her knees, gently tapping the fingers of her left hand across her pants. "He's his own person, right? And all he's thinking about is his own pain. It's consuming him. He has to process that. You shouldn't feel bad for processing things the way you need to, either, but it isn't going to change what's in his head. You can't *fix* him."

"You can support him while he figures himself out," Damien added. "You can be there for him. Knowing there's someone in your corner gives you the strength to fight the battles you have to face alone." Damien looked at Jessica, his eyes appearing black among the shadows created by the firelight.

Jessica couldn't interpret his expression.

We do what we can.

Dragging her gaze from Damien, Jessica softened her voice. "Do you want him in your life, Abigail? Because you're your own person too. You're under no obligation."

"I don't know," she whispered.

Jessica found it so strange how two people at odds could be loyal only because they were blood-related. Was there more to it? Some bond Jessica couldn't see? If they weren't siblings, would Abigail have walked away by now?

Abigail's face fell. "I don't know if I can connect with him," she confessed. "It's hard enough knowing he's been alive all this time, but then, when I finally understand why he never came back, he runs away again. I can't understand what he's going through if he won't tell me."

"He may never tell you," Damien admitted. "But if you won't give up on him, that gives him a reason not to give up on himself either."

With a heavy sigh, Abigail took off her glasses and dragged her other hand across her face. "I can't think straight right now."

"Let's get some sleep," Jessica suggested, eager to retreat from the tension in the air. "You can have your own tent tonight, Abby."

Abigail nodded. She dragged herself to her feet, her movements rigid and heavy, and grabbed her bag before disappearing into the tent.

Jessica watched her until the zipper closed. Then she turned to Damien, who was already staring at her.

"He's lucky to have her," he said.

Jessica nodded and pulled her knees into her chest to try and brace against the worrying thought that was nagging her.

"Damien?"

"Hmm?"

"Were you talking about Connor?"

His eyebrows pulled together.

"When you said 'he may never tell you'. Were you talking about your brother?" She swallowed the rock of emotion forming in her throat. "We don't have to talk about it if you don't want to, but we haven't—"

"I don't blame you for Connor's death."

"I know," she said, though it was still nice to hear. "But are you blaming yourself?"

Damien sighed, leaning back on his hands to look up. The dense clouds covered the night sky in a thick blanket of churning, dark-grey soup.

"I joined the military when I was sixteen so I could get out of the house. The uncle who raised us after our parents died was a fanatic. I'll never miss that man." Damien's jaw tensed as if he were looking at his uncle as he spoke. His gaze dropped to the dirt. "Serving was my way out. But Connor never left."

Jessica hugged her knees tighter, straining so she wouldn't miss a word.

"I did what I had to, to save myself. But I always wonder what would've happened if I hadn't left, or if I had come back sooner. Maybe if I had convinced Connor to enlist with me, things would have been different. Even though I know none of that would have worked."

"You can't feel guilty for taking care of yourself," Jessica said, leaning into her legs as an edge of desperation scratched her voice. "You're just as important."

A sad smile slipped across his lips. "It's not that easy."

They sat in silence. For the first time, the quiet tightened Jessica's skin. While nerves still made her stomach flutter, Jessica was rarely uncomfortable around Damien. Tonight, she couldn't shake the horrible sense that she was failing him if she didn't speak, but she couldn't think of a thing to say.

Damien stood with a soft groan and looked down at Jessica, his expression gentle. This remorseful side of the man she had come to know was foreign to her. She searched for his cheeky sparkle, wishing to see the familiar roguish grin or hear a joke about their sleeping arrangements, but Damien seemed too tired. "Come in when you're ready?"

She nodded, and he left the fire to turn in.

Once he was settled in the tent, Jessica's shoulders drooped and she rested her forehead on her knees. She was a Beata — she was supposed to be a leader, a change-maker. *How can I do that if I can't even think of the right thing to say to him?*

She sighed and stared at the tent where Damien had gone to sleep. She was lucky to have him at her side. If only she could find the words to tell him.

CHAPTER 25

Nathan

When Nathan blinked his eyes open, he saw a faint light speckled across the back of his hand. Despite protesting muscles, he pushed himself onto his back and stared up at the trees. The warm orange glow of sunrise created a backwash of colour behind the dense green canopy. The birds were waking up and saying hello to each other, unseen in the forest that surrounded him. Nathan listened to their conversation, wondering what they were trying to say.

Filling his chest with new air, he held it in until tiny pinpricks across his lungs reminded him that they were full. Nathan let out a burdened sigh and watched the fog of his breath waft up to the trees above. He felt like his brain had short-circuited and was still coming back online.

Nathan sat up with a moan and leaned back onto his hands as he stared into the depths of the forest. Abigail was back there. He couldn't hear them, and he didn't know how far he had run last night before collapsing. His heart flinched, pulling him toward the direction he had come.

No.

The memory of her horrified expression when he'd snapped at her — he couldn't even control himself enough to prevent that — was burned into his memory. The only thing he could bring her was more pain. He wasn't human, after all.

Nathan dragged his gaze away from the path of crushed leaves and snapped twigs he had left in the wake of his journey the night before. Pushing himself to standing, he turned in the opposite direction. She was better off without him.

As he dragged his feet through the debris, he turned his nose up to the sky and inhaled the fresh smells of the woods. The soft rustling of the leaves and the dense scent of the earth didn't bring the same comfort as they had before.

As long as he continued to hike down, he would eventually find his way back to town and his den. Back to his old existence and to being alone.

Trudging through the trees, Nathan noticed the absence of the wolf's protesting instincts.

Don't you have an opinion?

He expected a snarl but was greeted by a quiet rumble instead. It pawed at his consciousness, questioning.

Nathan paused between two large pine trees, his toes balanced on a large root that arched out of the soil between them. "This is your fault," he muttered to himself. His life was in pieces because of the wolf.

Rather than getting riled, the wolf instincts nudged him again, urging him to give it control.

Nathan buried his face in his hands and lowered himself to sit on the root.

Why aren't you angry with me too?

He expected a snarl in reply, but was met with silence. *Why are you acting complacent* now?

An image of the tiny purple flower from the intelligence trial popped into his mind.

"That was a stupid flower," he muttered, dismissing the memory of the one time they'd managed to cooperate. He had still snarled at his sister. He still wasn't human — she had said it herself.

A sharp pain stung his temple, almost as though the wolf had bitten him for that remark.

"It's true!" Nathan complained, shoving to his feet. A new thought stopped him in his tracks.

So?

The wolf's instincts pawed forward, more aggressively this time, making itself irritatingly impossible to ignore. It wanted to try again.

"Whenever I try anything, I hurt someone," Nathan argued. He had tried to stand up to Silas so many times and had always failed. He couldn't connect with Abigail; he pushed her away because he was too scared. He had attempted to fight the giant, but all he could do was give Jessica an opening to negotiate with it.

His heart rate picked up. That was a fluke, wasn't it? When he had tried to save Abigail during the trial with the Questing Beast, he'd gotten Jessica hurt.

But if he had trusted Jessica and Damien instead, maybe it wouldn't have happened.

Curious, Nathan eased his control and allowed the wolf to come forward. The instincts settled in the forefront of his mind, considering the smells and eyeing the dark leaves that rustled above in the chilled breeze. The wolf shared space with Nathan's human thoughts, just as it had been during the Trial of Intelligence and in the fight against the demons.

Nathan examined the forest with a new sharpness. *What are you trying to tell me?*

The wolf grumbled unhappily, but it didn't fight back as Nathan continued down the mountain at half the speed he had been travelling before. He focused on his feet, watching how the roots from the trees moved through the earth like dolphins crossing the ocean. Bugs collected in the shadows beneath tiny leaves, hiding from the predators lurking above. The rocks were marked with striations of different colours, their lines so defined it looked like someone had drawn on the different layers.

Nathan's pace slowed further when he caught the hint of a new smell. It was a deep, earthy scent, like the layer of dirt below the roots had been pulled to the surface. Mixed with the softness of grass and a tang of salt, all the scents intricately folded into each other. The scent was surprisingly welcoming, as grounding and ancient as the smell of the earth itself, but as it continued to grow stronger, the hairs on Nathan's arms stood on end. A soft metal chime danced through the air, reminding Nathan of the bracelets he had seen women wearing in town.

The light tinkling and grounded scent were at odds with the ominous energy in the air, almost as if the oxygen was being sucked away and the temperature was dropping. The skin on the back of his neck tightened.

Nathan stopped walking and bared his teeth as Supai stepped out of the shadows. His sleek black hair, smoothly combed across the top, was too perfect for a man hiking through the woods. The black tunic and straight pants were also out of place. Staring into Supai's black eyes made an ache pulse in Nathan's chest as if the god's magic had squeezed his heart and was trying to pull it out.

"*Buenos días.*" Supai scanned Nathan from head to toe and raised one thick eyebrow. "You aren't looking so good."

Nathan curled back his upper lip and bent his knees, ready to lunge.

"I can help your sister," Supai said.

Nathan froze and Supai's grin deepened. "I thought that might get your attention." He pulled his hands from his pockets and interlaced them behind his back. "Your sister has placed herself in a very difficult position, and you would like to protect her, correct?"

Nathan fixated on Supai's face with a hunter's focus, noticing swirls of grey smoke shifting across the god's black corneas. A shiver rippled down Nathan's spine. He kept his knees soft, willing to take the chance his speed could overtake the god's ability to cast a spell. "How could you help?"

Supai tilted his head lazily, drawing out the silence as he feigned a thoughtful pause. "You are not a simple animal, my friend. You understand my quarrel is not with you or Abigail but with the witch and her companion, do you not?"

Arrogant prick. Nathan's upper lip twitched. "Get to the point."

Supai's smile wavered. He readjusted his tunic and gave Nathan a pitying look. "You don't belong among them."

"What do you know—"

"But you already know that, don't you? Or else you wouldn't be here," Supai stressed, gesturing to the woods. "Alone."

Nathan's nostrils flared and his jaw tightened. When he couldn't come up with a retort, Supai lifted his chin.

"I have a much better offer for you."

"Get. To. The. Point," Nathan said with a snarl, dipping his chin and glowering at Supai. He was happy to see the god stiffen.

"You bring the Lupatus Stone to me, and I will ensure no one touches your sister."

Nathan paused, making sure he had heard the words correctly, and then he spat out a harsh laugh. "So you couldn't control Silas, and now you're looking for a replacement werewolf?"

Supai narrowed his eyes. "We had a difference of opinions," he said, his jaw tight. "Silas doesn't understand the bigger picture. He is obsessed with the wake he leaves behind him. You were meant to be part of that carnage, you know. Part of a legacy." Supai watched him appraisingly. "But you can be better than him, than what he tried to make you into. You do *want* the Stone, don't you?"

Nathan bit the inside of his cheek, his fists clenched tight at his sides. If he had been asked the question yesterday, Nathan wouldn't have hesitated to say *yes*. The Stone was supposed to be his salvation. Today, Abigail's pained words rang through his ears.

It doesn't change what you did.

The wolf let out a soft growl, cautioning him to tread carefully. The god's magical energy pressed into his skin. They needed to be sure they had the advantage before striking.

Relaxing his shoulders and listening to his wolf's instincts, Nathan pulled back his urge to attack. "I'm listening."

Supai smiled victoriously. "Silas is the biggest threat to your sister. But if you get the Stone first, she won't have to risk her life going after it, nor will Silas go after her. He'll come after *you*." Raising an articulate eyebrow, Supai took a step forward. "Your sister remains safe, and you and Silas may settle your little" —he swirled his hand through the air, as if trying to find the right word—"disagreement. And with the Stone, you will most certainly be victorious."

It was tempting. Nathan wouldn't have to be useless. He could do something good, for once, without having to see Abigail again. The thought left a sour taste on his tongue. But his desire to fight Silas couldn't trump his distrust of the god.

"What's stopping me from taking the Stone and running?"

The god shook his head with a condescending chuckle. "I'm not asking you simply to steal the Stone. I want you to join me."

"Join you?" Nathan's inner wolf raised its hackles. "Join you in what?"

Supai's lips pulled into a wide, thin grin as the smoke in his eyes swirled tumultuously. "In something *much* bigger. Do you honestly think I would come to the human realm for one little werewolf trinket?" His shoulders shook in silent laughter, but he didn't share what he found so funny. "It is true that the Lupatus Stone may only be acquired by a werewolf, so I require one to retrieve it, but I have many more plans. What I'm offering you, Nathan, is a place in reshaping the world."

Nathan's knees wobbled. Supai's eyes were dangerously sharp, and the veins in his neck pulsed. Other than the hushed sound of his tunic shifting and the hollow echo of his gold jewellery striking itself, Supai was silent. Surely even a god should have a heartbeat, and the disturbing absence of one made Nathan's stomach twist.

"I-I don't suppose you'll tell me what reshaping the world looks like?"

Supai's hungry expression eased into a professional, composed seriousness. "Swear your loyalty to me and, of course, I will share everything."

"How can I trust your word?" Nathan challenged. "You turned a woman's corpse into a demon puppet. Why would I ever believe you wouldn't hurt Abigail?" His skin tightened as the god's glare intensified.

"That woman was a witch hunter," Supai said, his words precisely enunciated. "She would have killed you if she had the chance."

"She was still human!"

Supai shook his head with disappointment. "Why do so many creatures have this absurd obsession with *humanity*?" he complained. "Why should you care? *You're* not human."

His words punched Nathan in the gut, but it didn't hurt nearly as much as when Abigail had said the same thing.

"No," Nathan agreed, the weight falling from his shoulders. "I'm not." All this time, he had clung to what he had lost, but it had only kept him in the past. He wasn't fully human anymore, and that was never going to change.

"I'm not sure what I'm going to do about that. But it's better than whatever you've got going on." Nathan gestured vaguely to the god. "If you want to work with me, then you gotta offer the same protection to Jessica and Damien."

Supai's nostrils flared. "Those two will receive no mercy from me. Surely you don't owe them anything."

"I owe them more than you'll ever understand." That truth hurt. Nathan wasn't a bad person because he was a werewolf. It made him irritable and irrational at times, and he had a long way to go before he learned how to fully control his power, but that didn't make him bad. It wasn't the … *his* wolf's fault, either. Nathan was the one who ran.

"I have a better idea," Nathan said, a sense of power bubbling up and sending strength throughout his body. At last, he and his wolf were on the same page. "How about I destroy you now? Then you can't get in their way anymore, and Abigail stays safe."

To Nathan's satisfaction, the god's composure cracked. He sneered, showing his teeth. "You would be wise not to make an enemy of me," he warned in a low voice.

With a feral smile, Nathan flexed his hands at his sides. "What's one more enemy?"

He lunged, driving a fist into Supai's diaphragm before the god could blink.

Supai gagged, his body folding inward as he grabbed onto Nathan's shoulders. Nathan drove his other fist toward Supai's chin but, before he could connect, the god shoved him back and an invisible power threw him into the air. His back struck a tree with a loud crack, the wood splintering on impact, and he dropped to the ground, managing to land in an awkward crouch.

"I gave you a chance," Supai growled. "But you will die like the worthless dog you are."

"Nice to see your true colours," Nathan said with an answering snarl. He lunged again, but a blast of hot air from Supai's palms collided with his chest. Nathan howled, trying to push through the wall of wind.

"Even if you get the Stone, I will be waiting," Supai threatened. "You will retrieve it for me."

"Not if I kill you first!" Nathan forced a step forward, slowly but surely walking up the tunnel of wind that Supai threw at him.

"Stay back!" the god demanded, his tone rising.

Nathan showed his teeth vindictively. He roared and shoved forward three more large steps as the gale desperately battered his skin. Through narrowed eyes, he could see Supai's figure, almost within reach.

The wind stopped so suddenly that Nathan fell forward onto his stomach with a loud thud. He jumped to his feet, spinning around to search the woods, but Supai was gone.

"Coward!" he shouted at the forest, before scoffing at himself. *Look who's talking.* He had to find Jessica and Damien and warn them that Supai was planning an ambush — but that would mean facing Abigail again.

With his wolf lending him strength, Nathan retraced his steps, his nose searching the wind for any indication of their scent. His heart was already pounding before he started running, and his mind buzzed as he tried to think of what to say to his sister. There was no forgiveness; he knew that. At the very least, he should apologize properly. Abigail deserved that much.

CHAPTER 26

Jessica

When Jessica woke the next morning, Abigail was already packed up. The dawn light broken up by the leaves' shadows twinkled like stars across the snowy ground and the mud-caked toes of her boots as she stood in quiet stillness at the edge of the forest.

"Ready to go?"

Abigail jumped and hugged herself tighter. "Yes," she said, with none of her usual spark.

"Are … are you sure you want to keep going?"

With a weak but grateful smile, Abigail nodded. "The most important thing is finding the Lupatus Stone."

Despite how she held her head high, her tone remained unconvincing. Her gaze was focused on the forest.

Unable to offer anything better, Jessica nodded silently and went to help Damien clean up their things. Once they were set, Damien led the way as they continued their hike north.

After the first few minutes of hiking in silence, Jessica was surprised to find she missed the usual noise made by their crew of four. It felt like the energy of the entire forest had diminished.

"Abigail?" Jessica asked hesitantly over her shoulder, hoping that talking about Abigail's interests would lift her mood. "Do you have a guess about where the Stone's hiding place is?"

The riddle had said, 'Where the shadows swallow the sun, and the earth roars at the sky, the giant guards the power born from weakness.' Jessica had never been a fan of riddles. Magic was much more straightforward. The amount of magic exerted impacted the results of the spell, and the harder the spell, the more magic-output was required. It was a simple problem-solving equation. Riddles made Jessica feel inept.

Abigail's expression remained solemn. Evidently, not even puzzle-solving could raise her spirits. "I think it's a cave."

Damien's eyebrows lifted. "'Where the earth roars at the sky could be the opening to a tunnel. And the giant could be the rock it's made of?"

"Or the mountain itself," Abigail suggested. "Maybe it's another giant."

"I hope not," Jessica muttered, pushing back a low-hanging branch and holding it for Abigail to duck under. "I've had my fill of giants for a while."

They'd hiked most of the morning before the terrain changed, giving way to exposed rocks on the mountainside. Jessica kept the magical tracker hovering in front of her so she could check it regularly. The needle held steady, leading them around a high crag with trickling tendrils of water running across the rocks. The water pooled at their feet, sloshing as they walked.

"I hope we're getting close," Jessica muttered, mostly to herself, her attention fixed on the ground to avoid tripping.

"Getting impatient?" Damien asked, raising an eyebrow.

"Even you must be a little impatient by now," she complained. It was probably close to midday.

With a sympathetic smile, he gave her a small nod. "I'm sure we'll reach it today," he said as they rounded a bend.

The forest terrain levelled out, spanning the size of a football field. The other end of the plateau hit the base of a peak that rose dramatically before them, with valleys lining either side. Soon they would have to either climb down the ravine or climb over the mountain.

With a frustrated sigh, Jessica stopped and checked the navigation spell. The compass mirage was pointing directly at the mountain. "*Great*," she said, showing Damien.

He examined it closely, and then scanned the woods. "It has to be close," he muttered.

"What about that?" Abigail grabbed Jessica's forearm as she pointed to a series of rock formations at the base of the peak. "That has to be the answer to the riddle."

"What are you talking about?" Jessica asked, but Abigail had already taken off across the plateau, forcing Jessica and Damien to jog after her.

Once Jessica reached the base of the peak and saw up close what Abigail had been pointing at, her eyes widened. "*Oooh.*"

A cave opening jutted out at an angle, pointing toward the clouds, and jagged rocks that looked like fangs lined the floor and ceiling at the entranceway. It looked like a set of jaws roaring at the sky.

"'Where the shadows swallow the sun, and the earth roars at the sky, here the giant guards the power born from weakness,'" Abigail said excitedly.

Jessica nodded. "The cave swallows the shadows, and the giant is the mountain." She had a new appreciation for ancient werewolf poetry.

Abigail readjusted her glasses. "The Stone must be inside."

"Well. We made it," Jessica said. It didn't feel like a victory. She scanned the woods, imagining Nathan suddenly jogging through the trees to join them again. Her hope quickly dwindled. "I guess we better get going before Supai or Silas catch up with us."

Facing the entrance, Jessica was stopped by Abigail's quiet voice. "Can we wait?"

Jessica clenched her jaw. "Abigail, we're running out of—"

"I know." Her gaze sharpened as she came to a decision. "Can we wait? Just a few minutes?"

"There's only so much …" Her voice trailed off as Damien placed a hand on her shoulder, and with a heavy sigh, Jessica nodded. "We can wait. But only for a little bit." She crossed her arms over her chest and leaned into one of the stalagmites at the mouth of the cave.

Abigail remained standing in front of the cave as though guarding the entrance. She shifted her weight from side to side occasionally, her eyes never leaving the woods.

Fifteen minutes passed, and Jessica silently decided to push it to thirty. Then forty-five.

After an hour, Abigail's head dropped.

"I'm sorry, Abby." Jessica placed a hand on the girl's shoulder. "I don't think he's coming back."

Abigail swallowed. "I wish …"

Jessica squeezed her shoulder. "We get the Stone," she told Abigail confidently. "We finish what we started."

Abby lifted her chin. "Or I could go look for him."

"What?"

Pulling away from Jessica's hand, Abby turned to face her, her expression determined. "You two get the Stone. You have to stop Silas and Supai from getting it."

"Abigail," Jessica said firmly, "you shouldn't go hiking this deep in the woods alone, even without the demons and werewolves and angry gods chasing us."

Abigail adjusted her glasses and shook her head stubbornly, the curls of her ponytail swishing across the back of her jacket. "You were right, Jessica. I'm angry. I'm furious that he left me behind. It's so much easier to be angry, to go back to being alone. But he's been in as much pain and felt as much grief as I have. He's had it *way* worse. He's hurting and blaming himself, and I *let him*. Now I'm the one who's abandoned him." Her conviction was unwavering. "I don't know how to fix this, but I have to try. I-I don't want to lose him a second time."

Sympathy eased Jessica's frustration, but not the urgency of their situation. "Abigail, please be reasonable," she said. "You've made it this far. After all the research and hard work, after you've dreamt about discovering one of these treasures, don't you want to see this to the end?"

There was a long pause until Abigail gave a subtle shake of her head. "My brother is more important than the Stone."

The words hung in the air for a lingering moment before sinking into Jessica's pores. She glanced back at the cave. They were so close.

"Alright then," Jessica said with a heavy sigh, "let's go look for him."

"What?" Abigail's eyes widened. "But what about Supai and Silas and—"

"We've stopped Supai once, we can do it again," Jessica said, waving away the idea despite how the words twisted her stomach. "Even if they get the Stone, we'll have Nathan to help us get it back." They had come this far together; to go further without Nathan and Abigail wouldn't be the same.

She was worried about Nathan too.

Abigail's expression brightened. "Really?"

"Let's be quick about it," Jessica said, giving her a teasing look. She clapped her hands and rubbed her palms together. "I have a few tracking spells we could try. Usually, I need an item from the person, but since you're related, maybe there's a workaround."

"Jess," Damien interrupted. He came to their sides, a tense expression on his face and his gaze on the forest to the south.

"Wha—" But then her skin tightened at the back of her neck and the needle-like sensation ran down her spine. She pushed Abigail behind her as she faced the direction of the approaching energy. Someone—or something—with power was heading straight for them.

Jessica had loosened her knees, her hands raised and ready to fight, when Nathan burst through the trees at full speed.

CHAPTER 27

Nathan

Nathan skidded to a halt, digging his heels into the soil when he saw Jessica, Damien and Abigail. They were huddled next to a cave that looked like a gaping jaw with spiky rocks for teeth. He bent forward and braced himself on his knees, panting.

"Sorry ... sorry. I sprinted here," he explained against his laboured breathing. When he straightened up with a big inhale, they were still staring at him in shock.

Immediately, he forgot all the things he had planned to say. Then he made the mistake of catching Abigail's gaze, and his lungs seized.

"I'm sorry," he croaked. His mouth gaped a few times, but the words stopped. Silence filled the forest. Nathan's back stiffened, his feet glued into place.

Abigail stepped out from behind Jessica, looking at him like she was seeing a ghost. "You came back?"

"I, um, I—" He met Jessica's gaze. "I ran into Supai. He tried to recruit me, and then I tried to gut him, but he got away, and now he's planning on ambushing you whenever you get the Stone." He sucked in another deep inhale, his heart still hammering against his ribs. "I … thought you should know."

"Uh, thanks," Jessica said, her eyes darting between him and Abigail.

Nathan rubbed his sweaty palms down the sides of his pants, his eyes focused intensely on the ground. He paused, the adrenaline quickly fading and leaving him to stand on his own strength. Suddenly his legs felt like they were made of jelly. There was nowhere he could hide now.

"I'm sorry I ran, Abigail. I shouldn't have … What I mean is I-I should have told you what I was from the start. I shouldn't have put you in danger. Again. And again." He took a deep breath and lifted his head to meet her gaze.

"My wolf and I don't get along," he said, keeping his hands in tight fists at his side. "We've been fighting since I got cursed, and I've never dealt with that. I've tried to bury the instincts instead of listening to them. And I know I've been a pain — I wouldn't like me either, with the way I've been acting. But I have to be okay with the fact that I-I'm *not* human, anymore. I have to figure out what that means."

He let out a heavy sigh, freed by the release of the truth. "I came to say goodbye. I won't put you into danger anymore, so you … you don't have to worry about me."

There, he'd said it. Nathan wasn't sure what he'd anticipated feeling, but it wasn't this hollowness. His shoulders slouched forward, struggling to bear weight. "I'm, um … Good luck."

He turned to leave.

"Stop!" Abigail shouted.

Nathan jumped, the noise rattling his brain, and turned sharply to meet the wild-eyed stare of his sister. His heartbeat pounded in his ears as he scoured his thoughts for what she could possibly want.

"Don't leave. Please."

Nathan squared his shoulders to her, searching her gaze for the anger from the day before and finding none. Only fear pulled at her features, but this time, that fear wasn't of him.

"You want … Why would you want me to stay?"

Abigail's jaw dropped. "You're my *brother!* We finally have a chance to regain a piece of what we lost." She wrung her hands together. "But you ran away. *Again.* And that scared me, Nathan. I'm sorry for what I said, but I don't want to lose you! Not for anything."

Nathan's face paled, and his lungs trembled. The desperate hope that had been hiding in a deep corner of his heart rushed forward, ravaging through his chest and bringing with it gratitude and relief that left his head spinning.

Abigail's expression eased. "This is messy, Nathan, but I want to figure it out. I'm sorry I hurt you, and I can't promise I won't say the wrong thing again—I have no idea what might upset you—but you can help me figure it out, right? I don't care if you're a werewolf. I just care that you're *here*." She watched him for his reaction, the desperation in her eyes unwavering.

He shook his head, his face slack, and took an unsteady step backward. "But … Abigail. The fire—"

"I don't want to talk about that right now." She shook her head forcefully. "Not while I'm still processing this." She gestured to him and Jessica and the woods as she spoke.

Nathan struggled to find his voice. Once they found the Stone, once she had time to think about it, she might never want to see him again. And he wasn't sure he could put himself through that; he couldn't risk getting his hopes up. "I'm dangerous, Abby."

"I don't think you are," she said. "But we're also up against a maniacal werewolf and some crazy god of death, so maybe … maybe we need dangerous right now." She gave him a hopeful look, but when Nathan couldn't pull himself out of the shock, her expression fell. Sliding her hands into the pockets of her jacket, Abby stared at her feet.

"But if … if it's too painful for you to be here, then … that's fair. You've been through a lot, and maybe … maybe you don't want me around. But can you at least *tell* me that?" She met his gaze with a tense jaw. "Tell me that this is too hard for you before you run away again."

She was giving him an out? After all that he'd … she was giving him an excuse to run. It would be so easy.

"You … you think I don't want you in my life?"

"I honestly don't know," Abigail confessed. "You keep pushing me away. What am I supposed to think?"

Nathan shook his head. "I don't want to lose you, Abigail. I thought … I thought you must hate me. Everything that's happened to you is my fault."

There was a long pause where Abigail stared at the ground, holding herself tightly. Nathan's throat tightened, wishing he could take his words and swallow them back down.

"I don't hate you, Nathan," she said quietly. "I don't think it's all your fault, either, but I know you won't believe me right now. This is a lot to take in, but I hope … I want you to give me a chance."

"You want me to give *you* a chance?"

"Let's get to know each other." Abigail took a tentative step forward. "We can find the Stone. It's designed for werewolves; maybe it will even help. Once we're through this trial, we can revisit the past. Okay?" Her voice cracked as she met his gaze, her eyes flickering desperately to his.

He nodded, barely able to find the words. "O-okay."

Relief washed across Abby's features, and after another long pause, her cheeks reddened. She turned to Jessica and Damien. "I'm sorry—"

They held up their hands to stop her. "I'm glad you're both sticking around," Jessica said with a weak smile. "But we really need to get going."

Oh, right. The dizzy joy in Nathan's head slowly faded as they turned to face the cave entrance together. When they stepped up to the jagged rocks, Nathan heard Jessica's heart rate spike. Her wary look at the crevices around the ceiling of the cave made his nerves twist his stomach.

"Are you scared?" Nathan asked in disbelief.

"No," Jessica said curtly, and at the same time, Damien replied, "Yes." She glared at him, but that didn't stop his cheeky grin.

"What could you possibly be afraid of?" Abigail asked.

Jessica waved away the question. "It's nothing."

"Bats," Damien said, winking at Jessica. "Don't worry, I'll protect you."

"Don't make me laugh." Jessica rolled her eyes for emphasis, which made Damien's smile grow stronger. Shaking her head, she faced the entrance of the cave, and the rest of the group followed her lead. "Alright, let's—"

"I'll go first," Nathan said.

Jessica gave him a wary look. "Are you sure?"

He nodded, his mouth tightening at the corners. "That's the reason I'm here, right?" His gaze flickered toward Abigail, who smiled her reassurance. Nathan looked at Damien and said, grudgingly, "You focus on covering our backs."

"Got it."

Nathan marched into the cave. Abigail followed next, leaving Jessica and Damien to bring up the rear.

They crept down the narrow tunnel single file. Nathan had to hunch to avoid hitting his head on the ceiling. Either this Arthurian werewolf had been really short, or this tunnel was not built for werewolves. Although Nathan would fit if he were in his wolf form.

The tunnel continued straight for what felt like centuries. The only light they had to guide them came from the entrance of the cave. He could navigate fine in the dark, but he heard the others tracing their fingers across the walls to keep their balance.

When he saw the end of the tunnel dip down into a set of stairs, he slowed his pace to look over his shoulder. "There are stairs up ahead, with some torches on the wall. Could you light them, Jess?"

"She could, but that would alert anyone else in here to our presence," Damien cut in.

"Yeah," Jessica agreed apologetically.

Nathan grumbled. "Watch your step."

Abigail reached out and gripped the back of Nathan's shirt. "Slow?" she asked cautiously. Nathan gave her a shallow nod and led the way down.

"At least the bonus of Nathan being so tall is he'll block the way if anyone falls," Jessica whispered.

"I heard that," Nathan said with a scoff. "And if you think I'm catching any of you, you'd better think again."

Jessica snorted out a laugh, accompanied by a shy giggle from Abigail. The laughter floated behind them as they descended into darkness.

With the tight walls surrounding him and not enough room to even stretch his arms overhead, it didn't take long for Nathan to get impatient. He kept his hands on either wall so he would stop anyone who fell. The stairs were carved into the rocky floor of the cave, and their creases melted into each other, steps merging like cascading water.

"How long do you think it took to make this?" Abigail murmured wistfully.

"Hard to say," Jessica replied. "It's definitely old. I can't feel magic in the walls."

"Should you be able to?" Nathan asked warily. He wasn't keen on the idea of being surrounded by magic.

"Usually places like this would have veins of magic running through them. At least, that's what my Nonna told me. But either there isn't any, or it's too deep for me to feel."

"That doesn't sound like a good thing," Abigail murmured.

There was a noticeable pause from the witch. "Hard to say."

They continued in silence until Nathan stopped again.

"What is it?" Abigail asked pensively.

He whispered, "There's light up ahead."

With that warning, they inched their way down the remaining stairs. A faint light crawled up the walls toward them. The dents and bumps across the stone came into focus, and as they got closer to the light, Nathan could see claw marks on the stairs reminiscent of the ones covering the floor of his cave.

When they reached the opening at the end of the stairs, Nathan leaned forward and checked the area. It was an oval room with a low ceiling and torches already lit along the walls. Three new tunnels awaited them. "It's clear," he muttered, stepping off the stone steps onto the soft dirt floor.

Jessica shuddered. "There's strong magic in here."

"Torches don't usually light themselves."

Jessica shot him an unimpressed look, while Abigail stepped away from the group to examine the tunnels on the other side of the room.

"Which way do we go?" she asked quietly, looking at Jessica. Nathan and Damien also turned to the witch.

"It's my first time here too," Jessica complained as she turned her attention to the tunnels, frowning as if she expected them to tell her something.

"It could be the markings," Nathan suggested. Standing in the opening of the tunnel on the left, he reached up and brushed away the dirt from the wall, revealing a small X carved into the stone above the entranceway.

Jessica's face lit up with recognition. "That's a territory marking."

Nathan undusted the other two tunnels, revealing a pair of vertical lines over the centre tunnel, and a square with another X inside it carved above the tunnel on the right. "What do they mean?"

"Malcolm taught me. Had I known them then, I probably could have avoided crossing paths with his pack in the first place. The *X* means 'do not cross,' and the vertical lines mean 'safe passage.' The last one …" She hesitated, biting her lower lip. "The last one essentially means 'do not cross or you'll be considered a threat'. It's warning people that if you pass, you could be killed without question."

"That's likely the one we want," Damien muttered darkly.

"Can't it be the 'safe passage' one?" Abigail asked in a small voice.

"Who knows where that'd take us." Nathan turned to his sister. "Maybe … maybe you should turn back here, Abby?" He tensed, expecting a fight, but instead she was silent.

"You did promise that you'd follow orders," Jessica reminded her gently.

With a heavy sigh, Abigail nodded. "Yeah. Threat of immediate death is a bit over my head."

Nathan's upper body sagged with relief. Jessica looked to Damien, and the witch hunter nodded. "I'll go with you," he offered. "Let's go back the way we came."

She gave him a grateful nod, and they headed back toward the stairs.

Jessica turned to the tunnels. "Alright, Nathan. What do you—"

"Wait!" Nathan turned sharply and sprinted after Abigail and Damien, who hesitated on the first step. He grabbed the handle of Abigail's backpack and pulled her back, shoving past Damien to stick his head up the stairwell.

"What are you doing?" Abigail gasped, stumbling as she tried to regain her balance.

"Shh!" Nathan said. "Just hold your breath for a second."

After a panicked look to Jessica, who nodded urgently, Abigail did as she was told, her cheeks puffed out.

Nathan listened intently. His stomach dropped when he heard the sweeping sound clearly coming down from higher up in the tunnel. It was the same sound that the demons' smoke had made when they invaded Abigail's house.

"Demons are coming down from the entrance."

"Are you sure?" Damien asked, but Nathan was already ushering Abigail away from the stairs.

"We have to get going," he urged.

"But we don't know which tunnel," Abigail reminded him, her heels digging into the ground.

"It has to be 'threat of death,'" Jessica said grimly. "There's no way a dangerous treasure is hidden on the safe path."

"Abigail and I could take the safe route?" Damien offered.

"No way!" Abigail cut in, finally getting her feet under her and shrugging Nathan off. "We stick together. That's basic horror movie rule number one."

"Are you serious?" Jessica said, exasperated.

"No time," Nathan snapped. "Let's go!"

He led the way as they rushed down the tunnel marked with the threat of death, which quickly swallowed them in darkness. A second later, once all four of them were in the lower tunnel, a torch twenty feet down the path ignited.

"Definitely the right way," Jessica muttered.

Using the dim lighting of the torches self-igniting every three metres, they moved as swiftly as they could down the tunnel, weaving back and forth as it led them deeper into the mountain. Dirt swirled at Nathan's feet, a hush sound emerging with each step. Dust coated his fingers when he trailed his hands along the wall.

"I don't like this," he muttered. His head scraped the roof of the tunnel as he tried to straighten his back. "The tunnel's getting smaller."

"Nathan, watch out!" Abigail grabbed the back of his shirt, yanking him back before he could topple forward. His heart leapt up into his throat, and he thrust both hands out to brace himself against the walls. The familiar tingling of Jessica's magic coated the back of his neck, stronger than Abigail's tiny hands as it pulled him back from the ledge.

The tunnel abruptly stopped at the edge of a pit so vast the light from the torches was unable to penetrate even a hint of the chasm. As far as he could see, there was no tunnel on the other side.

Abigail gasped behind him. "There's writing!" She dusted off the wall to her left with both hands, silt lingering in the air and trapping them in its cloud.

Coughing into her fist, Jessica squinted through the dirt. "Can you read it?"

"Quickly," Nathan urged, pressing his body into the wall across from the inscription to give Abigail more room.

"I think I can," Abigail said. "But it's not … it's more of the Celtic–Latin fusion but—not quite. There are some similarities."

Damien glanced over his shoulder. "Nathan, how much time do we have?"

Pressing his lips into a thin line, Nathan squinted up the tunnel. "Three minutes. Maybe."

"I'm working as fast as I can," Abigail muttered absently, readjusting her glasses.

Jessica turned to Damien. He already had his hunting knife out and ready. "Damien, let me?"

Nodding, he shifted out of the way so Jessica could take up position behind the group. It was a narrow space with one line of attack. She cracked her knuckles.

Nathan ground his teeth. "Abby, now's the time for that big brain of yours to work *faster*."

"I've almost got it. I think."

"I can hear them," Jessica warned, her brow tightening.

"Any time now, Abby," Nathan pressed.

"*Almost!* I have to be sure."

A flicker of shadow made Jessica's fingers tense. "They're here!" she shouted as she shoved her palms forward, sending a ball of green fire barrelling down the tunnel.

Abby pushed herself back from the wall. "I got it!"

Three demon shadows slipped across the tunnel walls, avoiding the fire and manifesting right in front of Jessica. She waved her arm across the path, using a gust of wind to push them back. "What does it mean?" she snapped.

"Everyone but Jessica can jump!"

"What?" everyone exclaimed.

"And let the demons through!" she shouted back. Then Abigail took two large steps, jumped into the chasm, and was instantly swallowed by the darkness.

"Abigail!" Jessica screamed.

A combination of a yelp and a scream screeched out of Nathan's throat. One of the demons shoved past him, but as its wispy body dived toward the pit, a sudden flash of blinding white light erupted. Nathan threw up his forearm to protect his eyes as the demon's wail assailed his ears with a sharp, burning pain. When he blinked his eyes open, the demon was gone.

The tunnel filled with the sounds of hissing demons and crackling fire. On the walls, the shadows shifted and jerked in all directions. It was impossible to tell which was light and which was monster. Nathan didn't linger long enough to sort it out. He jumped headlong into the chasm after Abigail, with two more demons on his heels.

CHAPTER 28

Nathan

Nathan landed far more quickly than he thought he would. His knees buckled and smacked the bottom of his chin before he fell sideways and rolled across the ground. On his hands and knees, he searched the dirt, coughing as it swirled up and filled his lungs. "Abigail?"

His right knuckles knocked something light and thin, and a faint metal sound echoed in the darkness. Glasses. He grabbed them quickly. "Abby!"

"Over here," she replied in a strained whisper.

He crawled toward her voice until his hand hit her ankle. She flinched, but he grabbed her tightly so he wouldn't lose her. "It's me," he rushed the words out. "I got you."

Awkwardly swatting the air until he found her hands, he placed the glasses into her trembling grip. Not that they would do her any good right now, but he figured she would feel better having them.

"What were you thinking, Abby?" His body was shaking, adrenaline still thundering in his blood.

"Don't growl at me!" she snapped in a voice as tight as a bowstring about to break.

"You jumped headfirst—"

"It wasn't headfirst!"

"—into the dark without thinking!"

She huffed. "The translation said the wolf's journey required a leap of faith and only creatures of the earth could pass."

"Are you kidding me?"

There was a long pause. "Well … it was *something* like that."

"You based your jump off a guess?"

"An educated guess," she argued. "And it destroyed the demons!"

He bit his tongue before arguing further and turned his hearing toward the air above them. Silence lingered overhead. That blinding light had eradicated the demon that tried to follow Abby—had it destroyed the rest?

"The choice of vocabulary was fairly clear. Obviously, werewolves can jump in because it specified the *wolf's journey*, and I figured humans would count as creatures of the earth since lots of creation myths involve them being moulded out of clay and dirt, but I didn't know if Jessica would be okay, being a witch, so——"

"Abby."

She stopped, her words catching on an awkward gulp.

Nathan let out an exhausted sigh. "How did you get so smart?"

Abigail was silent. He sensed no movement from her.

"Next time give me … give me a heads up, will ya?" he pleaded. Her curls swished against the back of her jacket, which he interpreted as a nod.

Suddenly Jessica's voice called out, "Are you guys alive?"

Nathan made a mental note to have a talk with Jessica about her word choice. "Yeah, we're fine. You?"

"All good," Damien replied.

Nathan's werewolf hearing picked up the rest of their conversation.

"You call that 'good'?" Jessica whispered sharply. "Your arm is bleeding. *Again.*"

"You can make it better," he mused, his voice dropping.

She huffed. "Did you do that just so I'd have to patch you up?"

"Call it a fantasy."

She snorted. "You're a barbarian."

"You seem to like it."

"Stupid witch hunter."

Nathan rolled his eyes, and Abigail reached out to squeeze his forearm.

"Is everything okay?" she asked nervously, reminding Nathan she couldn't hear everything he could.

"They're fine," he assured her. "Tell them what you told me."

Abby shifted her weight, keeping a hold of his forearm to steady herself as she got to her knees. "The inscription said only creatures of the earth could pass. I guessed demons were probably made of magic, so they'd get destroyed, but I wasn't sure how a witch would be affected," she explained, projecting her voice.

"That sounds about right," Jessica said disdainfully. "The demons that tried to follow you got evaporated. We took care of the rest, but there'll probably be more soon. Witches are part human, but our ability to manipulate raw magic classifies us as magical species. I doubt any exception applies to me." She paused. "Next time, don't give us a heart attack, Abigail."

"Sorry! I thought we were in a rush."

Nathan furrowed his brow, looking up at the darkness above them. "Jessica, can you break the spell?"

A scuffling sound suggested Jessica was on her knees, her jeans scratching across the dirt. "There's a barrier over the pit. I'm guessing it's a magic-destruction spell of some kind. But it's ancient. It would take me too long to even *try* to undo it."

Before Nathan could respond, Damien beat him to it. "Jess and I will go back and find the exit. Don't let us beat you there." Soon the rustling of their footsteps faded to the distance, and the air overhead was silent again.

"We're on our own," he told Abigail. "Did the carvings say anything about what to do once we're down here?"

"No," she admitted in a quiet voice. "I should have thought this through."

"Well, being chased by demons kinda forces you into making choices," he said with a shrug. "Don't move, okay? I'm going to look for an exit."

"I can help too," Abigail told him sternly.

He was about to object but caught himself. Abigail had already proved how capable she was. Trying to do everything alone certainly hadn't worked up to this point. "Thanks."

Nathan pulled away and swept his hands across the earth as he crawled on his hands and knees. The darkness was eerie. They hadn't fallen far, and yet the torchlight from above couldn't reach them.

Since he couldn't see, Nathan used his nose instead. All the scents were muted, covered in a layer of must and dirt. Abigail's soft honey and paper hovered to his left, where she was crawling around trying to find a clue to escape the pit. Underneath the dust were tendrils of decay and rot—the scent of death coated the floor.

"Can you smell me?"

Abigail's voice was so quiet Nathan almost missed the question. It would have been easy to ignore it, but he didn't want to deny his wolf any longer. Nathan inhaled musty air, tensing his gut. "Honey and paper," he admitted.

To his surprise, she giggled nervously. "That makes sense."

The pause weighed on him like a heavy blanket. Pressing his lips together, he turned his nose back to the task at hand. He picked up the stench of stale, thick air. It wafted up from the ground in an isolated spot, like a puff of steam steadily seeping through the ground. It was denser than the air in the pit.

"Abigail, come toward my voice."

She crawled across the ground until she hit his hand, and then she gripped it tightly. He used his free hand to search the ground near the scent until it abruptly hit a rock. It was the first rock he had come across, as the rest of the ground was covered in sand-like dirt.

He grabbed hold of the stone, fitting it perfectly into the palm of his hand, and pulled it up. A creaking noise broke through the quiet, followed by the rusty sound of hinges trying to open. A trap door collapsed in front of him, revealing a new tunnel beneath them, awash in a dull yellow light. The hatch was so old and unused that it shattered to pieces on the ground below. The musky air rushed up to coat his face, leaving a layer of grime across his skin.

He gripped Abigail's hand tighter. "I'll go first," he told her. Then he let go and lowered himself into the tunnel beneath the pit, which was a hair taller than he was.

The walls were carved to form a rectangular hallway. He couldn't identify where the dim light in the tunnel was coming from, but it was enough for him to see the layer of dust on the walls. Once he had his footing, he reached up and helped Abigail down to his level.

"I hadn't thought about how dense the air would be," she said quietly, her forehead wrinkling. "How far down do you think we are?"

Nathan gritted his teeth. "I'm trying not to think about it." He eyed the walls as if they were about to close in on them.

Abigail gave him a sympathetic smile. "For a place meant for werewolves, it doesn't seem very well designed."

"Or it's designed to keep werewolves out," Nathan guessed.

"Maybe it's a test of will."

Nathan frowned. That would fall in line with the other trials they had endured. They continued down the hallway, dirt swirling around their feet. Nathan listened intently to the thin, raspy sound of their breathing growing stronger.

"Can I … can I ask you questions about it?"

"About being a werewolf?"

She hesitated. "Yeah."

Nathan sighed, trying to calm his racing heart. It was time to be brave. No more running from the truth. That didn't stop the nervous sweat from pooling at the back of his neck. "Yeah … okay."

"Can you control the transformations?" Her quiet voice echoed off the walls.

Nathan nodded. "Most of the time. I can turn when I want to, which took a couple of years to learn. The full moon does make the … it makes my wolf stronger. The instincts are too powerful to ignore, so I have to shift then. Otherwise, I control the transformation."

"Why do you think the riddle calls it a power born out of weakness?"

"I'm not sure," he admitted. Jessica had been right when she said the first transformation was excruciating. While the pain became manageable with practice, and was exhilarating now that he could control it, he could still remember the agony of that awful night. The curse stripped a person down to their weakest state, but then they gained superhuman strength and senses in return.

"A power—the wolf, born out of weakness—that is the curse," Abigail said, her words taking that steady rhythmic beat that she had when she was rattling off history facts. "It's the classic *what doesn't kill you makes you stronger*, right?"

"It's still a curse," Nathan muttered.

Her tone wavered. "Nathan—"

"This is painful, Abby," he confessed. "It's hard to talk about 'cause I can't stop thinking about how this curse has destroyed so much of our lives. Mom and Dad are dead because of me. Whether or not this is some kind of superpower," he muttered, looking down at his own hands, "everything you've lost—that we've lost—is because of me."

There was a long pause before Abigail spoke again. The still air was filled with the soft shuffling of their feet as they continued down the hallway. The dim lighting continuously faded away to shadows thirty feet ahead, making it feel like they were walking in place. Nathan was acutely aware of the sound of his breathing, his mind spinning with what Abigail might say … if she said anything at all. *Does she regret asking me to stay?*

"What would you have done differently?"

Nathan scoffed. "How about not setting the hospital on fire?"

"The brother I knew wouldn't have done that on purpose."

Glancing at her over his shoulder, he wondered if she had hit her head on the way down into the tunnel. "You said I wasn't the same person anymore, Abigail."

Abigail's curls shook as she shook her head, frustrated. "I'm talking about the kid you were, Nathan. On that night, you were still the boy who hated killing spiders and used to … used to hide little gifts in my room so I'd smile." Her hands clenched at her sides. "As terrified as you must have been, you wouldn't have hurt anyone. Not on purpose. And I don't think your wolf would have done it either. It's still *you*, right?"

Nathan's mind felt fuzzy. "How can you not blame me?"

"Honestly?" She hesitated, her gaze dancing across the wall. "Maybe I'm in denial, but it doesn't feel right."

"There's no other explanation, Abigail," he said, the words leaving him nauseated. "I'm the only one who survived."

"That doesn't mean you started the fire."

"The wolf took over," he told her, turning away. "It lashed out."

"And blew up an old furnace?" Abigail grabbed his arm and pulled him halfway to face her. "How is that even possible? Doesn't it seem the least bit strange to you that, while in agony and panic, you sought out the furnace room, broke a heavy piece of equipment, and still managed to survive long enough to be found by the crazy man who put you in the hospital in the first place? Everything you know about that night, Silas told you, right? And you take his word for it?"

"Why are you so determined to find an excuse?"

"Why are *you* so determined to hate yourself?"

He tried to respond, but the words wrapped around his throat like a noose and tightened until he strained to fill his lungs with the musty air. The walls grew tighter around him.

Abigail stuck out her chin. "You can keep trying to justify your guilt, but I'm not going to stop proving you wrong."

He scoffed, but despite the heaviness in his chest, he couldn't help but smile. The statement was so incredibly Abigail. He turned back to their path ahead and led them on. "I guess siblings have to fight about something."

CHAPTER 29

Jessica

Jessica's knees buckled as she jumped over a rock that jutted out of the steep mountain, landing on the precarious, slanting earth. Her muscles burned, but she could feel every second ticking by and refused to slow down. Stray baby hairs were plastered to her forehead, soaked by a mixture of her sweat and the moisture that hung the air.

"Jess, slow down," Damien said behind her.

The calm command made her want to push faster, even as she slipped and skidded a foot lower down the sharp incline that she and Damien were crossing to make their way around the peak that Nathan and Abigail were currently somewhere underneath.

She gritted her teeth, sneering at the snow-soaked soil that crumbled under her weight. It would be easier to search for the exit to the Lupatus Stone caves if they had flat ground to walk on. Instead, they were stuck on the side of a valley between two mountain peaks, and she didn't want to risk going to the bottom of it in case it took her too far away from her goal.

"If you hurt yourself, then you won't be able to help them," Damien said, his tone sharper this time.

"Well, I'm not about to go backward," she said curtly.

She caught a whisper of Damien's frustrated sigh. "We don't know where the exit is, or if there even is one. We could be going in the wrong direction already."

Spinning on her heel to face him, Jessica's ponytail whipped around and smacked her opposite cheek. She brushed off the hairs and glowered at him as if it was his fault. "That doesn't help either."

He stopped out of arm's reach. A sharp pang of guilt poked her in the gut, but Jessica wouldn't apologize. She was anxious, stressed, and, frankly, irritated that the cave had been guarded against witches. Her usefulness was her magic, and she couldn't use it to help. There was no spell she knew for finding cave exits.

"At least this way you don't have to deal with the bats," he offered gently.

"Read the room, Damien."

He grimaced.

"How can you be so calm about this?" she asked, genuinely concerned. "Yes, it was their choice to come, but they're both in vulnerable states *and* alone in a cursed tunnel in the middle of a mountain, and Silas could be right on their heels." The guilt returned with a vengeance, gnawing at her insides.

"Because panicking doesn't help," he replied firmly. "If you act irrationally, you put others into more danger."

The sharpness to his words made her flinch, her frustration shifting to concern as she watched his gaze flicker across hers.

He focused his gaze on the trees. "If you're a leader in a high-pressure situation, you can't afford to freak out."

Jessica pursed her lips and glowered at her feet. "Maybe that's easy for you," she mumbled, wishing she had his composure.

Noticing his drawn-out pause, she looked up to see a tense expression on Damien's face as he eyed the sea of trees around them. A moment later, his low-toned voice washed over her, his words silencing all the other sounds of the forest.

"The two years before I moved back to Toronto, I was working for Interpol."

Jessica stilled in surprise. "I thought you were in the military."

"I was." He was choosing his words carefully. "I served for a few years before Interpol recruited me. They employee a handful of people from global militaries and security forces who know about magic to work for their department that focuses on supernatural threats." His gaze was wistful, thinking back to a different time.

"I was in charge of a three-man team, and just over a year ago, we heard about a suspected vampire coven based near our location. I was so proud of my position that I didn't think twice about investigating despite the lack of intel on their numbers. It was a small house in the countryside; it shouldn't have been a big threat. But the coven was over thirty vampires strong and was actively targeting humans. We were ambushed. My friend Beckett was killed, and I nearly lost Eli too."

Jessica remembered Eli from Toronto, a white-haired witch hunter with a British accent. He had always seemed to have the closest relationship to Damien, aside from Connor.

When Damien met her gaze again, the strength in his expression was firm and unshakable. He stepped toward her, causing her pulse to jump, and placed his hands on her arms. "We agreed as a team to go in. It wasn't my fault alone." His voice hitched, and the words that followed were strained.

"I should have been wary that we were going in dark, should have voted to pull back instead. My friends were counting on me to lead them, and I failed. It was that incident that led me to getting let go, and after that, the military wouldn't take me back."

He shook his head, his hands squeezing her biceps before sliding down the length of her arms to gently envelop her palms in his, staring at their hands. "So, no, it's not always easy. It's taken a year of therapy to even ease the weight, and I know it will never totally be gone.

Accepting that I can't protect people from their own free will is the only way I can look forward."

Jessica exhaled carefully and squeezed his hands. "I can't imagine." The weight of his confession made her uneasy, like she had been given a delicate gift and she was afraid of dropping it.

His touch was so warm that she didn't want to let go. She glanced up at him through her lashes and found him watching her back. Her eyes fell to his lips. An urge in her stomach pulled her forward but she chose to look away as she pulled her hands back.

He tightened his grip instead. "Can I kiss you?"

Jessica coughed, startled by the blunt question, and looked anywhere but his eyes. "Now is really not the time."

"You've been avoiding getting this close to me since we left Toronto," he said, a heaviness in his voice. He stroked his thumb across her knuckles.

"You want to talk about that *now*?"

"It doesn't have to take long," he said with a weak half-smile. "You're still avoiding the subject."

She gritted her teeth behind tight lips. Talking about it meant facing the feelings spinning in her stomach.

Damien's forehead creased. "Talk to me."

Jessica sighed, staring at their hands. "The night we kissed, you turned on me and held a knife to my back." She didn't want it to sound like it was his fault, but there was no other way to say it.

"Yeah. Guess I haven't really apologized for that either."

When he didn't reply, she knew he was waiting for her to look at him. He never let her get away with hiding. With a deep breath, she met his gaze.

"I'm sorry," Damien said. The words made her heart palpitate. "I wish I had thought of a better way out of that situation, one that didn't involve hurting you. And I'm asking a lot for you to forgive me for that, but ..." He dipped his chin, his curls brushing her forehead. "I'm also kinda selfish. Will you forgive me?"

She understood why he had done it. She couldn't imagine the situation at the gala could have gone any differently for Damien, not when his brother's soul was on the line. Jessica hadn't anticipated how much that apology meant to her.

"I forgive you for what happened at the gala," she said, the words sliding a weight off her shoulders and leaving room for the intense attraction to bubble to the surface. "But I'm still trying to sort out ..." She twirled a finger in front of her temple. And that didn't address the flutter in her heart or the tightening of her stomach. She needed more time to find the words. She gestured between them. "What is *this* to you?"

He made a small *hmm* sound. "What do you want it to be?"

"No, no, no," she squeezed his hands in protest. "Don't turn it back on me. I'm no good with words."

"Neither am I," he said with a chuckle. "Just say what you're thinking. You don't need to filter anything with me."

I'm not the one who's impossible to read. "I was thinking that dating while hunting demons sounds like a ridiculous idea." She bit her lower lip, hesitating. "Though, *honestly,* I've been using that as an excuse to not deal with the way you make my heart freak out, which is kind of scary because it's more intense than anything I've felt before. I want …" *What do I want?*

"I want more time with you. I want to explore what *this* is, but it's also overwhelming, and that makes me freeze up." Jessica braved a look at him.

Damien was serene, and the faint smile at the corner of his lips told her nothing. "You're right. Dating while demon hunting is ridiculous." He teased her with a lift of his eyebrow. "I don't think it's all that weird given the lives we lead, but if we both want each other, what more do we need? We go with what our emotions tell us. But promise me, if you—" He paused, his gaze shifting with uncharacteristic nervousness. "You'll tell me if that changes. Right?"

"Deal," she agreed readily. "Same to you."

"Agreed." His smile stretched as he lowered his forehead to hers. "You're special, Jess."

"That's a good thing, right?" she asked, chuckling nervously as he pulled her a fraction closer.

An amused smile spread across his face. "Let me show you what I mean," he whispered before lowering his lips to hers.

Jessica melted into him as she closed her eyes, luxuriating in the warmth that spread through her body and the tingling that followed. Time always evaporated when Damien was near … at least, until the skin on the back of her neck tightened and sent a warning chill down her spine.

Jessica broke away with a start, her attention on the woods behind her. "A strong magical presence is coming this way."

Damien stiffened and pulled his knife from its hidden sheath on his lower back, standing shoulder to shoulder with her as they stared at the endless sea of dark trees.

The long seconds of silence were filled with the sound of Jessica's heart knocking against her ribs. Keeping her knees relaxed, she readied herself for a fight.

Her heart flinched when Supai stepped out from behind a tree, a twisted smile on his face. His black eyes narrowed on her as he held his hands behind his back. His posture had lost its stiffness from the previous day, and a lock of thick black hair was hanging carelessly down his forehead. If he felt the cold snow beneath his sandaled feet, he didn't show it.

Jessica could close the distance between them in ten steps.

"Lovely to see you again," he murmured, eyeing her up and down.

"Wish it was mutual," she retorted, crossing her arms over her chest to try to hide the nerves making her heart race.

"Yes," he said, reconsidering his earlier statement. "You have proven to be quite the nuisance."

"That's my favourite compliment," Jessica said with a humourless grin. "I'm guessing you're here to teach me a lesson? Nice of you to take us head-on."

Supai sucked his teeth, and Jessica's skin crawled. "I had planned an ambush while you too were *busy*," he said in disgust. Jessica's cheeks burned, mortified. "However, you detected me." His harsh tone made his frustration clear. "Not that it makes a difference." Supai tilted his head slightly, his gaze fixated on her. "It will be more fulfilling to look you in the eye as you die."

Jessica lunged. A fight could be decided by who struck first, and she knew Supai wouldn't see it coming. She closed the gap in five fast strides. Supai's eyes widened, but before she could reach him to strike, he thrust out the heel of his hand. Jessica threw up her forearms just as an invisible force of magic slammed into them and threw her backward.

Damien caught her with a grunt, his heels skidding across the snow as the force drove them back.

"Constantly surprising me," he muttered, holding Jessica's biceps as she steadied herself.

"I had to try," she grumbled, rubbing her right forearm, where she could feel a bruise forming.

Wisps of smoke churned across Supai's irises. The temperature of the forest dropped as ominous energy pulsed outward from the god, striking Jessica and sending a chill down her spine.

"You are nothing more than a thorn in my foot on the path to greater things," Supai said, his words tense.

Jessica swallowed, clenching her fists to ready herself for the next onslaught. "What 'greater things'?" she taunted, hoping to give herself time to think of a strategy. "We heard Silas betrayed you, and you failed to manipulate Nathan. You have no one to get the Stone for you."

Supai rolled his eyes. "A minor hiccup. I no longer have the time to waste chasing after dogs or their toys, and more artifacts can serve my purpose. My plan remains unchanged."

Cursing to herself, Jessica's mind kicked into overdrive. What was he trying to accomplish?

Smile returning, Supai took a step back and swept his hand forward like an invitation. "I can, however, spare a few moments making you suffer." He coaxed his finger toward the woods to his left.

Skin tightening on the back of her neck again, Jessica sensed the dark magical energy approaching them through the forest. Her throat turned dry when the corpse demon stepped out from the shadows.

Mariel. She'd had a name before Connor had killed her and turned her body into a puppet for Supai to use. Damien tensed at Jessica's side. His expressionless face worried her.

"Too afraid to face me yourself, Supai?" Jessica taunted, but she couldn't keep her nerves from slipping into her tone.

The demon's black hair was matted and messy, barely moving as her body swayed with each gangly step she took, until she reached her place between Jessica and the god. Her once copper skin had faded to grey and caved in where the muscles had deteriorated. Twitching red eyes were the only part of her that seemed alive, and those red eyes weren't hers. They belonged to the demon wearing the skin of Damien's friend.

Jessica swallowed the lump in her throat. She had destroyed the other demons; she could take care of this one. Then Damien wouldn't have to face that horrid creature—that terrible memory—any longer.

A firm hand on her shoulder stopped her from jumping into action. "What are you doing?" she asked Damien.

"Let me do it."

"Are you kidding?" She searched his gaze, but his eyes were unfocused.

His Adam's apple bobbed as he lowered his hand. He'd already taken off his backpack and drawn his hunting knife with the other. "I need to do this."

"Damien, it's not like she … *it's* gotten any weaker." The shadow demons were difficult enough, and he hadn't stood a chance when they'd faced the corpse demons in Toronto.

Damien stepped around Jessica and raised his knife.

The demon charged. Damien lunged to intercept. Claws clashed against the knife as the two collided, but it was Damien who stumbled back. The demon quickly followed with another strike, catching Damien in the face.

Jessica cringed, her body flinching forward as she wanted to step in, but Damien threw out his hand to stop her. A thin trickle of blood dripped down his cheek where the skin had been split, but his gaze was focused solely on the demon. "Watch my back."

Jessica glanced warily at Supai, but the god seemed as intrigued by the fight as she was terrified to take her eyes off it. If she attacked the god now, they could get in Damien's way. Even if she ignored Damien's request and tried to intervene, Supai would likely stop her. Biting the inside of her cheek, Jessica's body vibrated as it took most of her willpower to keep herself in place.

The creature swung its forearm like a sword. Damien barely had enough time to raise his knife to guard himself. The blade pierced an inch deep into the demon's skin, releasing the repulsive stench of rotting meat into the air.

The black stringy hair fell forward to frame the demon's face as it stabbed its other hand toward Damien's neck. He ducked, yanked his knife free, and drove his elbow into the demon's gut to knock it back.

Jessica caught a glimpse of the knife before he charged in again. The blade was disturbingly clean, aside for a few clumps of black dried blood. The wound on the demon's arm didn't ooze. The blood must have stayed in the body after Mariel died, drying up inside the corpse and giving the body structure.

Damien should have been hanging back, waiting for an opening—or so Jessica thought. He knew the demon was stronger than him, and he couldn't risk taking too much unnecessary damage. But he charged in without hesitation, his conviction surprising her. She wasn't sure whether she should be impressed or disturbed that he could fight even though the demon wore the decaying face of his once-friend.

The demon also seemed to be getting slower. Damien started to dodge its powerful strikes with greater frequency. His expression had shifted from tense to unfazed.

Jessica's blood pounded in her ears. She didn't recognize Damien fighting like this. She had never watched him as a spectator before, and she hoped the different perspective was the source of her discomfort. A part of her wondered if it wasn't the demon slowing down but Damien getting faster. It was like he was on autopilot, and the back of Jessica's neck tingled as foreign energy lingered in the air like a sour smell.

Damien ducked beneath another of the demon's strikes, slid behind its back, and reached across its throat with the blade. Jessica closed her eyes as the demon's eyes widened, realizing what was coming.

The squish of thick, rotting blood, followed by the rancid smell of death and the dull thud of the demon crumbling to the ground told Jessica it was over.

When she opened her eyes, Damien was standing next to the body, his chest heaving. He stared down at the demon, eyes flickering with disbelief. Supai was silent.

"Jess." Damien's voice cracked.

Still stunned by the body of the corpse demon that had crumbled to the ground, it took her a moment to respond. "Get over here," she said rather forcefully.

Her tone must have gotten through to him. Damien stepped around the body to come to her side. She stared at his face the entire way, but he didn't meet her gaze.

Questions swarmed her mind but now wasn't the time. The threat wasn't gone.

Rolling her shoulders back, Jessica positioned herself in front of Damien, blocking him from Supai and the demon's body. She snapped her fingers, producing a small flame, and then flicked her wrist toward the demon. The body caught fire immediately. When the heat of the flames reached Jessica's skin, she coated the body in a barrier to protect the rest of the forest. In a minute, the body had been turned to ash, and Jessica used the barrier to swallow the residual fire. As the barrier burst, the fire's energy and the demon's ashes scattered softly, staining the snow black.

"I think you'll find we're a bit more than a nuisance," Jessica told Supai, turning her fear into malice and forcing it into her voice as she watched the god.

The lines on his face tensed, his eyes appearing darker than before, popping out against pale skin.

"Now, are you brave enough to fight us yourself?" She kept her hands ready at her sides. "Or are you going to hide behind your shadows again?"

The god stiffened, holding his head high. The smoke in his eyes swirled, but the brightness of the wispy grey was dimmer than usual.

Jessica took a brave step forward. "What's the matter, Supai? Did you run out of demons? Tired yourself out by summoning so many?" If she could rile him, maybe she could set him off balance.

His eyes widened a fraction, nostrils flaring in anger, but no demons appeared. Instead, Supai's expression softened to an eerie calmness. Jessica took another step forward and the god mirrored her, taking a step back.

Supai focused on Damien past Jessica's shoulder. "I commend you, witch hunter. I did not believe you capable. As for you," he said, narrowing his eyes at Jessica. "I look forward to the day when I will cut out your tongue and burn it as a sacrifice to my power. It is your fortune that today is not that day. I have other things to attend to. But you can be sure that when I'm through, you will have my name carved into your soul."

The cold air tightened around Jessica's body and squeezed the air out of her lungs.

Taking another step back, closer to the shadows, Supai adopted a blasé expression. "You may have the Stone," he decided, as if they needed his blessing. "Kill Silas if you can. You'd be doing me a favour, ridding the earth of that ungrateful dog. Whatever you manage, you will soon find this *small* victory is the start of the path that leads to your deaths." With his final word lingering in the air, hovering like a ghost refusing to leave, Supai melted into the darkness of the woods and vanished.

The tightness in Jessica's neck relaxed, and the magic coursing through her veins eased, no longer reacting to his presence. She let out a controlled exhale. "Did he look different to you?"

"Dishevelled."

Jessica didn't think gods could be tired, though, admittedly, she was relieved he had chosen not to fight. While she knew his demons were conquerable, she wasn't confident she could beat the god himself. She hadn't even been able to land one punch.

Turning to Damien, Jessica quickly scanned his body. Other than the bruise and cut on his cheek and the rips in his jacket from the demon's claws, he appeared uninjured. "Are you alright?"

Damien hesitated. "Yeah," he said, his voice strained. "Thank you. That was …"

"I get it," she assured him. He needed to be the one to put Mariel's body to rest. It didn't erase the memory of the emotionless gaze and strange sureness in the fight that made her feel queasy. "But are you sure you're okay?"

She watched him closely, looking for any sign of distress, but Damien's expression remained steady and composed. Indifferent.

"I'm fine, Jess."

She wasn't sure how to express her concern. "You didn't look like yourself when you were fighting."

Damien's eyebrows tensed for a moment, a brief hint that there was something more than what he was saying, but the concern was gone so quickly that Jessica questioned if she had imagined it. "I was focused, that's all," he explained. "If I thought too much about it, incapacitating the demon would have been impossible."

But you could *beat it.* She didn't want to doubt his capability, but this fight had been so different from when they'd faced the corpse demons in Toronto.

Before she could press her worries, Damien said, "We should get going. Even if Supai is backing off, there's still Silas to worry about."

"Right." Jessica took a cleansing breath. They could talk about the fight later. She handed Damien his backpack. "Let's get moving."

"*Carefully*, this time," Damien said with a scolding tease.

Jessica picked her way across the slope, this time balancing her pace with the purposeful placement of her feet.

"What strategy would help us find them?" Damien asked.

Jessica pursed her lips. That was the problem. "The cave doesn't have any magical signature I can trace, because it's the whole ..." She gestured in frustration at the mountain.

"Could you trace Nathan instead?"

Hope stirring, Jessica rapidly shifted through the tracking spells she knew. If she could track Damien across Toronto, surely she could find Nathan in the forest. Even if he was inside the mountain. "The problem is that I don't have anything of Nathan's I could use to track him with."

When she glanced back at Damien, his eyebrows had knitted together, his gaze off to the side in what she recognized was his thinking face.

She needed a substitute of some kind, so she could rewrite the spell to search for Nathan without using something of his. Until she thought of an alternative, they would keep marching through the woods.

Hold on, she urged Nathan and Abigail. *We're coming.*

CHAPTER 30

Nathan

"Do you know how long we've been walking?" Abigail asked, her voice strained.

"No," Nathan muttered. The air was old and stale in the tunnel. Sense of time was nonexistent, but the scratchiness of his exhales worried him. Werewolf strength was useless against asphyxiation. A second later, he stopped in his tracks and scowled at the tunnel ahead. "We have a problem."

Peeking around his shoulders, Abigail groaned as she saw the giant boulder that filled the tunnel, blocking their path. "Now what?"

Nathan placed his hands on the boulder and scanned its edges. His pulse jumped. "It's an exit." The boulder was blocking the end of the tunnel like a door.

"Can you ... can you move it?" she asked, a wheeze trailing after the words.

There was no other choice. Wetting his lips, Nathan cracked his knuckles. "Stay back."

He braced himself against the boulder and pushed with a loud groan. The boulder didn't budge. Baring his teeth at the rock, Nathan summoned all his strength, his muscles flushed with energy, and tried again. The boulder groaned as it moved a few centimetres, and a fine shower of dust rained down on Nathan's head.

The wolf instincts surged forward, bringing a calm focus to Nathan's mind. With his jaw clenched and toes digging into the earth, Nathan heaved the rock slowly but surely, until there was half a metre of space between the tunnel wall and the boulder.

Nathan collapsed against the boulder with a gasp as crisp oxygenated air flooded the tunnel. "Abby, hold on. I'll go—" He stopped when he saw her staring at him, slack-jawed.

Looking away, he swallowed despite his tensing throat. "I'll go first." He flinched when she placed a hand on his back.

"Be careful." She gave him a gentle push off the rock, and his body teetered on jelly legs as she guided him into the new room.

Nathan looked up, searching for the source of the cold air, and found a small hole on one side of the domed ceiling. The curved walls of the circular room were smooth, covered with the same thin layer of grime as the rest of the tunnels. Light spilled in from the skylight, and Nathan's stomach sank as he realized he might be looking at the room's only exit. The chamber was empty except for a large stone box and four identical statues standing at equal distances from it, like the points of a compass facing a geometric centre.

Abigail sucked in a deep breath and released it with a heavy exhale as she pressed her hands on her knees. "I forgot what fresh air feels like." Straightening her back and scanning the room, she flinched when she noticed the statue closest to her.

It was a stone wolf standing on its hind limbs, snout gaping open to show its blade-like teeth. In human hands with nails grown long like claws, it carried a sword and shield. Each wolf statue had a different weapon, and all were frozen at the moment before jumping into battle.

"There's magic in here," Nathan mumbled, the hairs on his neck tingling.

To his surprise, Abigail murmured in agreement. "I think I feel it." She wrapped her arms around herself as her focus fell on the stone box. "Is that a casket?"

"There are markings on it," Nathan noted with a grimace, hesitant to get close enough to examine the engravings.

Suddenly, the earth rumbled beneath their feet. Abigail yelped and toppled over. Nathan bent his knees, absorbing the shock, and his eyes darted around to find the source. He doubted it was an earthquake. A light shower of dust shook loose from the ceiling, but the walls weren't shaking.

Motion drew his attention to the left, and he flinched as one of the stone statues raised its knee. The head tilted down, then jerked to the right to stare at Nathan. The other statues followed suit, shifting their stiff limbs as if waking up after a long sleep. The weapons ground against the stone and joints creaked as they came to life.

"Abigail," Nathan warned, waving his hand behind him as he ushered her toward the tunnel. "Don't scream." He wouldn't be able to fight properly if she broke his eardrums.

A high-pitched *eep* slipped through her lips, which transitioned into a weary moan as she shuffled backward with him. When her hands pressed into his back to stop him, Nathan cursed. There was nowhere for them to run.

The statues stepped off their pedestals, and the ground quivered as they landed. They all squared their shoulders to Abigail and Nathan and lifted their weapons. The warning growls grew louder as the statues inched closer, one robotic step at a time.

"Abby, hide behind the boulder," Nathan ordered, turning and pushing her toward the tunnel as he spoke.

"What about you?"

"I'll be fine." He met her alarmed gaze with a firm nod. "Stay there." He hesitated. "But if anything happens to me, run back the way we came."

"Nathan!" Abigail tried to grab him, but he stepped out of reach and turned his back to her, staring down the statues.

The wolf soldiers had positioned themselves in a straight line, forming a barricade between Nathan and the casket that reached from one side of the room to the other. They marched forward as one unit, their broad frames making Nathan feel short for the first time in ages.

He gritted his teeth and sneered at the statues before charging at the one on the left. The soldier raised his weapon, a stone club twice the size of Nathan's head. As Nathan was about to run past him, the club came down with alarming speed and caught him across the abdomen. He hadn't anticipated the heavy statues being able to move so fast.

The air rushed out of his lungs as he wrapped both arms around the club to stop the soldier from striking him again. The deep ache of a bruise rapidly forming blossomed across his abdomen as he twisted his body underneath the club to regain his footing. He tried to wrench the club away, but it wouldn't budge. The soldier turned to face him, and in his peripheral vision, Nathan noticed the others following suit.

Giving up on the club, Nathan leaned his upper body against the cave wall and, using it for support, shoved both his feet into the stone wolf's torso. The soldier teetered on its heels as the weight of the raised club pulled it back. The next statue got caught behind the falling one, taking time to steady its comrade, but the other two redirected themselves toward Nathan, who had dropped off the wall and sprinted to the other side of the tomb.

With space between them, Nathan had a good view of the soldiers. A club, a sword, a spear, and a crossbow were all now aimed at his head.

Nathan ducked as a stone dart from the crossbow caught the tip of his ear, leaving a burning pain in its wake. The statue paused to reload its weapon from the quiver on its hip while the other three stepped closer.

Energy built up inside Nathan, bubbling in his gut and rising up like steam through the rest of his body. Wolf instincts and human desire blurred as he snarled at the statues. The soldiers growled back. Their mouths never moved, but the vibrations of their anger rattled his bones.

The powerful noise tempted Nathan to dip his head and cower, but only for a moment. He kept his chin lifted, refusing to bow. He had come too far and dealt with too much to be bullied by some old hunks of rock.

He leapt onto the casket to stand a hair taller than the statues. Curling his toes and flexing his fingers, Nathan tilted his chin back as he filled his lungs. Nathan let the energy course through him, up his throat and across his lips, and released a long, low-pitched howl to the soldiers, to the sky, and to anyone else who dared to listen. The sound swelled in his ears until he could no longer hear the warnings of the stone guards. Goosebumps prickled his skin and his hair stood on end as the cry carried with it all the pain and anger he had been harbouring since he'd first been cursed.

Nathan was powerful. He felt it in every part of his being.

Cutting off the howl, he lowered his chin and bared his teeth at the statues again. "Who's first?" he asked, his voice deep and gravelly.

The statues remained still. Nathan straightened his knees, tilting his head. *Did they break?*

He crouched low on top of the tomb and was about to launch himself at the stone wolves when the statues moved again. Their joints creaked in unison as they lowered their weapons and marched back to their respective pedestals. He turned his head constantly to watch as all four stone wolves took up their posts, readied their weapons, and froze once again.

Nathan's heart pounded against his ribs until enough time had passed that he was sure the statues wouldn't move again. With a relieved exhale, he leapt from the tomb. When he found his balance, he caught Abigail's tense gaze from across the room.

Nathan dipped his gaze. "You sure you're not scared of me?" he asked, his voice emerging like a croak.

She shook her head, her expression softening. "I think I get it now." She took careful steps across the room, eyeing the statues. "And *that* was pretty awesome. I think that was the Trial of Strength. They must have deemed you worthy." She gestured at the statues. Then she looked Nathan up and down, her eyebrows knitted together. "Are you hurt?"

He cringed and lifted the hem of his shirt. His stomach was mottled shades of deep purple. "It'll pass," he assured her, gingerly lowering the fabric. "Are *you* okay?"

She nodded, but her attention had drifted past him to settle on the coffer at his back. "What do you think is in there?"

"Probably the Stone," he muttered.

They held their breath as Nathan wiped the dust off the lid and Abigail traced her fingers gently across its surface. "I don't understand this writing," she said, remarking on the inscription carved across the centre of the tomb's lid. She leaned back and examined the sides of the stone casket. "It's awfully bland to have all these traps protecting it."

"Wolves don't care for fuss," Nathan explained absently. His focus was transfixed by the casket as he moved around to its other side.

"Nathan?"

"Hmm?" He looked up at Abigail's concerned face and heard her nervous swallow.

"Do you think he's inside?" She took a subtle step back.

Nathan tilted his head. "'He' who?"

"The first werewolf. The one who created the Lupatus Stone." She was struggling to keep her composure.

"Why are you acting like that?" Nathan asked accusingly, his words pained. She just said she wasn't afraid of him.

"You … your eyes have changed."

His jaw tensed. "Changed how?"

She searched his face, pressing her lips together. "Sharper."

Nathan rubbed his knuckles against his eye sockets, but when he met her gaze again, Abigail shook her head. He frowned, looking at the tomb. When he placed his hand again on the stone, he could feel energy beneath it, like a warm heat that tingled his skin and crawled up his arm.

"Whatever's in there is making my, um, *abilities* feel stronger," he told her. He bent his knees to get his weight beneath the lip of the lid.

Abigail squeaked. "Are you crazy?"

"He's already dead."

She looked like she was going to be sick. "Are you sure?"

Nope. But he was certain the Lupatus Stone was inside the tomb. With Abigail on the other side of the casket, shielded from the contents by the lid, Nathan pushed it up far enough to let some light in.

He coughed violently as dust rose like a cloud of smoke, accompanied by the smell of rot. Swatting away the dirt, his lungs aching against the inescapable musty scent, Nathan peered inside the casket.

The bones were as brown as the dirt they lay on. A human skeleton was perfectly intact, exactly where the body had been laid to rest. The mouth was open, revealing all the teeth minus one of the canines. The remaining canine was sharpened to a point. The jaw resembled a vampire with only one fang.

"What is it?" Abigail's question broke through Nathan's fascination.

"A skeleton," he explained. "There's no flesh or anything. Just bones."

Hesitantly, she made her way to his side of the tomb as he slid the lid until it rested half off the casket. A shiver racked Abigail's body as she held herself tightly, looking down at the body.

They shared a moment of silence, partly out of respect for the dead, but also out of a lingering fear that the body might decide to move.

Convinced the skeleton was nothing more than bones, Nathan scanned the rest of the tomb. "I don't see anything that could be the Stone, do you?"

"What?" Abigail's eyes scanned the casket until her expression turned cross. "That doesn't make sense. It *has* to be here. Maybe there's another clue."

Nathan pointed out the missing tooth. "That's the only thing of the skeleton that seems to be missing. You think that's important?"

Abigail peered closely at the bones, expression bright with curiosity. "I think that's it," she said, pointing to the ribcage. "It's around his neck."

Now that Abigail had pointed it out, he spotted the piece of soft twine looped around the skeleton's neck, attached to a canine tooth resting peacefully inside the ribcage. The tooth was nearly ten centimetres long; Nathan couldn't help wondering how he would have measured up to the werewolves of Camelot.

"Oh!" Abigail exclaimed, clapping her hands together and making Nathan jump. "How did I not figure that out before?"

"What are you talking about?"

"There is no Stone!"

Nathan's forehead wrinkled as he frowned at his sister. "Why do you sound happy about that?"

"Because we were never looking for a *rock*." She shook her head again, marvelling at her own words. "The hint is in the name. One English translation for *Lupatus* is 'wolf's tooth.'"

It took a moment for Nathan to register her words. "*Oh.*"

They looked down at the skeleton simultaneously, the tooth suddenly prominent among the other bones. "You think the Lupatus Stone is the tooth?"

Abigail shrugged one shoulder. "It makes sense. There's nothing else here."

Reaching into the casket, Nathan grabbed hold of the tooth and gave it a firm tug. The bones clattered and cracked, one rib crumbling, giving little resistance as he pulled the tooth out of the casket.

Nathan held the tooth up to the light pouring in from the rough skylight above. A rush of power flooded his veins. His instincts sharpened and his mind went strangely quiet.

"N-Nathan?"

Nathan let out a shaky exhale. "That's definitely it." The heat of the power swelling through his body made him feel like he could run for a day and still not tire.

His wolf growled, low and steady, and a sense of worry licked at Nathan's mind. His human side understood immediately. Ever since Abigail had first told him about the Lupatus Stone, his sole drive had been the desire to use it to rid himself of the werewolf curse. Now he held the potential for that freedom in his quivering hand.

His wolf slid to the back of his mind, like it was giving up, but Nathan gritted his teeth and pulled its consciousness forward again. He shoved the tooth toward Abigail. "You keep it. That's too much power for me right now."

Eyebrows lifting in brief surprise, Abigail cradled the tooth in her hand. "Are you sure? Y-you could try and remove your curse. If that's what you want?"

Nathan shook his head, staring at the Stone. "I don't want to." He wanted to learn how to understand the wolf side of him and find the peace of mind he got a taste of when he and his wolf worked together. *That* was the freedom he wanted. He lifted his gaze to meet Abigail's. "Is that ... is that okay?"

Abigail nodded, a proud smile on her face. "Being a werewolf doesn't change anything in my eyes. I want to get to know you as you are now. The *real* you."

Warmth spread through Nathan's chest, easing his soreness with a rush of relief. He wasn't sure what he would have done if she had wanted him to remove the curse, but he was so grateful she didn't that it made his knees feel wobbly.

Abigail looped the twine around her neck, turning the tooth between two fingers thoughtfully while Nathan scanned the room.

"Now we have to get out of here," he grumbled.

"Do you have an idea?"

"You may not like this," he warned her. "But I think our way out is up."

Her chin jerked up toward the skylight in horror. "You're joking."

Even if another way out existed, the skylight would take them directly outside. It was the best shortcut they had. "I should be able to lift you high enough to grab the edge."

"But then how will you …?" She gestured up at the hole.

He shrugged. "Run and jump? If I get enough momentum and launch myself off the casket, it should work." It might take a few tries, but he was confident he could make it. His wolf rumbled in approval, excited by the challenge.

Abby's eyes widened, searching his face for a different answer. Then she scoffed in disbelief and smiled, still fiddling with the tooth. "I guess you *are* like a superhero," she said with a chuckle. "With the super strength and all that."

Nathan's expression went slack as he stared at Abigail, waiting for her words to turn cruel, for her fear to take over.

Her expression shifted to worry, but instead of scorning him, she asked, "Do you think Silas will be out there?"

Muscles tensing, Nathan paused to listen for movement outside but heard nothing. "I'm sure we'll run into him soon, so we'll have to be ready," he said grimly. Abigail shivered. Instincts guided him forward, and for once, he listened to his gut and put his arm across her shoulder, pulling her into his side for a tight hug.

"I won't let him hurt you," he promised, feeling her nod. "I owe you a lot of apologies, Abby, but I—"

She placed a hand on his ribs and wrapped her other arm across his back, squeezing him. "It's okay," she interjected. "Remember, we'll figure this out. I promise to work on forgiving you if you promise to be patient with me getting used to this whole wolf-slash-*Superman* thing."

Nathan huffed out a surprised laugh. "Deal," he agreed, squeezing her one more time before releasing her.

Abigail eyed the tooth around her neck. "Are your wolf teeth this large?" she asked, following Nathan as he positioned himself beneath the hole.

"They might be," he admitted. He had never taken a close look at his teeth, and the forest wasn't exactly littered with mirrors.

Abigail blew out a gentle whistle. "That will definitely take some getting used to."

"I'll show you my wolf form if you want. When you're ready," he added, not in a rush to cross that boundary. He crouched down and held out his hands. "I'll have to hold your foot and your calf. Keep your legs strong as you go up. I'll give you a shove so you have the momentum to pull yourself up."

With a stiff nod, Abigail placed her hands on his shoulders. She hesitated before lifting her foot. "The wolf form," she asked quietly. "It's still *you*, right?"

"It's still me," Nathan assured her.

And for the first time, he believed it.

CHAPTER 31

Nathan

Both Abigail and Nathan were covered in scrapes and bruises by the time they were back in the fresh air of the mountainside. The elation of being free from the underground caves waned when Nathan realized Jessica and Damien hadn't yet arrived.

"Can you smell them?" Abigail asked, her face twisting in a strange expression. Questions like that still sounded strange to both of them.

Nathan inhaled deeply. His wolf instincts had relaxed now that they were out in the open, making it easier to sift through the complex layers of scent. Among the dirt and pine, animal droppings and snow, he found no hint of Damien's dense musk or Jessica's magical, fresh-rain scent.

"They could be too far downwind for me to find them, but I've got nothing so far." He wasn't sure how long they'd been in the tunnels, but he had expected Jessica and Damien to be waiting for them. Of course, he had no idea how they would have found the exit to the cave, but the chance that they wouldn't find them at all hadn't crossed his mind.

"Hey," he scolded Abby when he saw her crestfallen expression. "They'll be fine."

"But what if—"

"No buts. For now, we'll focus on what *we* can do."

Abigail eyed the vastness of the forest around them. "And what's that? Stay put until they find us?"

Nathan surveyed the landscape. They could try hiking to the top of the mountain or following the slope down to the valley. Given how Abigail's shoulders were sagging with exhaustion, Nathan didn't want to take her far.

"Let's move away from the opening and wait," he suggested, pointing to a fallen tree some fifty feet away. "If we stay in one place, they can find us more easily."

Once they arrived at the tree, Abigail plopped down with a tired sigh. "How are we going to hike all the way back?"

"Maybe Jessica can teleport us," Nathan said. He meant it sarcastically, but the idea didn't sound so bad.

He put his nose to the air again and caught the intense scent of musky cologne and blood intrinsically mixed.

Nathan spun around, positioning himself protectively in front of Abigail, and snarled at the forest.

"You're getting sloppy, Nathan," Silas called out, his voice echoing off the trees. "You should have scented me at least five minutes ago."

"Where is he?" Abigail whispered, now on her feet. Nathan reached a hand behind his back and relief rushed through him when she clasped it.

"You're only caught when you want to be," Nathan shot back.

"Which is why I haven't been caught yet. I'm having too much fun." Silas materialized into view, strolling among the trees until he was within throwing distance, and close enough that he could lunge in the blink of an eye. Nathan's blood rushed to his head at the gleam of excitement in Silas's eyes.

Abigail squeezed his hand, and Nathan's feet steadied. "No demon lackeys to do the work for you this time?"

"I don't need demons to deal with you," Silas said, a grin stretching across his face. He glanced to the side, where Abigail peeked around Nathan's frame. "Lovely to see you again, my dear. You're a far more engaging prospect than Nathan ever was."

Abigail sneered at him.

Silas raised an eyebrow, unimpressed. "I'm starting to see your similarities."

Nathan's nostrils flared. "This is between you and me, Silas."

"Then you shouldn't have involved her, Nathan," Silas tutted, shaking his head. "You seem to have a talent for getting the people you love *killed*."

Nathan's heart spasmed, but before his thoughts could scatter, Abigail squeezed his hand painfully tight.

"Shut up," she snapped. "You are not going to hurt him anymore."

"Me? Hurt him?" Silas laughed mockingly. "My dear, I've got some sad news for you. You see, Nathan is a—"

"He already told me." Silas's expression stiffened, and Abigail's tone grew bolder. "He told me about you hunting him through the woods to curse him, and about the fire."

"And you think *I'm* the villain?" Silas mused, looking off into the distance as if deeply considering her words. "Even though it's your brother's fault all those people in the hospital burned to death?"

Abigail's hand flinched in Nathan's, but she didn't let go. "That's a family matter," she said curtly. Nathan could hear her pulse racing and smell the sweat beginning to seep from her pores. "But you have no place in his life anymore, so ... go away!"

"Abigail," Nathan whispered, his cheeks burning.

Silas broke the moment, throwing his head back and unleashing a laugh that tightened Nathan's skin.

"I'm surprised at you, Abigail." Silas slid his hands into his pockets. "You sound proud to have a murderer for a brother."

"Shut up!" Nathan snapped, his voice cracking.

"Don't listen to him, Nathan," Abigail whispered forcefully. "You're bigger and stronger. He's just trying to mess with your head so you won't fight as well."

Silas's eyes narrowed. "I think you should keep out of matters that don't concern you, *my dear*," he remarked, his lips bordering on a sneer. "This is between Nathan and I, isn't it?" He arched an eyebrow. "But if you're so determined to protect your sister, hand over the Stone and we'll call it square."

"There's no Stone," Nathan said.

Silas chuckled, but when Nathan's composure didn't crack, the sound died quickly. His expression shifted to a pout. "Do you honestly think I'd buy that?"

"I'm not lying," Nathan said, a victorious smile spreading across his face. Finally, even if just for a moment, he could outsmart Silas. "There. Is. No. Stone." Since it was technically true, Silas wouldn't be able to sense the double meaning in the words. Nathan held onto his grin as Silas's expression slowly faded into a malicious glare.

Nathan released Abigail's grip and took a step forward, his hands hanging loose and ready at his sides. "But you're right; this is between you and me. So let's settle things."

"Nathan," Abigail whispered.

"He's not going to let us go, Abby." Nathan turned his chin as far as he could without taking his eyes off Silas. "Get back and hide."

"*Nathan—*"

"It'll be okay." He risked a quick glance to show her he meant it. "Please don't watch, okay?" After a moment's hesitation, she nodded and crawled over the fallen tree. Satisfied, Nathan faced Silas's fierce glare.

Death — that was what Silas's eyes reminded Nathan of. Even as a child, he had known not to trust the piercing blue eyes that had shone through the darkness and made goosebumps crawl across his skin. Maybe that was what had saved him from Silas's offer, what had given him the strength to run when he had nothing else.

He was done running.

"You're hiding something, aren't you?" Silas asked in a threatening voice as he removed his jacket. "You have no idea what chasing this treasure has cost me."

Sweat trickled down Nathan's neck as he kept his head high. "Yeah, I'm sure you're real upset."

"You are so disappointing." Silas cracked his knuckles. "Had you not been so stubborn, had you taken my offer when you were new, you would be so—"

"Happy to disappoint," Nathan cut in. "Are you going to prove you're not all talk or what?"

Silas charged at inhuman speed, aiming straight for Nathan's legs. Nathan swiftly blocked a kick and received a fist to his cheek.

Jumping back a step, Silas tutted. "I could have taught you to be better than that."

Nathan ignored the jab and went for the werewolf's gut. Silas caught the tackle with ease and hit Nathan with a stone-like fist across his back. Grunting against the pain in his bruised muscles, Nathan twisted to get out of the hold and back onto his feet.

Silas kept aiming for his knees, trying to get Nathan to the ground. A strong sense of déjà vu settled into Nathan's mind. *Was this always Silas's strategy?*

Nathan kept on his toes, always moving, trying to get Silas off balance. Sticks and leaves flew in all directions as they scuffled across the earth.

Silas aimed a kick at Nathan's ribs, but Nathan turned and caught the werewolf's foot, using it to shove him back with a deep grunt. Silas stumbled and hit a tree, knocking the air out of him. As he gasped, Nathan caught a brief look of concern on Silas's face. It vanished just as quickly, and before Nathan could lunge, Silas was charging at him again.

It took a few more punches to his abused ribs before Nathan finally found a good opening. Silas dropped his shoulder, lowering his guard in frustration, and Nathan sliced out with clawed fingers, cutting Silas across the cheek.

The growling stopped and both men retreated, their breathing equally laboured. Silas was the first to move, reaching up to touch his cheek. His eyes widened as he took in the blood on his fingers.

A surge of strength pulsed through Nathan; he had never marked Silas before. The cuts were already healing, but the damage had been done. He had made the untouchable Silas bleed.

Silas's temple throbbed and the veins in his neck swelled. Keeping his focus locked dangerously on Nathan, he spat out a bit of blood that had trickled into his mouth.

Despite the aches pulsating from every part of his body, Nathan smiled. He knew he couldn't let his guard down, but elation made him pause and savour the moment. This was how it was supposed to be: man and wolf, working as one. There was a hunger in his stomach now. The desire to win, to walk away without crumbling to the ground, to see tomorrow was palpable on Nathan's tongue.

"How did it go so wrong?" Silas muttered, straightening. His hair flopped to the left, covering the shaved sides as his hair product lost its hold.

Nathan's smile dropped. He narrowed his eyes and loosened his knees, ready to lunge.

"You were supposed to be perfect, a prodigy I could mould. A child always in the woods, secluded, already strongly connected to the natural world, with no regard for rules and restrictions." Silas shook his head, glaring at Nathan in frustration. "You would have been perfect."

"And yet here I am," Nathan taunted, spreading his arms wide. "Damaged and too desperate to be human, right?"

Silas's lips pulled back as he began to retort, but Nathan cut him off. "You can say whatever you want, Silas. I don't care. I'm not the one who hides behind demons and can't fight his own battles."

"I've put you down numerous—"

"When I was a child!"

Silas filled his lungs, his words coming out with strained control. "The demons were insurance. And how can you insult me when you hid behind that stupid witch? Had I my full strength in that trial, she would be dead, and it would be *your* fault."

The words sank into Nathan's mind like claws, and he swallowed past the thick lump of guilt threatening to swell in his throat. *Jessica can handle herself.* He wouldn't fall for the taunt. "Maybe you've rubbed off on me after all."

"Ha!" Silas's nostrils flared. "If that were the case, you would have *some* sense of self-preservation — a quality you constantly lack."

"I've survived this long by myself. Fighting's what got me this far."

"You can't fight a fire, Nathan, yet you were stupid enough to try."

Nathan's eyes widened. "I … what?" His lungs struggled to fill with air.

With his lips pulled into a thin line, a low growl slipped from Silas. After a moment's pause, he collected himself, and his jaw relaxed as he rolled his eyes. "I suppose it doesn't matter now. I was sure that, disoriented, you would run for the woods, but after your first shift, you stayed with *those people.*" He spat to the ground and then lifted his chin and glowered down the length of his nose. "If I hadn't pulled you from the fire, you would have died alongside them."

Nathan could barely hear Silas's words through the blood pounding in his ears. Memories flooded back, brushing past his vision as his mind released a heavy sigh: the flames crackling around him, the echo of their burning heat digging into his fur, using his teeth to drag someone by the pant leg. The images were fuzzy, but the truth settled onto his skin. His wolf had been trying to tell him for years. From the beginning, it had recognized what was important to Nathan.

He gasped, desperate to fill his lungs. "You ... it was your fault. You caused the fire."

Behind him, Abigail sucked in a gasp.

Silas sneered. "What's a hundred lives to someone who can live for centuries? If you were to be my legacy, nothing could survive that might hold you back."

"You killed my family!" Nathan roared, charging at Silas, moving so fast his tackle landed with full force, and he took the other werewolf to the ground. A red haze coated his vision as anger seared through him. He barely sensed Silas's cheek crunch under his fist.

Silas shoved him off and rolled to his feet. He shifted into his wolf form, and Nathan followed suit. The sounds of tearing clothing and joints popping crackled through the air.

Nathan shook his golden-brown fur, settling into his skin, before leaping at Silas with his jaw open, aiming for the throat. In the ensuing storm of claws, fur, and fangs, the wolves each struggled for the upper hand. Nathan managed to roll beneath the snap of Silas's jaw and clamp his teeth around the other wolf's thigh. Silas howled in pain and swiped his front paw, scraping the underside of Nathan's flank. Warm blood met cold air, but Nathan hardly noticed the pain. He lunged again, barely missing Silas's knee as he leapt away.

In the tangle of bodies, Silas's expression grew frantic. He swiped carelessly, more cat-like than wolf, as he attempted to tackle Nathan to the ground and managed to scratch the edge of Nathan's jaw as he jumped aside.

Nathan was unfazed—he trusted his wolf's instincts. He took the blows to find an opening where he could get Silas in his jaws. When Silas stumbled, trying to regain his footing, Nathan lunged and clamped his teeth into the other wolf's other thigh. Nathan thrashed his head to the side, tearing into Silas's flesh. Silas howled in pain, and when Nathan tried to adjust the grip of his jaw, he wrenched his body away.

Silas faced Nathan nose-to-nose, lips curled back in a fierce snarl, his chest heaving. Blood dripped from both his hind legs, staining the snow.

The sharp metal taste of Silas's blood coated Nathan's tongue. If he could get Silas by the neck, he would win. He would be free.

Silas feinted going in for a bite, but instead used the weight of his body to shove Nathan to the side. Nathan stumbled one foot over the other, struggling to regain his centre of gravity. Silas, smaller and lower to the ground, stabilized first. He took off into the mess of trees. At first, Nathan hesitated, unable to believe that Silas had run. Then he spotted Abigail in the distance, scrambling to get away as the black wolf charged toward her.

Nathan sprinted after him, his claws churning up snow and dirt. Stretching his neck as far as he could, Nathan caught the end of Silas's tail between his teeth. Digging his paws into the ground, Nathan pulled back as hard as he could. His knees popped from the strain, but Silas had already gotten close enough to strike.

Abigail's scream split the air.

With a guttural groan, Nathan wrenched Silas back, throwing the wolf away from Abigail. His sister's abdomen was coated in blood, and her hands clutched the wound as her pale face twisted in agony. Before Nathan could do anything to help her, Silas moved behind him. Nathan spun around to face the black wolf. Silas's ears were pricked forward and his tail was straight up as he stared Nathan down. Nathan's heart rate spiked and panic turned the skin beneath his fur cold.

Abigail was still conscious; her crying filled the forest. He desperately wanted to transform back to his human form so he could help her, but doing so would leave them both vulnerable to Silas. But if Nathan didn't act quickly, Abigail could die. He didn't know how bad the wound was or how much time she had. His ears rang with the sound of her sobs.

Nathan's ears flattened against his head as he snarled at Silas. *I will kill you.*

"Nathan!"

Jessica's voice cut through the trees and the sound of her stomping feet, accompanied by Damien's heavier gait, drew closer. "We're here!"

They stopped right behind Nathan. Jessica muttered a curse when she saw Abigail.

"I can help her," Jessica said firmly, her knees squishing in the snow as she dropped to the ground. "Go. We'll take care of her."

Silas snarled, his eyes slitting as he threatened Nathan, warning him to stay back. Nathan didn't think twice as he sprinted forward and leapt at Silas.

Nathan tackled the wolf to the ground, pinning him on his back as he clamped his jaw on the flesh and fur of Silas's collarbone. Silas writhed beneath him, his claws scratching and catching pieces of fur as he flailed.

Twisting his body, Silas got his back paws up and kicked Nathan in the ribs. Racked by coughing, Nathan released him. Silas got to his feet and leapt back, drool cascading from his jaw. Nathan didn't slow; the pain was merely an irritation compared to his rage.

The wolves thrashed, their bodies intertwining as each got a hold of the other for seconds at a time. Silas kept trying to create distance, and Nathan refused to give him any. The ebb and flow of their fight moved them steadily across the mountain.

As Silas retreated, his wrinkled snout coated in blood, Nathan spotted the hole to the underground cave directly behind the other werewolf. Nathan stopped and voiced a low, sharp bark to warn him, but Silas continued to back away. His blue eyes shone like ice that had been struck by light, sharp and livid and so different from the malicious, hungry glare stained into Nathan's memories.

Nathan barked again and took a step back, trying to urge Silas toward him so they could continue the fight, but the black wolf only growled. With flattened ears and his tail curled down in fear, Silas took another step and his back paw slipped into the hole. Silas's eyes stretched wide in horror and his jaw snapped at the air as he slipped backward. He let out a high-pitched yelp as he scrambled but was unable to find purchase on the snow. Nathan lunged, aiming to grab the scruff of Silas's neck, but he was too late. The black wolf dropped down to the tomb below.

Looking into the tomb, Nathan spotted Silas on his side. The fall wasn't enough to hurt him. With a shake of his head, Silas pulled himself up to standing. His blue eyes cut through the darkness, staring up at Nathan for a moment before they narrowed. Nathan huffed in frustration, figuring he would have to wait for Silas to find his way out, when he heard stones shifting, grinding together.

The statues.

Silas whipped around, his warning growl filling the tomb as the stone wolves stepped off their pedestals. Each raised its weapon and began its slow march toward Silas.

The black wolf backed up, his snout turning sharply to each statue. He barked, snapped his jaws, and bared his teeth, but nothing slowed the encroaching guards. The one with the crossbow shot a dart, which Silas barely escaped by lunging to the side. Regaining his balance, Silas threw his head to the sky and unleashed an echoing howl. The sound rattled Nathan's ribs, but he heard weakness in it. His wolf instincts were stronger, and the fear from the past was gone. The stone soldiers formed a semi-circle around Silas, trapping him against the wall.

Nathan pulled away, leaving Silas to his fate. A part of him was frustrated, and adrenaline still coursed through his body. After seven years of fear, Nathan was sure he could have defeated Silas this time. He huffed, and his instincts prioritized the scent of Abigail's blood still hanging in the air. A wolf never lingered on a fight—once it was over, it was over.

As Nathan loped back to Abigail, Silas's howl rang through the air. The tone was heavy, a sad cry for help.

Then the howl was silenced.

CHAPTER 32

Nathan

Nathan let out a soft whimper as he approached the log the others were crouched behind. Jessica's gaze was fixed on the ground and a film of sweat coated her brow. Damien knelt next to her; he looked up as Nathan approached and eyed the wolf warily.

Nathan put his front paws on the log and yelped when he saw Abigail lying in the dirt. Her face was so white it blended into the snow. Tight lines creased her forehead and the skin around her half-closed eyes. Damien was pressing a large padded gauze dressing to her abdomen; Jessica held her hands over his, and green light glowed beneath her palms.

The metallic scent of Abigail's blood surrounded them like a cloud, souring her usual honey and paper scent. It crawled down Nathan's throat, twisting in his stomach. *This is my fault.* His vision blurred with the threat of tears.

"Nathan?" Abigail croaked.

He leapt over the log, landing on silent paws on her other side. He nudged her limp hand with his muzzle. She lifted it enough for him to tip it onto the top of his head as he lowered himself to his belly to lie next to her. His heart raced.

"It is you," she whispered with a sigh of relief, her hands trailing across his fur. Her fingers slipped for a second before she gripped the scruff of his neck. Nathan whimpered as her face contorted with pain.

Nathan growled softly at Jessica, urging her to try harder.

Abby thwacked his muzzle lightly. "Stop that," she scolded.

Did she seriously just bop me?

"She'll be fine," Jessica assured him. "We would have been here sooner, but we got delayed." The green light beneath her palms flickered.

Damien picked up the story. "Supai and his corpse demon attacked us."

That explained the fresh cuts and bruises covering their bodies. Damien's cheek was sliced, a bruise darkened the brown skin under his right eye, and his clothing was especially tattered. When Damien caught him staring, he added, "We destroyed the demon, but Supai got away."

Abigail coughed violently and moaned through gritted teeth. Her breathing deepened and, slowly, a hint of colour returned to her face.

"Jess, you're pushing yourself too hard," Damien warned, motioning to Jessica's hands. Her fingers were shaking.

"I'm fine." Her voice lacked its usual strength. "The bleeding has stopped."

Abigail groaned.

"If she's stable, you should stop," Damien insisted.

Reluctantly, Nathan nodded, hating that Abigail was hurting but reassured by her steady heartbeat. He didn't want the witch to hurt herself too.

Jessica looked at Nathan, and it wasn't until he nodded again that she let out a heavy sigh and pulled her hands away, sitting back with a heavy thud. Then Nathan saw the wound, clearly exposed as the bottom half of Abby's shirt had been cut away.

Four clear claw marks raked across the left side of Abigail's abdomen from the bottom of her ribs to the top of her hip. The area was covered in gummy blood, halfway to dried, and the skin surrounding the wound was purple.

Fluttering her eyes open, Abigail whispered her thanks.

A weak smile creased Jessica's face. "When I get some strength back, I'll keep going. You'll have a scar, but we've prevented any major damage."

While Damien bandaged her wound, Abigail focused on Nathan. Gently, she stroked the fur between his ears and down to his shoulders. Nathan's muscles tensed beneath her touch, but he didn't dare move if Abigail was this comfortable with his wolf form. Shifting his attention back to her wound, a whimper slipped across his teeth as his insides twisted with guilt.

Pulling at his fur, Abigail forced his attention back to her gaze. "If you blame yourself, I will smack you again."

Her scolding didn't stop the *what-ifs* from swarming his mind. What if he had been faster? What if they had walked farther, to more favourable terrain? What if he had dodged a different way or forced their fight back right from the start?

Abigail took in a fresh inhale and promptly gagged, cringing as her stomach muscles flexed. "Can we get out of here?" she pleaded. "All I can smell is blood."

Definitely.

Jessica hurriedly agreed and was the first to get unsteadily to her feet. "Damien, can you carry Abigail?"

Once Abigail was situated on Damien's back, she let out a pained groan. "It'll be over soon," Damien promised softly as she buried her face into his shoulder.

Nathan whimpered, but there was nothing he could do. Even if the injury was no longer life-threatening, every step Damien took was going to hurt Abigail's wound.

Jessica walked side by side with Nathan, their pace slowed by her fatigue.

Once they found their rhythm, Jessica's quiet voice fluttered into his ears. "You killed him?"

Nathan stilled, numbness consuming his body. Even though he hadn't taken the final blow, the responsibility for Silas's death weighed heavily on him. He nodded. There was a lightness in his body that he had hoped would come with finally being free of Silas, but it didn't feel as *good* as he thought it would.

"I get it," Jessica said quietly. "You can do the right thing, and sometimes it still feels wrong." She shuddered, perhaps remembering such a moment from her past.

"But you did it. By yourself." She gave him a gentle smile. "Not to mention, you saved your sister. She would be dead if you hadn't fought Silas off."

His responding grumble made Jessica wince. "Sorry, maybe I shouldn't have said it like that," she admitted, looking at him sheepishly. Then her expression tightened. "What happened to the Lupatus Stone? You did get it, right?"

Nathan hesitated. He would be naked if he shifted back to his human form, and he was in no way comfortable crossing that personal boundary yet. Instead, he tried to communicate with her through miming. Nodding his head exaggeratedly, he pointed his muzzle up to her and showed her his front teeth.

Jessica scowled. "What? It's a fair question."

Shaking his head, Nathan tried again, pulling back his front upper lip to show his front fangs.

Raising her eyebrows, Jessica searched Nathan's strange expression for the answer.

Teeth! Nathan thought desperately. *How can you not get this?*

"There is a Stone?" Jessica asked.

Nathan wobbled his head to say *no*.

Stopping abruptly, Jessica placed her hands on her hips and squared off with him. "There is no Lupatus Stone?"

Nathan shook his head.

"But it does exist?"

He nodded.

She frowned. "And you *got* it, right?"

He nodded again with a huff. Jessica responded with a deep frown. "Then why did you say you didn't have it? And where is it?"

Using his nose to gesture toward Abigail, Nathan then pointed his nose at Jessica and pulled back his front upper lip again.

"Why are you snarling at me?"

Nathan rolled his eyes and gave up, trotting after Abigail and Damien.

Jessica groaned behind him. "This would be much easier if you transformed back," she complained. "You could borrow a pair of Damien's pants."

I'd rather not. He had an extra set of clothes in the truck. He would have to stay as a wolf until they got back to the beginning of the trail, but that didn't bother him. He felt right in his fur, like his skin finally fit properly. It was hard to believe Silas was gone, but he had time to let that sink in. Abigail, though injured, was safe, and he had kept his promise.

But what do we do with the Stone now? He vividly remembered the sense of power that had surged through him when he'd touched it. Knowing that strength existed, that it could end up in the hands of someone like Supai, made Nathan queasy.

Once the air was free of the stench of blood, the crew settled next to a small stream that cut down the mountain. Nathan rinsed out his mouth, savouring the fresh, crisp water as it trickled down his throat.

Damien set Abigail down on a large rock and checked her bandages. Jessica sat at her side, rambling on about the different kinds of healing spells as a distraction, while Nathan remained at a safe distance to protect himself from Abby's high-pitched whimpering and moans of pain. That was the downside of being in wolf form—he couldn't cover his ears.

They rested among the trees until the sun dipped below the treeline and the chill of dusk settled onto their skin.

Then Jessica stood and stretched her arms overhead, rolled her head to loosen her neck, and cracked her knuckles. "Alright, are we ready to go?" she asked.

Abigail frowned, looking at Nathan—as if he had any clue what the witch was talking about.

"Should we set up camp?" Abby asked. "It's getting dark."

"Personally, I don't want to stay in this forest a second longer," Jessica replied with a mischievous look that made Nathan uneasy. The witch turned to Damien. "Do you remember the licence plate number of the truck?"

When he nodded, Jessica fetched a pen from her bag and handed it to Damien. Then she offered her open palm so he could write the identification on her hand. Reading it back to herself, Jessica smiled. "Alright, that should work. Everyone gather close."

Abigail and Nathan hesitantly came to stand beside her, even more suspicious thanks to the look of discomfort seeping into Damien's face.

"What are you going to do?" Abigail asked, her expression shifting between excited and nervous.

"I've got enough energy left for a transportation spell before I'm going to need a nap," Jessica said with a shrug. "Here we go." The witch mumbled the spell, which mentioned returning travellers to the licence plate number and a bunch of other rhymes, while she spun her hand in a circle.

Nathan's mouth filled with a metallic taste like he had licked an iron bar. He closed his eyes against the sensory overload.

When he opened them again, they were standing in front of the trucks, back where they had begun their journey into the woods.

Nathan flinched in surprise and checked his body over, relieved to see his tail was still intact.

"I hate that," Damien grumbled.

Jessica giggled. "Which is why it's my new favourite spell," she said, shooting him a devious look. A smirk creased his lips.

Abigail's eyes were frozen wide as she turned in a slow circle. "That was … incredible. How did you do that?"

"I used that as an indicator," Jessica explained, pointing to the truck. Then she let out a loud exhale and pressed her hands into her knees. "Alright, let's get going. I need to lie down."

"You gonna be okay?" Damien asked Nathan.

Nathan's lip curled at the witch hunter's condescending tone, and Damien chuckled and gestured at the truck. "Abigail, could you ride with us and fill us in?"

Abigail turned to Nathan. He hesitated, surprised by her worried expression, and then nodded. With a lingering look, Abby shuffled to the rental truck.

"Where should we meet?" Jessica asked as she helped Abby into the back seat.

Before Damien could reply, Abigail said, "We could go to Nathan's place."

Nathan's eyes widened, which earned him an amused look from Jessica. "Do you know the way?" she asked.

Abigail nodded earnestly. "I can give directions once we're back in town."

Nathan gaped, but before he could object, Jessica and Damien were already nodding. "We can head to the motel after," Jessica said. They piled into the car before Nathan could manage a weak bark.

"We'll meet you there!" Abigail called out the window, leaving Nathan sitting in the parking lot, alone.

He huffed and prodded across the cold cement to his truck, checking the surroundings to make sure no one was around before shifting. With an exhilarating mix of pain and adrenaline, his body reshaped into his human form.

After slipping into his jeans and a faded green t-shirt, Nathan stretched his hands overhead and enjoyed the invigorating pull of his muscles. He'd never felt more comfortable, more like ... himself.

CHAPTER 33

Nathan

When Nathan pulled onto the abandoned logging road that led to the base of his cave, his stomach began to do barrel rolls. Everyone was waiting for him. Nathan slipped out of the truck and struggled to meet Abigail's gaze. She frowned as if he were a stranger.

"It's weird," she confessed. "I understand the wolf was you, but it's hard to connect the two images."

"But we're … we're okay?"

"Yeah, we're good."

Nathan's expression relaxed until she said, "Could I see you shift?"

His jaw went slack as he struggled to respond.

Thankfully, Jessica came to his rescue, placing a hand on Abby's back. "You might want to wait for that one," she said.

Relieved, Nathan led the way up the steep incline to the entrance of his cave. Abigail insisted on walking, though she winced with every step. It took eons to get to the entrance, even with Damien helping her. By the time they slipped in through his den's back tunnel, Nathan had smoothed out the ratty sheets.

Jessica sat on the floor at the foot of the bed, while Abigail chose to sit on the mattress and prop herself up against that wall. Damien leaned against the wall opposite the bed. Nathan lingered by the door, scowling at how small his space looked filled with people.

"Now that we're up to speed, we'll have to figure out what to do with the Lupatus Stone," Jessica said, eyeing the tooth that still hung around Abigail's neck.

Abigail nodded, twisting the artifact between two fingers as she spoke. "We have to destroy it."

"It's not that simple," Jessica said, clearly disheartened. "It's ancient magic."

"What's the difference?" Damien asked.

"It's not just an object with a spell placed on it. The artifact itself is partly magic." She hesitated, her gaze lingering on Damien's pocket. "Similar to your compass, actually."

"Can we neutralize it?" asked Damien, his weight balanced equally between his feet. Even at rest, he was ready to jump into a fight.

Jessica pursed her lips, her head listing to the side. "That's not magic I'm familiar with. We could ask an elven mage."

"What's a mage?" Abby piped up.

Jessica leaned back on her hands as she stretched her feet out in front of her. "Mages are like wizards and witches, except their power comes from the earth rather than from within. Most mages are elves, but the occasional human or other creature has slight abilities. Because their power is based in nature, they usually have a deeper connection with magic like this. They might be able to identify how the magic works, and then we can figure out if it's possible to undo it." She didn't sound optimistic.

"More magic?" Nathan asked.

Jessica gave him a funny look. "You're a magical creature."

"I turn into a wolf. You've taken on an army of demons, saved Abby's life, transported us back here, and you're still standing." *Sort of.*

Jessica rolled her eyes and cast her gaze to the ground to avoid his accusing stare.

Nathan could sense Damien watching him intently, but he carried on: "How powerful are you, exactly?"

The witch stiffened.

"There's something you're not telling us." He'd been suspicious from the beginning, and having experienced Supai's magic, the demons, and even the giant, his gut insisted that Jessica was different.

At first, she didn't respond, merely letting out a sigh as she stared at her feet. After a quiet moment, she lifted her chin. "I'm a Beata," she said. "It's someone who, *essentially*, has more power than would normally be expected of their species."

Nathan's eyebrows shot up. "So you're what, a super witch?" *That would explain a lot.*

Damien snorted, hiding his laughter behind his fist as Jessica shot him a dangerous glare.

"A super witch?" Abigail parroted, a big smile on her lips.

Jessica's irritated exterior cracked. "Sure," she said, shrugging in defeat and chuckling at the new title. "I guess you could put it that way."

"Is that why you're doing this?" Nathan pressed, crossing his arms over his chest. That was the other piece of the puzzle he didn't understand. "I understand Damien's drive: Supai killed his friends. But why are *you* chasing after the god?"

Jessica hugged her knees. "It's the right thing to do," she said. "I can't walk away when I know what Supai is capable of, or what he'll try to do."

"Destroy the world?" Abigail guessed.

"Probably," Jessica scoffed. "Destroy, enslave, that sort of thing."

Abigail's expression darkened. "That's why he wanted a werewolf army."

"Supai told us he had greater plans, and that the Lupatus Stone wasn't the only artifact he could use. It worries me to think what his larger goal might be if he can so easily brush off the potential of having a werewolf army."

Nathan nodded. "He said something similar to me."

They all turned sharply to him, and the sudden attention made his cheeks burn. "When he approached me before I came back and found you at the cave, he offered me a place in reshaping the world."

"If I were him," Jessica said grimly, "I would target the elves next. They've got huge collections of books, treasures, artifacts—things they collect over their thousand-year lifespans. If he wanted other powerful artifacts, that would be the place to start. They'll probably have a few pieces from other species as well."

Damien nodded as if everything Jessica was saying sounded perfectly normal. "We can't dismiss the possibility of him trying to take the Lupatus Stone once he realizes we have it."

Determination set Abigail's jaw. "Well, someone has to stop him."

Damien nodded in agreement and looked at Jessica. "Where do we find an elven mage?"

"I don't have one on speed dial."

"But you know how to find one."

"What makes you say that?"

"Because you know everything," he replied with a twinkle in his eye.

She pursed her lips, fighting back a smile, and spoke to Abigail instead. "The elves are closely intertwined with the pulse of the human world, despite keeping their culture and society mostly separate. The largest sphere, which also happens to be the central sphere for all elves, is in southern Europe. If we can convince the council there to speak with us, they *may* be able to connect us with a mage. Hopefully, we can also persuade them to up the security of their archives."

Nathan was afraid to ask, but it had to be said. "Where, exactly, are they?"

"Valencia, Spain," Jessica replied.

Abigail's squeal of excitement overshadowed Nathan's groan. "We're going to Spain!" she said gleefully.

"What do you mean, 'we'?" Nathan asked, appalled.

Ignoring him, Abigail asked Jessica, "How do we get there?"

Twirling the end of her ponytail between her fingers, Jessica's eyebrows knitted thoughtfully. "That's a good question."

"I can get us there," Damien offered. They all turned to him in surprise.

"My friend Eli has his pilot's licence," he explained. "He's just got a new job with a buddy of ours who manages a jet charter company. I'll call them and see if they can give us a hand."

"Hold it!" Nathan cut in. He placed his hands firmly on his hips and turned to Abigail. "What do you mean, 'we'?" After everything she had gone through, she couldn't seriously be crazy enough to continue associating with these people.

"How can you not want to go?" she shot back, staring at him like he was the crazy one. "We have the chance to see the world. Learn more about magic," she said, gesturing to Jessica as an example. "So many people have told me my degree is useless in the real world, but they have no idea what the real world *actually* looks like. I want to see all of it. I want to help!"

"Your knowledge would be helpful," Jessica confessed. "We couldn't have found the Lupatus Stone without you."

Nathan looked helplessly between the two women. When he glanced pleadingly at Damien, the other man shook his head. The message was clear: Nathan was not going to win this fight.

"Fine," he grumbled in defeat. "I guess we're going to Spain."

Abigail gave him a sly grin. "'We'?"

Nathan growled, but it was weak compared to the grin on his face. "You can't get rid of me that easily."

"Then it's settled. We're going to Spain," Jessica agreed. She looked up at Damien. "What are the chances we could stop in France instead? One of the largest goblin clans is there, and it wouldn't hurt to let them know what's going on."

"Goblins?" Abigail asked. "Do you think they would help us?"

Jessica laughed. "Probably not. Goblins only fight *if* and *when* they've decided it interests them. But if we can plant the idea in their heads now, it may prove useful later. The Grieves clan in the French Alps is influential enough to spread the word to the other tribes."

Abigail readjusted her glasses. "What is their artifact?"

Jessica averted her gaze with a guilty expression. "Despite what some people might think," she said, glancing at Damien, "I don't know everything. There are hundreds of magical artifacts across the species, and it's hard to tell which are myth and which are real because magical history isn't always well documented."

"Goblins?" Nathan thought out loud, struggling to keep up.

"Your world is about to get so much bigger," Damien told him in that irritating, all-knowing tone. Nathan resisted the urge to snap at him. If he was going to be dragged along on another ridiculous quest, he was going to have to get along with Damien.

"What are goblins like?" Abigail asked, bright-eyed behind her glasses.

Jessica paused. "I haven't met one personally, but from what I've heard, they're … unpredictable. They live all over the world, and their morphology is different depending on where they're from. The goblin tribes only have two things in common."

"Which is?"

"Blue blood and a *work hard, play harder* attitude."

"Oh," Abigail murmured.

"Elves, on the other hand, live three steps ahead of everyone else. Rumour is that some of them can see the future." Jessica shrugged. "They're so busy thinking about what comes next, they don't always address the problems right in front of them. That's why I'd rather see the goblins first, because at least they'll have some current knowledge.

It will take more finesse to convince the elves to even give us a minute of their time."

"Imagine how different our histories would be if the records included magic," Abigail said blissfully. Her eyes glazed over, and Nathan was sure her mind had wandered off to envision an alternate history. He smiled and his muscles eased as gentle warmth spread through his body.

"Actually, I could use your help with research, Abby," Jessica said. She pushed herself to her feet and crossed the room to stand next to the mattress. From her enchanted backpack, she pulled out a large text.

Abigail gasped, her face lighting up at the sight of a book the size of a serving platter and as thick as a dictionary.

Jessica crouched, handing the massive text to the historian. "If you want to take a crack at this, I'd appreciate it."

The old hardcover was covered in blue and gold writing that Nathan didn't understand. The title was a bunch of runes written with cursive flare.

"I don't understand this," Abigail said with a frown.

"That's Elvish," Jessica explained, pointing to the title words. "Don't worry, the inside has been translated. You know Spanish, don't you?"

Abigail nodded.

Of course she knows Spanish.

"I'm going to call Eli." Damien excused himself, heading down the tunnel toward the logging road where the trucks were parked.

As Abigail settled in to read the giant textbook of magic, Nathan knew even an earthquake wouldn't be able to move her. From the corner of his eye, he spotted Jessica leave the room. After a final glance to make sure his sister was comfortable, he followed the witch.

He found Jessica sitting in front of the den's entrance, the dark forest silhouetted beyond the safety of the cave. Snow was falling steadily, creating a wall of flickering white flakes in front of her. She sat close enough to reach out and catch one.

Nathan watched silently as Jessica did just that. She pulled her hand back and stared at the snowflake as it melted in her palm, watching it intently, like it was telling her a story. After all that he had seen over the last few days, he wouldn't have been surprised if Jessica could talk to the snow.

"Thank you," he murmured.

She jumped at his voice. "How are you that quiet?" she asked, her pulse easing back to normal.

"It's part of the package deal."

Jessica gave him a small smile. She turned back to the snow, and Nathan crouched across from her.

"For saving Abby," he explained. *And me.*

"I didn't do all that much."

"You took out most of the demons. That wasn't easy."

Jessica nodded. "It is getting easier now that we know what we're facing," she said. She was focused, but not on their conversation.

Nathan stayed quiet for a while, simply watching her. Her hair was tied back in a ponytail, as always. Her hands were scratched and bruised, and her face marred with dirt. If Nathan had to assign her an animal, she would be a tiger. Her features were calm, but her big, expressive eyes held a barely contained fire. Even as serene as she appeared, he knew she was deep in thought.

"Are you really afraid of bats?"

Jessica looked up at him, startled, before her chin dipped away. "I had a bad experience as a kid," she explained sheepishly.

Nathan liked to see her personality come out; it brought light to her eyes that was so different from the cold, distant look of the moment before. Nathan wasn't sure where Jessica's mind went when she got that look, but it was the same expression she had worn when she'd fractured his wrist. The wolf didn't like it.

"What's the story?" he asked, settling down opposite her, one leg extended and the other bent so he could rest his elbow on his knee.

Jessica smiled. "Damien would never forgive me if I told you before him."

Nathan's frown must have been amusing because Jessica broke into a laugh. It surprised him, and his face softened.

When the chuckling subsided, Jessica glanced at Nathan thoughtfully. "Why don't you trust him?" she asked, her curiosity genuine.

The wolf had first raised its hackles because it saw Damien as a threat, but after they had fought alongside each other, he was satisfied Damien was an ally. But something was still off about the hunter.

"I don't trust anyone who wears a mask."

Jessica paused, thinking over his words carefully. When she spoke, it was with quiet confidence "You have to learn how to read him."

Nathan pursed his lips. "Whatever is behind his façade, you're the only one he lets see it."

"They say werewolves have flawless intuition."

"Heart rate doesn't lie." Nathan's ability made it easy to tell when someone was lying. No matter their composure, the subtle changes in their body like heart rate, sweat, and fidgeting would give them away.

Jessica raised her eyebrows. "He has a fast heart rate?"

Nathan shook his head. "It doesn't go up at the right time."

"What do you mean?"

"It's dead steady when facing off against a bunch of demons," he said. That wasn't natural, and it was the crux of why Nathan thought Damien must be hiding something.

"When does it go up?"

"When you're around."

When Jessica didn't reply, Nathan focused on the snow. He wasn't sure if having flawless intuition was a good thing. It meant he could be right about distrusting Damien, and for Jessica's sake, he didn't want to be.

There was a long peaceful silence before they spoke again.

"Are you prepared for what comes next?" Jessica asked. Her face was serious. "The risk is more than I would ask of anyone."

"You said you needed Abigail's brain."

Jessica gave him a guilty look. "I meant what I said, but I also don't want to put her into danger. If you have an alternative idea, I'm all ears."

"Once she's set her mind to something, nothing can change it," Nathan complained. "And I … I want to come too."

From Jessica's suspicious stare, she didn't buy it.

"Abigail made a life for herself in her studies and research. I want to find my thing, what I can live for. I'm sick of always fighting against myself," he admitted to the snow, to Jessica, and to himself. "If I can give others a chance to live their lives, a chance I didn't get, then that's a good purpose." He wished it didn't sound so much like a question when he said it.

"Who knew a werewolf could be so deep?"

Nathan rolled his eyes. She was joking, but he was fully serious. He was an emotional guy, and maybe by acknowledging those feelings, he wouldn't be so embarrassed.

"Don't worry." Jessica smiled. "I won't tell them you're a sappy puppy inside."

"Or demons will be the least of your concerns," he warned with a smile bordering on feral.

Jessica smiled back with fondness but despite the teasing, Nathan could see the darkness lingering in her expression. Her jaw was still tense and the gold that speckled her green irises was muted.

"So what are *you* not telling us?" he asked.

Jessica didn't seem surprised by the question. She didn't turn away from the wall of snow that cascaded through the trees in front of them.

"There're a lot of questions that I don't have the answers to yet," she explained. "Not all of which apply to you and Abby."

"But they apply to Damien?" Nathan caught the slightest hint of the red in her cheeks.

"What I don't understand," she said, angling her body to face him again as she leaned against the cave wall, "is why Supai? Of all the gods or demons, how is it that he is suddenly able to communicate with our world? How was he able to get the power, or even the brains, to pull this off?" She paused, choosing her words carefully. "I can't figure out why, of all the creatures he could have pulled from the magical realm, the summoner chose Supai."

"Who was—"

"He's dead," Jessica cut Nathan off. "But where did he get the idea?"

Nathan scrunched his face, unsettled.

"You think someone else is involved?" a new voice cut in.

Jessica and Nathan looked back to see Damien silhouetted in the light of the cave's entrance.

"That's what I'm wondering," Jessica admitted.

Nathan stood, wanting to give them some privacy in this moment of peace and quiet. "Maybe the goblins or elves can give us some ideas," he suggested. He stretched, linking his hands behind his head, and headed for the back of the cave. As he passed, he made eye contact with Damien.

Unreadable. Damien wore a mask, even if Jessica didn't see it.

Nathan would put up with Damien, even fight alongside him, but his wolf instinct warned him not to trust the hunter. Whatever Damien was hiding—and he was hiding something—Nathan would find it.

As he re-entered the bedroom area of his cave, Abigail raised her head. "It's fascinating," she told him with uninhibited eagerness. It eased Nathan's tension, and he came around the bed to sit on the other side of the mattress.

He kept a comfortable distance between them, not wanting to test the still-fragile balance they had developed. "When did you learn Spanish?" he asked.

"About six years ago, after I learned French. I needed a hobby." She shrugged, turning another page of the book. "Do you want to see?"

"How about you read it to me?" He didn't like reading English and didn't feel any desire to try his hand at Spanish.

She smiled and pushed up her glasses as she turned back to the book. "It's a history of elves," she explained. "It says their species originated on a floating island."

Nathan settled against the wall as she told him the story.

"They travelled the world on their island, using their connection to the ocean to make a magical orb that could move the seas as they wished and take them wherever they wanted."

Nathan let out a heavy exhale, fatigue pulling his muscles toward the ground. The story was interesting, and he listened as best he could while Abby told him about a massive earthquake that shook the earth. It created a wave, which Abby theorized was a tsunami, which swallowed the island into the sea.

"It reminds me of Atlantis," she said, covering her mouth as her words gave way to a large yawn. Shortly after, Nathan did the same.

While the elves in Abby's story were displaced and faced a perilous journey to find a new home, her slow pace contrasting the content of the story, Nathan's body relaxed. He listened to Abigail's voice get sleepy and smiled as she gradually began to drift off.

Maybe their lives weren't normal, but this felt pretty close.

To Be Continued

ACKNOWLEDGEMENTS

Welcome to round two, everyone! The further I get in my career as an author, the more I appreciate how essential a good support system is. This book holds a very special place in my heart, in a way that makes it hard to find the right words to describe. (Oh, the irony.) While I am so excited to share this story with you, I know that I would not be here if it were not for some incredibly important people supporting me.

As always, I want to thank my family for being both my conscience and sounding board – even when you had no idea what I was talking about.

Thank you to Jaz from Feck Creative. Your endless patience and support throughout the back and forth of creating this cover, with some very unexpected twists along the way, was a blessing throughout the process. I'm so grateful to have a cover I'm proud to show off.

To my wonderful copy editor, Tara Avery. I had such a fun time working with you, and your guidance helped shaped this story into what it is today. Thank you to Michelle Parker. You have been incredibly supportive throughout the entire process of this second book, and I cannot express how grateful I am to you for sharing your wisdom and expertise with me. I can think of no better editor to proofread this story to give it its final polish.

I have to express an extra-special thank you to Mallory McCartney. Thank you for so generously sharing your experience in publishing with me and for always being a friend, whether talking books or gushing about your adorable dogs. To Katelyn for your endless, unwavering support and belief in me. And to Dr. John Walsh, for providing the Latin translations for the story.

There were a lot of incredible people who generously donated their time to this story in the early stages. I can honestly say there is no way this book would have become what it is without your input. Thank you: Mitchell Hoyle, Leah Blackett, Emily Gray, Emily McClary, Anya Wyers, Michelle Bienkowski, and Cherise Ragoonath. Your feedback helped this book, and me as an author, to grow.

The Lupatus Stone was inspired by guilt—the guilt we carry for things out of our control and for the past we can no longer change. Sometimes we carry it for so long, life without it doesn't seem possible. Sometimes we don't get the answers we feel we need. Beneath that guilt, however, I believe there is a sliver of hope that something will change. It's hard to reach, and often we can't do it alone. Through the mess of the world, there's something inside you that shines. Whatever your fight looks like, I hope you do fight.

So this book is also for anyone who needs to hear this … *You matter.*

Rachael Bell-Irving is the author of the Wicked Conjuring young adult urban fantasy series and resides in Vancouver, Canada. After graduating from the University of Guelph with a Bachelor of Arts and Science degree, Rachael specialized in the unique combination of Zoology and Classical Studies, and currently moonlights as a school administrator. When not buried nose-deep in her writing, Rachael can be found watching British panel shows, exploring tidepools on the beach, or enjoying a large cup of tea and dreaming of adventure. Connect with Rachael at www.rbellirving.ca or on Instagram at @rbellirving.

CPSIA information can be obtained
at www.ICGtesting.com
Printed in the USA
BVHW030458160421
604859BV00004B/6